F

SO-AHL-010

DATE DUE

LONE
WOLF

LONE WOLF

SARA DRISCOLL

KENSINGTON BOOKS
www.kensingtonbooks.com

KENSINGTON BOOKS are published by

Kensington Publishing Corp.
119 West 40th Street
New York, NY 10018

All Kensington titles, imprints and distributed lines are available at special quantity discounts for bulk purchases for sales promotion, premiums, fund-raising, educational or institutional use.

Special book excerpts or customized printings can also be created to fit specific needs. For details, write or phone the office of the Kensington Special Sales Manager: Kensington Publishing Corp., 119 West 40th Street, New York, NY 10018. Attn. Special Sales Department. Phone: 1-800-221-2647.

Library of Congress Card Catalogue Number: 2016947679

Kensington and the K logo Reg. U.S. Pat. & TM Off.

ISBN-13: 978-1-4967-0441-2
ISBN-10: 1-4967-0441-X
First Kensington Hardcover Edition: December 2016

eISBN-13: 978-1-4967-0442-9
eISBN-10: 1-4967-0442-8
Kensington Electronic Edition: December 2016

10 9 8 7 6 5 4 3 2 1

Printed in the United States of America

To family and friends who gave me the time and space needed to write this book. And to Kane, working therapy dog and nose work competitor, and his real life canine friends, Saki and Rocco.

Acknowledgments

During the writing of this novel, several experts generously shared their time and knowledge with me to ensure my research around dog training, search and rescue, and the FBI was factually correct: Special Agent Ann Todd, FBI's Office of Public Affairs, for providing me with information about the FBI's Forensic Canine Program, which includes the Human Scent Evidence Team. Michelle Munson, certified personal dog trainer and nose work instructor, for teaching me how to train a dog for scent detection and competitive nose work. Officer Ryan C. Miller, a pilot with the Austin, Texas, Police Department's Air Support Unit, for his assistance with the helicopter rescue scene. Apart from their assistance, any errors or literary license taken in the name of storytelling are mine alone.

I was very lucky to work with an amazing group of literary professionals during the drafting of the manuscript: My agent Nicole Resciniti, without whom this book would never have been conceived, thank you for always standing in my corner and being ready to assist at all times. My critique team—Lisa Giblin, Jenny Lidstrom, Rick Newton, and Sharon Taylor, thank you for your willingness to jump in with your virtual red pens, challenging me to always reach for bigger and better things. And to my editor, Peter Senftleben, it was a pleasure working on this first book with you and I'm very much looking forward to our future projects.

Chapter 1

Tracking Canine: A search dog that will follow the ground scent of a person who has passed through an area where the dog is searching.

Tuesday, April 11, 8:02 AM
Monocacy National Battlefield
Monocacy, Maryland

The world whipped by in a blur of color.

The nearly translucent green of new spring lined the path. Sunlight trickled through the canopy, dappling the barely visible path beneath her pounding feet, while bursts of blue and pink flowers spotted the underbrush. To her right, the Monocacy River shimmered in the sun, water tumbling over shallow rapids as it ran toward the Potomac.

Megan Jennings ignored the water squelching noisily in her soggy hiking boots and focused instead on the black Labrador running ahead. Hawk ran with his nose skimming the ground, his thick tail held stiff and high. The chase was on, and he was in his element. Pausing briefly, he pushed through the broken underbrush, following a path that meandered through the trees, a path that nearly wasn't, unless you knew what to look for.

They were looking for a killer.

Meg swallowed hard, thinking of the body she'd left behind only minutes before with the crime scene techs. Partially buried in the soft river mud, the girl had been young, maybe only thirteen or fourteen. All fair hair and gangly limbs, still with that layer of baby fat all teenage girls swear they'll never lose, but often do in a rush of maturity that leaves them with curves in all the right places. Sadly, this girl would never reach that age.

Cases involving children were the worst. In all her time doing scent identification and tracking, it was the children—missing, or worse, dead—that tore at Meg the most. All that promise, cut brutally short; a life gone in an instant of misadventure or cruelty.

Her gaze flicked across the wide expanse of the Monocacy. About a hundred feet upstream, the navy of Brian's standard-issue FBI windbreaker was barely visible through the trees where he jogged behind his German shepherd, Lacey.

The call to the FBI K-9 unit had come at just the right time, Meg reflected. In fact, it was only the day before that Brian had perched on the corner of her desk while she was finalizing the report from her last case. Playing with anything he could lay hands on and generally interrupting her concentration, he'd complained for ten solid minutes that Lacey was bored. She cast a glance once again across the river at Brian's bobbing head. Lacey wasn't bored. *He* was bored. More than that, he needed a fix. Search and rescue was their addiction, and saving lives their drug of choice. She understood his pain—she also wanted to be out there. Besides, when cases followed in quick succession, it kept the dogs on their game.

So when a body was discovered on federal land by a predawn dog walker, both teams had been raring to go. Not their case of choice—no life would be saved here—but a part of their job. The body's location away from any convenient place to park a car, paired with faint boot prints leading into and away from the scene, gave the investigating agents hope that the killer had come and gone on foot, a perfect scenario for overland tracking. Lacey and Hawk were trained search and rescue dogs, but excelled equally at the kind of scent work required to track both criminal suspects and lost innocents.

The dogs executed a spiral search originating at the center of the scene before locating the outbound scent trail. Meg and Brian unleashed their dogs and the animals didn't hesitate. To their surprise, Lacey immediately trotted east down the wide dirt path hugging the river's edge, while Hawk headed toward the muddy bank. Without pausing, he plunged into the rocky rapids separating the south bank from the diminutive island that obstructed most of the channel under the I-270 bridge. Meg met Brian's eyes briefly before jumping knee deep into the water after her dog. They knew exactly what this meant: either they had two suspects on their hands who had fled in different directions, or a single perp had returned using a different path to revisit his kill.

The frigid spring water was a shock to Meg's system, and the murky, rocky bottom was treacherous underfoot, but she gamely waded after her dog. Hawk nimbly sprang forward, a water dog naturally at home in his surroundings. He scrambled onto the opposite shore, stopping briefly for an enthusiastic shake.

Meg raised a hand to shield her face from flying droplets as she clambered out onto dry land. She only had a few seconds to catch her breath, lost during the icy plunge, before Hawk had the scent and was off.

They'd followed the scent ever since, hugging the riverbank. But now Hawk abruptly stopped, giving his characteristic whine indicating he'd lost the trail. Meg jogged up behind him, hanging back a few feet to give him room to work. "Hawk, find it," she encouraged. "Find it."

Huge soulful brown eyes gazed up at her—a bond reestablished, a purpose cemented—then he started rooting through the underbrush surrounding a towering white sycamore, its tiny yellowish-green flowers draping in delicate chains through young leaves. Suddenly his body stiffened as he focused on an area to the left of the path, leading away from the river. Meg balanced on the balls of her feet. She knew this moment: this was when Hawk would take off in a leap of renewed energy on a fresh path and she'd have to strain to keep up.

As expected, Hawk bounded straight up the hill, tearing into a newly plowed field. Loose dirt slipping beneath her hiking boots, Meg glanced at the white, two-story farmhouse to her left, sending up a silent apology to the absent worker who was in the midst of planting this year's crop, only to have a woman and her dog jogging through his freshly tilled soil. She had visited this local battlefield with family previously, so she identified the farmhouse: the Best Farm, overrun by Union and Confederate soldiers alike on July 9, 1864. She and Hawk were ruining the efforts of some National Park Service employee who worked the land to re-create the look of that one-hundred-fifty-year-old tragedy.

Hawk made a beeline toward the 14th New Jersey Monument, gathered himself, and then sailed over the low rail fence separating the memorial from the plowed field. "Hawk, wait!" The dog froze and glanced back at his handler. Meg scrambled over the fence and jumped down onto neatly clipped green grass. "Good boy. Free. Find it!" Hawk darted across the lawn toward a stand of trees on the far side.

Shielding her eyes, Meg glanced up at the memorial. Wearing the traditional slouched kepi hat and full Union blues, the soldier atop the tall squared column leaned casually on the stock of his rifle while his free hand dug into the pouch on his right hip. The soldier's presence reminded

Meg that the victim at the riverbank wasn't the only person to have met a bloody end on this land.

Hawk was gaining speed now, as if the scent was stronger, allowing him the luxury of a faster pace without losing the trail. Her heart pounding, Meg paced herself, thankful those very painful jogging sessions with her dog at 5 AM were paying off. It was inhumane to jog before the sun came up and, more importantly, before she'd had at least two coffees. But, because of the habit, she and Hawk were fit and ready to take on any terrain for any length of time.

The radio at her belt crackled and Brian's voice broke through a haze of static. "Meg, we've just gone under the Urbana Pike and are still heading east. I've lost visual; what's your location?"

Meg tugged the radio off her belt as she and Hawk slipped into the cool shade of a stand of trees. "We're north of you, almost at the pike ourselves." She paused to drag air into her oxygen-starved lungs. "Looks like we're headed for the railroad track and the junction. Will keep you apprised."

"Roger that. Same here." A final click and the radio went silent.

Hawk scrabbled over the loose rocks lining the incline leading up to the sun-swept rail line. "Hawk, wait." Meg clipped her radio back onto her belt and studied the train tracks. The shiny metal of the rails told her this line was still in use. They could proceed but it had to be with caution. "Hawk, slow. Find it, but slow."

Hawk didn't try to cross the rails; instead, he hugged the edge of the track bed at a healthy distance from danger. Almost immediately, the track split at a switch, forking in different directions, but Hawk continued along the right-hand spur, heading south again. This was the Monocacy rail junction, one of the reasons the Confederate Army had wanted to seize the town—he who commanded the rail lines in that war held the upper hand.

In less than a minute, as they followed the curving track to the right, their next challenge came into view. "Oh, hell. Hawk, stop." The dog halted, but restlessly shifted his weight from paw to paw. He whined and looked up at Meg. She reached down and stroked his silky fur. "I know, bub, I know. He went that way. But give me a second here."

Ahead of them was the single-track trestle traversing the Monocacy River. Not a difficult crossing, unless a train came while they were stranded far above the water. Then there would be nowhere to go but straight down. Way, way down. This early in spring, the banks were near to overflowing and the river was a rushing torrent; if the fall didn't kill them, drowning would be a very real possibility.

She pulled the radio off her belt. "Brian, we have a problem."

"What's wrong?" Brian's words came hard through gasping breaths. He and Lacey were still on the move.

"The trail is leading us back to your side, but over the train trestle."

"Is it safe?"

"As long as we don't meet a train." She glanced back up the track. The fork Hawk had not taken stretched beyond them to the north, but the track they'd followed from the west disappeared from view into the trees. South of them, the track curved away into the forest. "I can't see the far side of the river. Hear any trains coming?"

"Lacey, stop." For a moment, all Meg could hear was Brian's labored breathing. "I don't hear anything. If I do, I'll warn you. And I'll call in our location to the railroad to tell them we're on the tracks."

"Okay. We're on our way; let me know if you hear anything. I bet we'll be over and clear before you even hear back." She eyed the narrow expanse of track. "But if there is a train, or if you don't hear from me inside of ten minutes, have a team scour the riverbanks downstream. In case we went over."

"Are you sure about this? I know how you feel about heights."

A vision of the young girl filled her mind—waxy skin, clouded, staring eyes, and brutally torn flesh. Meg owed it to that girl to give her best. Their best. She set her jaw. "Oh yeah, I know. Doesn't matter. We need to keep going. I'll contact you after we cross. Meg out."

"Good luck."

She cut contact. "Gonna need it," she mumbled.

One more quick look in both directions, one more moment of stillness with only the sounds of her dog panting and her own heavy breathing filling her ears. It was now or never. "Let's go, Hawk. Slow." There would be time to find the trail again on the far side; for now what mattered was getting across.

Hawk went first, picking his way carefully along the west side of the trestle where the offset track allowed extra room to walk. Meg was very conscious that while there was enough room to exit a disabled locomotive, were a train to speed by, the vortex of air produced would knock them from the narrow span and send them spinning into the abyss below.

A series of railroad ties over a steel base and stone pilings spanned the bridge, but the gap between the ties was easily five to six inches. Through the empty space, water rushed by forty feet below at dizzying speed. It was mesmerizing, that tumbling, swirling water, enough to make Meg's head swim. So far below. So very, very far . . .

With effort, Meg forced her gaze up toward the thick trees on the far bank. *You know the deal: you ignore the fact that heights freak you the hell out, and you get to enjoy a lovely walk on a rickety old bridge.* She took a deep breath and eased forward, placing her feet carefully to navigate the gaps. *Eyes ahead. Just think of it as a nice walk over the boards of the back porch.* She focused on Hawk and let his swaying back end guide her. Ten feet. Fifteen. *Doing great.*

Ahead, Hawk's paw slid on a creosote-coated railroad tie, still damp and slick from last night's rain, and he stumbled, all four feet scrabbling for purchase. Meg's fear of heights vaporized. She lunged forward to help him, but tripped over the raised edge of an uneven railroad tie. She landed hard on her knees and one hand, the other hand shooting through the gap between the ties and scraping a layer of skin off the inside of her wrist when the sleeve of her FBI windbreaker snagged on the upper surface of the wood. "Jesus Christ, Meg," she admonished, grasping her aching wrist. "Pay. Attention."

Two sounds struck at once—the piercing screech of the train whistle from the far side of the bridge and Brian's frantic voice bursting from her radio. "Meg! Meg! Train headed right for you. Get off the track!"

Her head snapped toward the sound of the whistle as her heart stuttered. No train yet—it was still buried in the trees—but the faint chug of the engine was swiftly growing louder. A frantic glance backward showed the north bank was closer to her, but Hawk had progressed enough that the south bank was closer to him. She lunged to her feet and started to run toward him. Right for the train. "Talon, go. *Go!*"

Years of training that demanded instant and unquestioning obedience in response to his "don't mess with me" name on top of an instinctive reaction to the panic lacing Meg's voice had Hawk bolting along the trestle, somehow keeping his feet firmly beneath him. Breath sawing, Meg pelted after him. One hundred feet. Adrenaline flooded her veins, making her feet fly. Her ears roared with the sound of her own raging blood. Eighty feet to go.

The whistle blew again. The grind of wheels against the rails sliced the air. Sixty feet. The tracks beneath her shook violently. It was nearly upon them.

Forty feet.

The locomotive barreled around the bend, a black monster snaking along the track, followed by tanker cars and loads of lumber. *Death on wheels. And they were headed right for it.*

"Run!" Even though Hawk was pulling away from her, she screamed to spur him on. But as the whistle blasted again and the squeal of wheels grew louder, she wasn't sure he could hear her.

Twenty feet.

Hawk leapt off the trestle, his lithe body stretching long and graceful as he hurtled into the tall grass on the far bank. Meg put on a final burst of speed, spurred by raw fear, the intense effort ripping a scream of agony from her lips as she dove for safety a second before the engine thundered past. She hit the ground with a cry, air slamming from her lungs. She tumbled over and over, through long grass and thorns and sharp fallen branches until she came to rest on her back, blinking up at the sunlight sifting through the leaves. The trailing cars flew past with a screech of wheels on steel, whipping the tall grasses into a wild frenzy over her head while the ground shuddered beneath her. Her eyes fluttered shut, sudden exhaustion overtaking her.

She was conscious first of Hawk's whine, then the warm lap of his tongue on her cheek. She slowly became aware of Brian's bellows through the radio. "Meg! Meg, are you all right?"

She reached for her dog, burying her face in the softness

of his fur and glorying in the heavy beat of her heart nearly banging through her rib cage. She was still alive, and so was Hawk. But it had been close. Too close.

She fumbled at her radio. With a groan, she pulled it off her belt, still feeling the imprint of the case in her bruised skin. "Meg—" Her voice was a raspy croak, so she cleared her throat and tried again. "Meg here."

"Oh, thank God. You scared the life out of me."

"I scared it out of me too. That was *way* too close. Like fractions of a second too close." She pushed up on her elbow to see Hawk already searching the area. He gave a sharp bark and looked back toward her. She could practically hear his thoughts: *Come on, already. What are you waiting for?* "Hawk's got the scent again and is ready to rock 'n' roll." The last car whizzed by, the rhythmic clacking of wheels on the track fading. "And we're clear."

"You up to finishing this?"

Meg rolled to her knees. Bracing one foot on the trampled grass, she lurched upright to stand, swaying for a second while she got her bearings. "Affirmative. We're on the move again. Meg out."

Pulling the hair tie from her now lopsided ponytail, she gathered up the long, dark strands with an experienced hand, tying them back once again. "Okay, Hawk. Find it."

Meg tried not to wince as she ordered her battered body to follow Hawk across the now empty track to reenter the forest. After a few minutes' jog over a faint path, she stopped at the tree line, squinting in the morning sunlight. On the far side of the wide clearing, a brick bungalow nestled into a clump of pines. A late model sedan sat in the driveway.

To her right, Brian and Lacey broke through the trees halfway around the clearing, Lacey bounding over some low scrub and Brian stumbling through with considerably less grace. He quickly took in the house and grounds.

Meg pulled the leash from her pocket, snapping it on Hawk's vest. They melted back into the trees, Brian following her lead to meet just inside the tree line.

"Two separate paths leading back to the same place," Meg said. "What do you think the chances are that this isn't the perp?"

"Exceedingly small." Brian squinted through the trees. "Car's in the driveway. No guarantee, of course, but the perp could be home. We need to see if there's a back door. Then we need backup. Don't know if anyone is armed in there and we can't risk the dogs."

"No way, no how." Meg unholstered her Glock 19, grateful for the FBI's requirement that the Human Scent Evidence Teams carry firearms in case of danger from a suspect while out tracking. She indicated the rear of the house. "Let's check it out."

Brian palmed his own gun and led the way, Lacey trotting at his heels. Staying deep inside the tree line, they circled to the back of the bungalow. They hunkered down behind a clump of leafy bushes to study the residence.

A large picture window framed with yellow gingham curtains looked out into a backyard scattered with children's toys. Smaller, bedroom-style windows dotted one end of the house, while wide, sliding glass doors led out to a concrete patio on the other end.

"Kids." Meg frowned at the toddler toys. "Young enough to be home at this time of day too. We definitely need backup. This can't go south with children around." She holstered her weapon and pulled out her cell phone to call for additional agents, outlining the location based on their current GPS coordinates and trail activity.

Meg pulled a compact pair of binoculars out of a jacket pocket. She scanned the back of the house, moving from the kitchen window to the glass doors. She was just about to scan back when a movement caught her eye. "Wait."

"See something?" Brian leaned in closer, as if he could look through the lenses with her.

Meg squinted in silence. *Come on, come on . . .* Then she spotted it again. "Yes! There's a guy sitting in an armchair on the far side of the couch. Maybe watching TV." She dropped the glasses. "Let's split up. I'll go back toward the road, intercept the incoming agents. You stay here and keep an eye on our guy. Make sure he doesn't rabbit out the back." She handed him the binoculars. "Let me know the second he moves."

"Will do." Brian took the glasses and settled onto his knees. He located and focused on their target. "Got him. Go."

"Hawk, come." Hawk shot to his feet, matching his pace to hers exactly as they slipped through the forest like shadows. Shadows intent on catching a killer.

Chapter 2

Overhead Team: A highly trained, quick response search and rescue management team that can respond to assist with search planning, coordination, and operations. The overhead team usually consists of a search manager and one or two assistants.

Tuesday, April 11, 3:06 PM
Jennings residence
Arlington, Virginia

"When he opened the door and saw the agents, you could see it in his eyes. He wasn't going to let himself get caught." Meg took a sip of coffee and sighed in contentment, sinking back into her favorite old recliner. It had been a long day, from the early chase, through the arrest, to reams of follow-up paperwork, and finally to coming home to clean up her dog, who still wore the muddy remnants of a plunge into the creek followed by a sprint through a freshly plowed field.

"Did the guy try to make a break for it?" Meg's sister Cara sat across from her, squeezed into one corner of the couch by a sprawled red brindle greyhound lying on his back against the cushions, all four feet in the air. The dog twitched in his sleep, one clawed foot raking lightly down Cara's bare arm. She rolled her eyes and gave the dog a gentle push. "Blink, for heaven's sake, stop poking at me."

Meg grinned at her younger sister. Separated by only eighteen months, the girls were often mistaken for twins with their towering height—nearly six feet was tall for a woman—athletic builds, ice-blue eyes, and long, straight black hair, a genetic gift from their paternal Irish grandmother. "You love him, and you know it."

Cara rubbed one hand over the deeply concave belly and the dog instantly quieted under her touch. "Big, dumb lug. Of course I love him." The blue pit bull, curled over her feet to spill onto the carpet, raised her square head. Cara scratched her behind her ears. "You too, Saki. Don't be jealous." Saki settled back down with a loud, breezy sigh.

Meg's gaze dropped to Hawk, fast asleep on his dog bed beside her chair, and then skipped up to her sister. It was moments like this that reminded her how lucky she was.

A year earlier, realistic in the face of skyrocketing housing prices in the Washington, DC, area, Cara had suggested they pool their resources and buy a house together in Arlington. Meg agreed and the arrangement had worked out perfectly for both of them ever since.

Their location put Meg fifteen minutes away from both her office at the Hoover Building in downtown DC, and just as important, Ronald Reagan National Airport for when she and Hawk were assigned out-of-town cases. However, the convenient location was only one positive aspect of their living together.

Raised by crusading parents who worked tirelessly at their central Virginia animal rescue and who never met a stray not worth saving, the sisters grew up with dogs as an integral part of their lives. Meg and Cara adopted animals from the rescue with an eye to turning them into working dogs. While between jobs, Meg had rescued Hawk as an abandoned and sickly puppy, nursed him back to health, and then trained him into a top-notch search and rescue canine. Gentle Saki was a runt found by the side of a road, the entire litter discarded by a backyard breeder because of birth defects and disease. She was now a certified therapy dog, enchanting both young and old with her mesmerizing blue eyes, cleft lip, and affectionate disposition. From AIDS hospice patients to the elderly, few could resist her charms, and nothing made Saki happier than curling up on a bed or couch with someone who badly needed her company. Their third dog, Blink, was a retired racing dog. Not a good candidate as a working dog—to say Blink was both dim and neurotic was a huge understatement—he was a companion to both dogs and never happier than when they all slept together in a tangled pile.

Once they settled in Arlington, Cara took the leap and fulfilled a lifelong dream of establishing an obedience and training school. She rented space in a strip mall a dozen blocks from home and set up both an indoor training area and an outdoor agility range for training during good weather. She'd already graduated half a dozen classes and word of mouth was making her quite popular among the DC set who wanted a well-behaved dog to show off to colleagues and friends.

Cara picked up the crossword puzzle book previously abandoned on the end table and started absently flipping through it, skipping over page after page of puzzles completely filled with blue ink.

"Don't tell me you've finished another one." Meg shook her head, bemused at her sister's ability for word games.

"These are all too easy. I need a better challenge." Cara tossed the book carelessly back onto the table and picked up her coffee instead. "So finish your story. Did the guy run?"

"He tried. Took off through the house for the back door, probably heading toward the battlefield again, since he seems to consider that a safe zone."

"Safe enough to drop the bodies of innocent girls . . ." Cara muttered.

"He got the surprise of his life when he reached the patio door to find another three agents standing there, guns drawn, waiting for him." Meg's smile was nearly feral, but then the mental picture of a broken child bloomed and her glee in the takedown faded. "His terrified kids and wife were home at the time. We tried to make it easy on them, but he refused to go down without a fight."

"He murdered a young girl but had kids of his own? Could you tell if he'd ever hurt them?"

"Too early to say, but they were young. The oldest was probably no more than four. I think his preferences ran a little older than that." Meg spit out words that left her with a bad taste in her mouth.

"But not much."

"No, not much. They might have been in real danger in a few years. What was brutally clear was the wife had no idea what he'd been doing in his spare time. There's no doubt Hawk and Lacey were right on the money. We found trophies of his kills tucked into a drawer in the bedroom. And not just from today's victim. There were indications of male victims too, so there may be some additional cases we'll be able to close from this."

"Guess this guy won't be getting out for a while."

"If ever. No judge is going to grant bail because he's a genuine flight risk. And it's going to be a slam dunk for the jury with what we have." She ran her fingers lightly over Hawk's back. He was so deeply asleep he didn't even twitch. "The dogs did a great job. There wasn't any other obvious evidence at the scene to link to the perp. We might have gotten DNA evidence downstream, but without the dogs we wouldn't have found him so quickly. And who knows who else might have died in the meantime."

Cara raised her cup in a toast. "You guys rocked it. Now that you're home—"

Meg's cell phone rang and she leaned forward to pick it

up off the coffee table. "Sorry, give me a sec. . . ." Her voice trailed off.

"What?" Cara set down her cup and shifted forward on the couch.

Meg stared at the caller ID on her phone: Supervisory Special Agent Craig Beaumont, her section chief at the Bureau. "It's Craig. Why would he call? He knows we've already put in a full day."

"Maybe you missed something in your three hundred pages of paperwork." Cara looked pointedly at the phone in Meg's hand. "Only one way to find out."

Meg answered the call. "Jennings."

"Meg, I need you to come back in." Craig's normally calm voice barked in her ear, his words unusually accentuated.

"Craig, we've just gotten off shift. Hawk is finally resting. Do you need the on-call list? I think—"

"I know who's on call. And I know you've just closed the Monocacy case, but I need you and Hawk. *Now.*"

The emphasis made Meg's blood run cold. She met her sister's eyes, seeing the question there. "What happened?"

"A bomb went off in the Department of Agriculture building. The courtyard in the middle of the north building appears to be the epicenter of the blast. It's the middle of the workday, so the building was full. To make matters worse, although it's not a public building, some rural school board from Virginia made special arrangements for its students to tour the facility and they were inside at the time." Craig ignored Meg's gasp of shock and continued. "I don't know how many are dead or injured, but part of the building collapsed and we have people trapped. Lauren and Rocco are still in New York City, Pat and Sadie are in Washington State with that landslide, and we lent Scott and Theo to the Louisiana Department of Corrections while they're trying to track down that escaped convict. Metropolitan PD are sending in all available K-9 units, but you know that unit is mostly tracking and detection dogs, not search and rescue. They need your skills and we're here to respond quickly. I called Brian; he and Lacey were on their way to Vermont. They've turned around and will be back in three or four hours, but I need another team now."

It was the truth of their relatively new and still fairly small unit—sometimes it was nearly impossible to rotate off shift depending on circumstances and existing national deployments. "It's okay. We're available for however long you need us."

Cara got to her feet and headed for the mudroom where Meg kept her K-9 gear. The sounds of her collecting equipment filtered into the family room.

"Thanks." Craig paused, the tension over the line growing as he seemed to be at a loss for words. "Meg . . ."

"Yes."

"I'm seeing early reports already." He cleared his throat roughly. "It's bad. Really bad. So hurry. And just . . . be prepared. I know you're no newbie, but . . ."

Dread curdled in Meg's stomach, all contentment and relaxation dissolving as if an intangible mist. "We're on our way."

Chapter 3

Mutual Aid Search: A large-scale search that cannot be handled by just one organization.

Tuesday, April 11, 4:17 PM
Washington, DC

The roadblocks were set up further out than Meg expected. In the distance, beyond the newly leafed trees, smoke was rising, black and sluggish, over the National Mall—a sign of what lay ahead.

DC cops were out in full force on the 14th Street Bridge, diverting all traffic away from Route 1, which led straight into the downtown core. Instead, they directed cars onto the Southwest Freeway toward the NASA building. Pulling onto the left shoulder, Meg glanced at Hawk through the mesh of the enclosure that replaced the backseat in her SUV. Dark eyes watched her steadily. "Hang on, buddy. I'll be right back."

She got out of the car, pulling her FBI identification out of her pocket when one of the DC cops moved to block her path. She opened her flip case and extended it. "Meg Jennings, FBI, Forensic Canine Unit. I'm under orders to proceed to the site of the explosion." She jerked a thumb toward her SUV. "I need to get my dog in there ASAP for search and rescue."

"Yes, ma'am." The officer turned and motioned to one of the other cops. "FBI search and rescue. Help her get through."

With a nod of thanks, Meg jogged back to the car. Within minutes, they were speeding along the deserted Route 1, the police car in front running with full lights and siren. Meg drove with her window down, the strong odors of sulfur and burnt plastic already permeating the vehicle, even from this distance. The smell was strong enough she could taste its bitterness, but she didn't close the window. This was only the beginning of getting them both ready to face the task at hand.

Just past the Bureau of Engraving and Printing, the road was clogged with emergency vehicles, so they shot down C Street to 12th and then onto Jefferson. The cop pulled over to the side of the road just past the Freer Gallery. He pushed out of his car and strode over to her as she climbed out of the SUV. "This is as close as I can get you." His gaze drifted to the west toward Jefferson Drive SW and the front of the building where firefighters ran inside, coiled hoses tossed over shoulders. "Good luck in there."

"Thanks." Opening the rear door of the SUV, she found Hawk crouched at the entrance. "Hawk, out." He leaped down with ease, and stood still and quiet at her feet while she snapped on his leash. Once they were on site, she'd let him run free with no risk of catching the lead on anything that could trap or hang him. But while they were about to enter the chaos of emergency vehicles, shouting first responders, and the power struggle of who was in charge, she needed to keep a hold on him. From the back hatch of the SUV, she grabbed her backpack, already filled with everything they might need—bottled water, a collapsible bowl, a first aid kit, dog shoes, a spare radio, and a selection of tools. She was already dressed for the location in her navy FBI coveralls and sturdy steel-toed boots. Tucking her hard hat and heavy leather gloves under her arm, she slammed the hatch. They took off at a light jog down Jefferson Drive SW.

To outsiders, rescue efforts at disaster sites always looked like chaos run amok. But to the experienced, there was order and hierarchy in the chaos. Even while weaving through fire trucks, police cars, and ambulances, Meg tried to locate the emergency operations center. She found it set up at the edge of the Mall, across the street from the Whitten Building. The District of Columbia Emergency Management Agency must have made it across the Potomac from their home base in the Barry Farm neighborhood in less time than the crow flies. Sturdy, portable tables were set up under the shade trees, with large building maps spread wide over them and men and women huddled around in groups. Meg spotted Craig, with his dark hair and craggy face, in his FBI windbreaker speaking to one of the local district fire chiefs. She headed toward him.

Craig glanced up from the map, relief fractionally relaxing the deep lines of concern around his eyes. "Good, you're here. Chief Campbell, this is Meg Jennings and Hawk, one of the search and rescue teams in the Forensic Canine Unit."

They shook hands. "What's the status?" Meg asked. "Can we get in right away?"

"Fire's extinguished." Chief Campbell studied the building from under the rim of his battered white helmet. "The blast took out some of the sprinkler systems in the building, allowing the fire to take hold, but we have it under control now."

"Is the building evacuated?"

"Of anyone who can walk. We got a dozen or more out while we extinguished the fire, but we know there are more inside. We've had cell phone calls from people trapped here"—he tapped a spot on the first-floor map with a heavy, gloved finger—"and here on the second floor. And no one has been able to reach the secretary of Agriculture."

"You know for sure he was inside the building?" Craig asked.

"He was. And the president knows it too. His chief of staff is breathing down Emergency Response's neck right now, looking for answers."

"Because if the secretary is dead, it's more important to the president than a bunch of dead kids?" The words slipped out before Meg could stop them, but one look at the furrow deepening Craig's brow told her she'd gone too far. She held up a hand to stave off a well-deserved rebuke. "And that wasn't fair. Sorry. I hate cases with kids. They never bring out the best in me. Do we know what happened here?"

"We've had reports of a drone flying over the Mall. Several people saw it go up over the Whitten Building ten or fifteen seconds before the explosion."

"A drone?" Turning, Meg considered the Washington Monument, the top of which speared majestically into the blue sky above the trees of the Mall. "Those things aren't legal inside DC's no-fly zone. Why the hell wasn't it taken down?"

"There are snipers on the roof of the White House, but they're not stationed out here on the Mall. Even if it was reported, there'd be no time to stop it. Not that most people would assume it was dangerous. They'd think it was just a stunt or someone shooting video footage."

Meg glanced toward the flashing lights of the emergency vehicles clustered around the Whitten Building. "Couldn't be farther from the truth. The drone delivered a bomb?"

"No one got that good a look at it, but that's our current theory," Campbell said. He outlined a wide rectangle on the map's ground floor. "This ground floor courtyard is surrounded by a balcony on the second floor. Overhead is a huge skylight, and the third to fifth floors of the building encircle the courtyard outside the skylight. We think the drone flew in from the top of the courtyard and either landed on the skylight or hovered just above it. When the bomb detonated, it shattered the skylight, brought down most of the balcony, and took out the offices lining the courtyard. It was damned ingenious. Central delivery for the most damage possible. The outside walls of the Whitten Building are solid white marble, but that inner courtyard was never meant to be seen by the public. It was just brick, which doesn't have nearly the same structural integrity. And there were a lot of windows. We're seeing significant glass-related injuries from in the offices surrounding the blast site."

"Deaths?"

Campbell's jaw hardened and he nodded curtly.

Shrugging off her backpack, Meg knelt beside her dog. After a moment of rooting inside the bag, she pulled out four mesh and leather dog boots with sturdy rubber soles. They only used Hawk's boots for the worst of scenes, when he was at greatest risk of injury, and this scene certainly qualified. Hawk lifted one foot at a time, allowing her to easily slip on the boot and Velcro it securely into place. "Where do you need us?" Meg asked, glancing upward.

"The courtyard, where the worst structural damage is. We know some people are trapped there, and we're already going after them."

She pulled her gloves out of her hard hat and jammed it firmly on her head. "What radio channel do you want me on?"

"Twelve."

"Will do." She started to step away, but Craig caught her arm. Her eyes rose questioningly to his.

"The courtyard. We're getting reports that's where some

of the kids were on their tour when the bomb went off. They were on the second-floor balcony or on the courtyard floor when it collapsed. They're fifth graders, Meg. Maybe nine or ten years old. They're going to be hurt and they're going to be scared. Bring home the ones you can."

His message was clear—some of the kids might be dead. If she found any, she was to move on. Concentrate on the living. "Got it." Meg pulled on her gloves and squared her shoulders. As well prepared as she might try to be, she suspected there was no way to prepare for this. "We're going in. Hawk, heel."

Tuesday, April 11, 4:34 PM
Washington, DC

It was like going through the gates of Hell.

The shock wave accompanying the explosion had blown out the glass-paneled front doors. Shards of glass were scattered over the front sidewalk and spilled into the front parking lot, now full of ladder trucks, snaking fire hoses, and lakes of water. Smoke continued to roll through the arched doorways of the three entrances, set deeply into the heavy stone of the ground floor.

Rising majestically to the fifth floor, twelve tower-ing Corinthian columns skimmed the classic Beaux Arts building, framing rows of windows, now shattered, cracked, or opaque with smoke and grime. The deeply etched words DEPARTMENT OF AGRICULTURE were carved above the portico.

Meg unsnapped Hawk's leash, coiled and stuffed it into one of the many pockets in her coveralls. After taking one last big breath of relatively clean air, she stepped through the center door and into a dim foyer leading directly to the center courtyard. In the distance, from deep within the building, came the shouts and reverberating crashes of a full rescue in progress. "Hawk, with me." Hawk fell into step at her side, stepping around the largest chunks of detritus.

They crossed the foyer, daylight receding as they moved into the building. As in any fire scene, all power to the building was cut, so the only light poured in from outside and was quickly snuffed out in the dark corners of the lobby. This peripheral area of the building wasn't in bad shape, as it was protected from the worst of the centralized blast by the bulk of the structure. Deeper inside, more and more debris littered the ground, hampering their progress. Papers had blown in from surrounding offices, concrete and brick dust coated every surface, and a crumpled wedding photo lay half buried in crushed plaster, one corner missing, as if ripped from its frame before coming to rest here.

The light grew stronger as they approached the courtyard, and then they were standing in the doorway, staring into a war zone. Time wound down to a stop, finally holding motionless as Meg's breath caught in her lungs.

Above their heads, daylight streamed in through the skeleton of the shattered skylight. Originally covering nearly the entire length and breadth of the courtyard as a series of small square panes embedded in larger panels, now only the edges of the skylight still held misshapen fragments of glass. The middle of the span was simply empty air, rent by the tangled steel trusses that once supported the weight of the arched glass. The brickwork of the inner walls had fractured and crumbled to litter the ground, rising in piles toward the outer edges of the courtyard. Sections of balcony still jutted from the wall, mere inches that wouldn't have been enough to prevent a child from dropping into the abyss.

The remains of a Grecian fountain still dominated the center of the room, but the tiered, scalloped bowls had toppled to the floor in shattered fragments. Water leaked from the cracked basins and ran in rivulets over the floor, washing the dust of destruction from shiny marble. Scraps of material, some bright, some charred black and crumbled, littered the floor or mixed with chunks of brick and concrete. In some long-disused portion of her brain, Meg recognized tattered sections of the state flags she'd learned in elementary school.

With a gasping indrawn breath, time abruptly snapped back, marching forward once again. All around were the shouts of the firemen—*"Fire department! Call out!"*—the sounds of power tools, moans of the injured, and weak cries of those still trapped. Meg bent down to meet Hawk's eyes. "Hawk, find them."

Hawk jumped into action, climbing the piles of rubble, his nose down, every inch beneath his feet sniffed before moving on with agility and sureness. Meg struggled behind him, acrid smoke rising from the wreckage in dark wisps to choke her. The air was filled with a particulate haze that coated the lungs and covered her teeth with grit. She thought of the mask in her pack, the one all first responders were supposed to wear in the post-9/11 era. Then she looked down at Hawk, unprotected in the environment. What was good enough for her dog was good enough for her.

Hawk was only four or five feet up the pile when he gave a whine and suddenly swerved left, pushing his nose frantically against ragged pieces of brick and chunks of plaster. Awkwardly balanced on the pile, he lowered his haunches in a half sit.

Meg clambered up behind him. "Good boy. Let me see." Grabbing a large chunk, she started lifting pieces out of the way as fast as she could. She nearly shrieked when a hand shot from under a section of wooden flooring to grab her wrist. "Hang on, we have you. Hang on." Turning to glance backward, she yelled, "I need some help here."

Two firefighters across the courtyard dropped the hoses they carried and ran toward her. Meg slid backward and watched them make quick work of the debris, carefully extracting a rail-thin boy. He was covered in dust and blood, and cradled his arm against his chest, struggling not to cry as the firefighters did their best not to jostle him.

"Wait." The boy's voice was a rough rasp, but carried enough urgency that the men froze. He reached out with his good arm and lightly grasped Hawk's fur. "What's his name?"

Meg knelt down near the boy. "Hawk."

Hawk, hearing his name, moved closer to the boy, who tipped his head against the dog's neck. Meg only heard the barest thread of his whispered "thank you" before the men carried him away.

Pulling off a glove, Meg ran a hand over Hawk's head. "Good boy, Hawk. Find them." She tugged her glove back on and their search continued.

Over the next hours, they found five more victims— three injured children and two women, one injured, and one dead—a blessing perhaps considering the extent of the burns on her body. One boy was in critical condition. The rescued woman, the children's teacher, was nearly hysterical when they pulled her free, asking about each child by name.

They'd been at it for nearly nine hours when they found a victim close to the west wall, near the World War I Memorial. Hawk alerted as usual, but then gave a frantic whine. The bottom fell out of Meg's exhausted stomach. That kind of audible signal could only mean one thing: Hawk sensed a critical victim. So far they'd been lucky and the only fatalities had been adults, but they all knew the longer the search went on, the higher the chances of losing a child.

Getting to the victim was not going to be easy. Close to the epicenter of the blast, large portions of structural steel had been ripped away when the balcony collapsed, and the bricks and rubble were trapped under and woven through dense sections of twisted metal.

Meg started digging while simultaneously calling for help. At the sound of heavy boots behind her, she looked up to meet the dark eyes of a firefighter who'd helped her several times already that day. Because they'd crossed paths a few times, she'd taken note of the name on the back of his turnout coat—Webb.

"Let me get in there." Not unkindly, Webb pushed past her, using his superior strength to lift larger pieces of debris out of the way.

While he worked, Meg shifted back to avoid getting in his way. To her left, part of a marble memorial showed above the tangled steel, brick, and concrete. A navy sailor stood facing an army soldier, each carrying a rifle. Between the two men were listed the names of the dead lost during World War I. A beautiful work of art, carved of stark white marble, a meaningful memorial to those gone before. Now it was defaced with splatters of blood and tiny bits of charred tissue hurled by the force of the blast. The honorable memory of war marred by the dishonorable remnants of a warlike act. She turned back to Webb, unable to look at the memorial any longer.

She frowned, studying Webb's progress. *This is taking too long.* Turning toward the courtyard, Meg glanced around to see if anyone else could lend a hand. Brian and Lacey were taking a very quick break by the fountain, Lacey thirstily lapping water from the collapsible bowl Brian held for her. She finished and Brian stuffed the bowl into his bag. Turning, he caught Meg's eye and gave her a nod before they

climbed the pile against the south wall, Lacey already searching for the next victim.

Across the room, a number of firefighters shored up one
of the walls in an attempt to free at least one hidden victim. No one was free; time to lend a hand, whether Webb
wanted it or not. A life could be in the balance.

Trying to stay out of his way as he strained to move
some of the larger chunks, Meg cleared some of the lighter
pieces, constantly checking to see if they could get a visual
on the victim. Between their efforts, in only a few minutes,
they could look into the framework of metal beneath the
rubble, light radiating from the portable rescue spotlights
filtering through to illuminate the space below.

Beneath them lay a girl, her huge eyes locked on them.
Her face was covered with dust and grime, several tear
tracks washing her pale skin clean.

Meg leaned closer. "Sweetheart, we're going to get you
out. Are you hurt?"

"My side." The reply was weak and shaky.

"Hold on." Without looking away from the girl, Meg
held out a hand to Webb. "Hand me your flashlight." She
waited while he pulled a flashlight from one of the pockets
in his heavy pants and laid it across her palm. Flipping it
on, she shone it down into the gloom, only allowing herself a brief moment to take in the crimson stain spread
over the girl's torso and the jagged edge of the metal support beam nearby covered in a dark gleam that could only
be blood.

She's watching you. Don't stare or you'll scare her more.
She forced her voice to stay steady and to calmly meet the
girl's eyes, even as adrenaline rushed like ice through her
system. "Hang on, honey. You're doing great. You're going
to be fine. Just hang on, we're almost there."

Meg pulled back and turned to Webb, the harsh beam
of the flashlight illuminating his face and highlighting the

gold flecks in his brown eyes. "How's your medical train-ing?" She kept her voice low, so only he could hear her over the ambient noise.

"Great. I'm dual-trained as a firefighter and EMS." He matched her volume, his eyes narrowing on her face. "Bad?"

She nodded. "I think so."

Webb took back the flashlight and leaned in. "Hi, honey, my name's Todd. What's yours?" His gaze slid from one end of the void to the other, taking in the girl's condition.

The girl's weak voice floated up. "Jill."

"Okay, Jill. We've just got to figure a few things out up here, but we'll have you out real soon." He turned off the flashlight and pulled back. He caught Meg's arm, drawing her away from the opening.

"What do you think?" Meg whispered.

"She's under a lot of debris." He kept his tone low and even, but the flat press of his lips and his pinched forehead clearly conveyed his concern. "And she's been sliced pretty badly by that support beam. The question is how deep the laceration goes and whether it's hit any internal organs."

"If it has, could she bleed out before we get to her?" Meg's attention jerked back to the gap at a painful keening from below.

"It's a possibility." He pulled his radio off his belt and relayed the situation, then asked for additional men and several pieces of equipment.

Still sitting near the opening, Hawk gave a whine. Meg touched his shoulder. "What's wrong, boy?"

Hawk pulled away to pace back and forth as well as he could over the uneven surface around the gap.

"What's wrong with your dog?"

"He's distressed that she's hurting. He feels useless and wants to be down there."

"Could he get there?"

"Could he—" Meg pulled back. Send Hawk down into

the rubble? If he tried, it could be a disaster should he get stuck or the area collapsed. She and Hawk were bonded; if anything happened to him, it would be a devastating blow. To lose a dog through old age or illness was one thing, but to purposely send him to his possible death?

Not again.

Icy cold washed over her at the thought of losing her dog, and her fingers involuntarily rose to touch the necklace she always wore . . . except when working difficult recovery scenes. Her gloved fingertips touched only the flat cloth of her coveralls. In her mind's eye she saw the necklace where she'd left it laid across her jewelry box—a flat glass pendant of electric blue and midnight black, interspersed with twining lines of powdery gray. It was a remembrance necklace, and only her family knew the secret of those lines—they were all she had left of her first K-9, Deuce. A glass artist had taken some of his ashes and made the keepsake for her so she always had a piece of him close.

Deuce. Her first heart dog. Her K-9 partner on the Richmond, Virginia, police force. Fallen in the line of duty, cut down by a bullet during a suspect's desperate bid for escape. Even fatally wounded, Deuce had brought down his man. And then never risen again. She'd known the agony of other officers' deaths while on the job, but losing Deuce had just about killed her. It had certainly driven her off the force and in search of a new career.

Regular people simply didn't understand the bond between a dog and their K-9 handler. She hadn't really even understood it fully herself, thinking that bond could never be repeated. Until Hawk came into her life and set her on her new path. Into search and rescue, into the FBI. And now to think about sending Hawk possibly down to his death? "I don't know. . . ." She trailed off, uncertain.

"He'd probably do her some good. Right now, she's

panicking, elevating her heart rate, and increasing the bleed rate. If he could get in there and calm her down, it might just buy us enough time to get her out alive. We have other dogs on site now. Can you spare the time away from the search to have him concentrate on just one victim?"

"We were supposed to be done an hour ago, so my replacement's already here." Her gaze flicked to Brian and Lacey to her right. "We just kept working anyway. You really think it will make a difference?"

"I think it might save her life."

Meg flipped on the flashlight again, analyzing the narrow path between the metal supports into the gap. She was too big to fit through, but Hawk could make it. She turned to find Hawk's gaze locked on hers, his desire obvious to her in their depths. He needed to be down there. It really wasn't her decision.

"Let's see if he can make it through." She shone the flashlight down into the hole, steadying the hand that wanted to shake with nervous tension at the risk Hawk was taking. She pointed down at the girl with her free hand so there was no mistaking her command. "Hawk, beside."

He didn't need to be told twice. Picking his way into the gap, he snaked his body through the metal trusses and over tumbled piles of brick and concrete.

"Jill? Hawk's coming down to keep you company while we work to get you out."

For the first time, the pale face raised in something akin to hope, a slender shaking hand reaching out to touch fur gray with dust and grit. Hawk settled beside her, tucking his body gently against her uninjured side. Jill wrapped one bloody arm around him and buried her face against his neck.

Meg turned back to Webb. Beyond him, three other firefighters climbed the rubble toward them.

Webb leaned into the hole. "Jill, we're going to have to cut some of the metal to get to you. Keep your face down, okay?" He gave Meg a gentle backward push. "You need to step back now. Let us work."

With a roar, one of the firefighters started a circular saw and began cutting through the metal trusses.

It was slow work as they systematically cut trusses and removed sections from the pile, careful to not weaken the structure around them and further endanger the girl and dog below. Every minute or so, they'd stop and Webb called down into the hole. "Jill, honey, how you holding up?" The first few times, the girl replied, her voice getting weaker and weaker. By the fourth time, only Hawk's whine greeted them.

"Can't you go faster?" Meg asked, sotto voce.

"We're going as fast as we can." Webb's words ground through gritted teeth as he lifted a section of metal beam and heaved it down the pile. "If we rush and cut through one of the support beams, the pile will collapse and they'll both die. And maybe take one of us with them." His face was grim as the saw roared to life again.

Nevertheless, the men worked with an added level of urgency. Time was running out and they all knew it.

"That should do it." A large, African-American fire-fighter pulled the last section of truss that blocked the way out of the gap. "You'll have to get in there to see what else you'll need."

"Going in." Webb set his helmet off to the side. He threw a last glance at Meg and went head first into the hole, army-crawling down into the pit, flashlight clutched in one hand to light his way. Up above, the other men shone their lights down, watching his progress. Finally at the bottom, he squeezed past Hawk with a murmured, "Good boy. Jill? Jill!" He tossed off his gloves, fingers sliding over her throat, searching for a pulse. "Pulse is weak and thready, but she's still with us. I need Hawk out of here before I move her; we're too short on space otherwise. Can you call him?"

Meg leaned over the gap. "Hawk, come."

Hawk gently pulled away from the girl. The upward footing was precarious, but he scrambled back up toward Meg and then out onto the pile, carefully avoiding the razor-sharp metal ends left by the saw.

"Here she comes." It was difficult maneuvering in tight quarters, but Webb managed to lift Jill's limp body and pass it up to the ready arms above. Two firefighters hurried as fast as possible to the courtyard floor and then ran for the ambulance waiting at the back door.

Webb hauled himself out, his face coated with grime.

"What do you think?" Meg asked. "Is she going to make it?"

"She's lost a lot of blood, but she's young and strong. They'll be running fluids already. I think she's got a chance as long as she hasn't lacerated her spleen or liver." Turning away, he spat out a mouthful of the stone dust he'd breathed in the pile. "God damn whoever did this. Little kids shouldn't have to live through something like this." He spoke quietly, but every syllable was filled with rage. He gave her a tight-lipped nod, then shouldered his equipment and trudged back down the pile to help the next victim.

Meg's tenuous hold on the emotion that bubbled just below the surface wavered at the vehemence in Webb's tone. Unspeakable fury filled her as her control slipped, fury at the person or persons who did this, fury at a God who would put children and adults in the path of such madmen. Fury that because of someone's selfish actions, once again her own dog was in jeopardy. Red hazed the edges of her vision and her hands balled into fists, short nails biting into her palms. She wanted to hurt the person who had done this. No, hurt was too gentle, too mild for the type of person who would harm the young and kill the inconsequential. She wanted to rip him limb from limb, and watch him suffer like his victims.

Hawk's low whine brought her back to the present. Back to sanity. Back to the world of those who helped, and who saved when they could. That was her world. Retribution and punishment were not her job. She was about life. True, part of life was death. There were always those they couldn't save, but knowing that, experiencing it time and again, never made it any easier.

There was more to do. Time was ticking since the blast, and the longer victims were lost, the less chance there was of saving them. Craig had told her more than an hour ago to go home, but she needed to be here. Needed to find the missing.

Focus on the ones you haven't found yet. They're depending on you.

Meg pushed purposefully to her feet. "Hawk, find them."

He immediately put his nose down, searching for a scent trail.

Wednesday, April 12, 2:41 AM
Washington, DC

Meg and Hawk stepped out of the building and into the chilly night. After the heat and closeness of the disaster scene, the early spring night air was so clear and sharp it almost hurt to breathe. She stopped, taking a few steadying breaths. Out with the smoke and haze, in with the fresh and clean.

They started across the parking lot. It was ablaze with spotlights, but the number of emergency vehicles had scaled down. The rescue efforts continued, but the estimated head count indicated there were only a dozen or so people still missing and they had mostly been in close proximity to the blast epicenter. No one was sure how many of them would be left to rescue.

"Meg!"

Meg looked up to see a tall, rangy blonde in coveralls accompanied by a border collie in an FBI vest speed-walking toward them.

"Lauren." Meg halted in surprise, Hawk automatically stopping at her side. "I thought you were in New York City."

"We were." Lauren looked up at the Whitten Building. For a moment, anguish sketched across her lovely face; too many years of facing this kind of scene had taught her what to expect before she even set foot inside. Then the mask was back in place, determination squaring her shoulders. "We were done there, so I caught the first train back as soon as I heard, knowing Rocco would be needed." Lauren reached down and stroked a hand over her dog's silky black and white fur. "Fucking bastards who did this. I hear we've lost nine so far, with more still missing. And Craig said kids were caught in the blast."

"Only adult fatalities so far. But twenty-one kids injured, some critically." Meg swallowed harshly. "Three are still missing. I wanted to keep going, but Craig finally ordered me out."

"How long have you been at it?"

"I lost track of time. We started around four-thirty."

"Over ten hours. You know very well Craig was right to get you out of there before you got so exhausted you made a mistake, or you or Hawk got hurt."

"There are still people trapped in there." Meg could hear the frustration and banked grief in her own voice and tried to bear down to steady herself. "And family members waiting to hear about the fates of their loved ones. Some of who did nothing more terrible than go to work this morning to earn money to put food on the family table. And now they won't ever be coming home." She closed her eyes, but dull, staring eyes, charred flesh, and blood-splattered marble soldiers followed her into the dark, so she opened them again, and forced herself to focus on light. On life.

Lauren laid a hand on her arm and gave it a gentle squeeze. "You've done your part for today. It's time for fresh teams to take over. Go home. Rest. Come back later today to help again if they still need us." She stepped back, Rocco moving as one with her when she turned and headed into the bomb site.

Meg and Hawk trudged down Jefferson toward the Freer Gallery. Every passing step seemed harder than the last as the adrenaline that had kept her going all night trickled away, leaving her wrung out and empty. Passing one of the deserted park benches at the corner of 12th Street, she finally admitted defeat. "Hawk, wait. I need a minute."

Meg made it to the bench where she collapsed, burying her head in her hands and letting her hard hat clatter to the ground. She clenched her eyes closed, but she couldn't shut out the images of what she'd seen today. *Dismembered bodies. Blood smears on concrete and steel. Desperate reaching fingers. A child's charred and torn backpack, ripped from her body by the force of the blast.* She shuddered while horrific images played through her mind in a never-ending loop.

The nudge of Hawk's damp nose against her fingers reminded her she wasn't alone, not during the search, not now, not ever, so long as Hawk was with her. Looking up, she found him at her feet, squeezing his sturdy chest between her knees. She wrapped her arms around him, taking comfort in his warmth and solid strength. Ignoring the grit covering them both, she buried her face in the fur of his neck.

And there, finally away from the death and destruction, she wept out her despair.

Chapter 4

Initial Planning Point: The starting point from which any search is planned; often it is the "axle of the wheel" and the search spreads outward from that point.

Wednesday, April 12, 8:01 AM
Outside Moorefield, Hardy County, West Virginia

The man hunched over the crude wooden table, bent low over the pieces methodically placed on the scarred surface—electronics, bundles of rainbow-hued wires, zip ties, rotor blades, and a soldering gun.

The muffled *boom* of a recorded explosion drew his gaze and he looked up, his fingers still holding the un-mounted camera against the body of the frame. Across the small, dim room, a flickering tube television showed the image of fiery clouds of crimson and orange blooming over the white marble columns and roof of the Jamie L. Whitten Building. The explosion of color fading into inky black smoke brought a satisfied smile to his thin lips.

Can't help themselves. Gotta keep playing it over and over. Now all the news agencies'll ramp up people's fears by saying Islamic terrorists did it. Because surely no American would do something like that. He shook his head at their tunnel vision. *Oklahoma City didn't teach them anything.*

He picked up several zip ties with his free hand and

deftly bound the camera to the frame and then set the drone down in the middle of the table on its short legs. He scanned the parts, finally selecting a small, squat motor. He bolted it onto one of the eight spidery legs of the contraption, before reaching for the next. Head down, he single-mindedly worked his way around the device, attaching the motors.

He loosed a low, guttural curse when an unsanded piece of razor sharp metal on the frame sliced his thumb. Dropping the screwdriver, he sucked the blood from his thumb while tamping down the urge to throw something at the nearest wall.

Cool it. Save your fury for the people that deserve it.

He wiped his thumb off on ripped, faded denim and looked back toward the TV, allowing the imagery of the blast, the rubble left in the aftermath, and the babble of the talking heads to cool his temper.

Pride slid over him like a cool balm. *He was the most important thing in their universe right now.*

But then the picture on screen shifted. It was clearly a shot taken during the blackest part of the night and without the knowledge of the participants. In it, a young woman sat on a park bench, a yellow hard hat tipped on its side beside a dark backpack at her feet. Between her knees stood a black dog wearing a dark vest that clearly spelled out "FBI" even in the dim light of the streetlamps. The woman's face was hidden from view, buried in the side of the dog's neck, her hands clenched in the thick fur.

There was no audio to accompany the visual, but none was needed—the pair radiated exhaustion, grief, and heartbreak. The talking head was expounding on the long shifts the FBI search and rescue dogs were working, the tragedy of finding the dead, and the waning hope of finding anyone else still alive trapped in the rubble.

He rose from the table to stalk across the room, his narrowed gaze fixed on the image of the woman and her dog, anger burning anew. The heartbreaking pain of the rescuer drew viewers' attention away from the point he was trying to make. That wouldn't do.

Wouldn't do at all.

This journey was just beginning. And it was time to bring attention back to his cause.

Chapter 5

Firedamp: An old coal-mining term for pockets of flammable gas that can explode when mixed with air.

Wednesday, April 12, 10:16 AM
Washington Post
Washington, DC

Clay McCord swore under his breath as the chime of yet another incoming message sounded from his computer. *Damn alerts. If I could take the time to figure out how to turn you off, you'd be gone gone gone.* He ran his fingers through hair going gray more rapidly than he'd like for someone in his midthirties, taking an extra moment to curl his fingers in the strands and tug in frustration before letting go. The sharp dart of pain brought him back to the present and to the story staring at him from his computer screen with frustrating brevity.

He'd just come back from the Whitten Building. Again. He and every other investigative reporter on the eastern seaboard had tried to get on-site yesterday, but the DC cops had been vicious in their determination to keep the press out. He'd even found a few officers he was on good terms with and attempted to sweeten the deal for them turning a blind eye as he slipped in close to the blast site. For once, not even tickets to Saturday's Nationals season opener could get him through. Real regret shone in their eyes at turning down such a tempting offer before they shut him down. No exceptions.

So he had stood on Constitution Avenue, on the far side of the Mall, one man in a crowd of onlookers, eyes fixed on the inky smoke still billowing skyward, feeling helpless. Yes, there was a story to be had, and everyone wanted it. But for him, beyond that lay the grinding desire to *help*. He didn't just want to report the story. He wanted to be in it. Because to report it was to be part of the inevitable media circus. To be in it was to make a difference.

It took him back to his days as an intern. Back to his second day on the job when his world had exploded and Americans learned the meaning of terror. Every able-bodied reporter had been sent out to get the story that day. There he'd been, wet behind the ears, disbelieving and shell-shocked, his heart in his throat, standing shoulder to shoulder with the veteran journalist he was shadowing in a similar crowd barricaded outside the Pentagon. They stood looking at the smoking wreck of the building that represented the military might of the United States, knowing three other planes had gone down that day, taking too many innocents and the security of America with them.

That day the crowd was stunned silent.

Yesterday, the crowd had been a living thing surrounding him, a many-headed monster with whispering mouths. *Terrorism. Islamic extremists. Al-Qaeda. ISIL. Retribution . . .*

He dropped his head into his hands. It wasn't even clear at this point who was responsible for yesterday's attack, but already hotheads were pointing fingers and wanting to strike back with all available force.

The whole thing made him sick.

He looked back up at the screen, at the faces of the men

and women who had died in the blast. At the faces of the children in critical condition. And all he could do was print their names and repeat the same scant recycled details as every other reporter because no one knew anything more. The FBI had the scene locked down tight and were saying almost nothing. None of his contacts inside the Hoover Building would return his calls. And his story, whatever he could cobble together, was due in fifteen minutes.

Maybe his mother was right. Maybe he should have joined the Peace Corps after graduation after all. Instead he went to a war zone.

In the end, 9/11 had informed his entire career. After standing so helplessly on the sidelines, he was never satisfied to sit back and wait for the story to happen; he needed to be there when it did. Three years in Iraq as a war correspondent, dodging bullets and IEDs, had temporarily taken the urge out of him as he had watched friends—both military and reporter alike—lose their lives during the conflict. But after a handful of years back home, his inability to be complacent was once again rearing its ugly head. Too much time watching ridiculous Hollywood A-listers and NFL thugs made him question the purpose of much of the media.

He took a gulp of the bitter, black coffee at his elbow— cold, as it so often was—and brought up his mail for a quick scan of his inbox on the very remote chance someone had answered one of the hundreds of e-mails he'd sent out since yesterday. It was always 97.8 percent junk, but every once in a while there was a diamond in the rough.

His gaze went flat at the top message prompting the latest alert: *SecureDrop message for C. McCord.* Not a returned e-mail.

He repressed a sigh. He understood the concept of the *Washington Post*'s SecureDrop service—a completely secure and private means for the public to communicate anonymously with reporters and staff. But it brought out all the crazies, every one of them aspiring to be the next Deep Throat, or more often than not simply complaining about a neighbor who partied too late or some new municipal regulation they opposed.

Setting his teeth, he logged in to the SecureDrop system and opened the anonymous message.

His blood froze as he scanned the message, his eyes moving faster and faster. He made himself stop, turning his head away to stare out the door of his cubicle across the aisle at Glen, one of the sports writers, pecking at his keyboard with two fingers.

You may never deal with something more important than this, McCord told himself. *Slow down and get your bearings.* He turned back to his monitor, reading the message a second time.

> Mr. McCord,
> Your employers get it all wrong, sir, when they said the bomb on the National Mall was terrorists work. Thats just the first grenaid lobbed at a tyranical government by a man whose been crushed too long under its jackboot heal. Im sorry some kids got hurt, but there parents only learn how they hurt others when they lose there own precious brats. I atatched a photo to let you know I know of what I speak. If your interested, talk to me.
> Sincerely,
> ~ Just One Angry David taking down his first Goliath

McCord didn't know why, but the bomber was talking to him personally. His gaze fixed on the final line of the message and a chill ran down his spine. "His first Goliath." Not the words of a man who felt his mission was complete, but the words of a man who is just beginning his reign of terror.

"I atatched a photo." McCord opened the JPG file attached to the message.

For a moment he wasn't sure what he was looking at. It was an aerial view of a building showing a flat gray roof with several protruding structures. Centered below the camera was a rectangular void, a fuzzy grid pattern far beneath disappearing into the gloom of shadows at the edges.

Like a poleaxe to the gut, McCord realized he was looking at the Whitten Building from above—the drone hovered over the courtyard skylight, only seconds before dropping into the sheltered space and detonating the bomb it carried, killing people in the surrounding offices and maiming children in the atrium below. He imagined people at the windows, looking up from their desks and daily grinds to see a drone hovering at eye level, not realizing they were staring into their own mortality. Just before the blinding blast. Then nothing ever again.

The pointer he slid over the printer icon shook slightly as he printed the message and the photo. His hand froze, suspended, over his printer momentarily. Not indecisive, just knowing everything would change the moment he touched that printout.

This was his chance to help. To make a difference, because the war zone had come home.

He snatched the papers off the printer with a sweaty hand, sprang from his desk chair, and sprinted down the line of newsroom cubicles.

McCord didn't even take the time to knock on the door, but wrenched it open and took two steps inside before stopping dead. His boss and editor, Martin Sykes, froze with his Washington Capitals mug halfway to his mouth, his eyes narrowing on the open doorway. "In a meeting,

McCord." He ended the growl with a head tip toward the leggy blonde in the chair opposite his desk.

"So I see. Sorry. This can't wait." When Sykes's eyes slitted further, McCord extended the printout. "The bomber contacted me."

Narrowed eyes shot wide. "The Whitten Building?"

"Yes."

Sykes shot out a hand, his fingers reaching. "Julie, we'll have to continue this later." He snatched the papers and didn't even look up when the door shut behind the woman. She was already forgotten.

McCord paced to the window to look out across K Street at the sunbathed footpaths and fountain in Franklin Square. Behind him, Sykes was absolutely silent as he read; McCord swore he wasn't even breathing.

Sykes finally broke the silence. "He's going to do it again."

McCord turned from the brilliant daylight, back into the gloom of the darkened office and the message contained there that seemed to increase that darkness. "I know. There's no doubt it's him. The picture proves it's legit."

"Unless it's just some schmuck looking to co-opt attention by using a satellite overview of the building with Google Maps."

"I thought of that already. He couldn't do it with that level of clarity. Whatever took that picture was close enough for excellent detail. Look closely, you can see right into the courtyard."

Sykes leaned into the picture, staring intently. Without taking his eyes from it, he opened one of his side drawers and rummaged through it with one hand, only glancing over quickly when he didn't immediately find what he wanted. He pulled out a magnifying glass and held it over the photo, studying it intently. "Shit."

"What?"

Sykes handed him both photo and glass. "Look at the windows."

McCord held the magnifying glass over the photo, focusing in on the windows, scanning along the row. His stomach rolled when he saw it—the form of a person, standing at the glass, looking up into the sky above the courtyard. He echoed his editor's curse.

"Yeah. I bet that person didn't make it."

"Not that close to the blast, and in front of a pane of glass." McCord put the photo and magnifying glass down on Sykes's desk, pushing them away, needing some distance from the horror that remained trapped in his mind anyway. "We can't assume that other papers got this message as well. We need to contact the FBI and pass it along."

"Of course we do. Doesn't mean we have to like it though."

"You think they won't let us publish it?"

"There's always that chance."

"But we're acting in good faith bringing it to them."

"True, but if they feel releasing it will compromise their case, they'll slap a gag order on us so hard it'll make your head spin."

"Unless broadcasting this message helps them."

Sykes leaned back in his desk chair, steepling his hands and tapping his fingers together as he considered McCord over them. "Like the Unabomber in ninety-five."

"Right. The *New York Times* received his manifesto stating that the killings would stop once it was published. And what does the FBI do? Agree to publish it in case anyone recognizes the views and the writing style in the manifesto."

"We publish it along with the *Times* and what do you know? The guy's own brother identifies him from the writing and turns him in to the FBI. All we need to do is remind them of that and it falls back to us." Sykes drilled an index finger at McCord. "Good thinking."

"Just trying to steer it back to us with as little hassle as possible. We know we have to take it to the FBI, but do we need to clear this with the brass?"

"It's simply a technicality, but imagine the hell to pay if we didn't. Remember, they like to think they're in charge, even when they aren't. As far as getting to the FBI quickly, I have a contact who will make sure this goes right to the director. We'll have his full attention because this has to be top priority for them today."

"After seeing this letter, they won't be pursuing any other cases for a while." McCord picked up the printed message and scanned it again. "Why do you think he sent the letter anyway? Besides being a pissed-off son of a bitch, which we already know."

"No one really knows but the bomber, but after years of working with people and covering stories, I can guess. Call it editor's intuition. His reaction is overkill and does nothing but build evidence against him, so it indicates some real control issues. Now, assuming he's only sent it to the *Post* . . ." A few short mouse clicks and McCord was looking at his own article. Sykes tapped the picture that accompanied the story. "Everyone else had the bare basics along with a distance shot of the Whitten after the bombing and a stock photo from better times. We also had the girl and her dog."

Over Sykes's shoulder, McCord considered the woman. Hunched over her dog, her face hidden except for one soot-covered cheek, her dark hair tumbled over her shoulder to drape over her dog's side. She looked young. Exhausted. Heartbroken. Even at this distance, she seemed diminished by the experience. "We gave the rescue efforts and the surviving victims a face."

"We also took the attention off whoever did this. Right now, everyone and their uncle is thinking Islamic extremists for this. Including us, because it was proposed as a possibility in your article. But it was a sideline, just a brief thought with no substantiation." Sykes picked up the letter, scanned it again. "This sounds homegrown to me. Not a single 'Allāhu Akbar' to be seen. It's more like a single unhappy guy who's going to make everyone pay, not some group of jihadists looking to destroy all nonbelievers. If so, everyone is looking at the wrong suspects right now. Far worse, as far as he's concerned, the public is only looking at the victims and this girl as the face of the rescue effort."

"The FBI needs this ASAP. They need to refocus their suspect profile before he feels he has to make his point again."

"Yes, they do." Sykes picked up his phone and stabbed out a number from memory. "Pauline, I need Allan right away. No, it can't wait." He covered the mouthpiece with one hand and looked up at McCord. "Drop whatever else you're doing today. I want you to follow this angle only. I want you to take it to the FBI personally." He whipped his hand away from the mouthpiece. "Al, it's Martin. We have a situation."

Chapter 6

Consensus Methods: A type of mathematical strategy developed to combine the knowledge and experience of multiple people to define probable search areas.

Wednesday, April 12, 1:54 PM
J. Edgar Hoover Building
Washington, DC

Meg took her usual seat in the conference room beside Brian, Hawk settling at her feet in the long aisle that stretched across the room.

Brian gave her a nod of greeting. "You guys okay?" His gaze cut down to Hawk as he contentedly flopped down beside Lacey and the dogs exchanged friendly sniffs. "You worked a long shift yesterday."

"Like you didn't," Meg replied. "Lacey's good?"

He gave her a dirty look. "I'm fine, thanks for asking."

She flashed him a grin. "You're always fine. I never worry about you." She reached down and ran a hand over Lacey's luxurious brown fur. "It's our girl here I worry about. You know she tends to push herself too hard."

"All heart, my girl." Brian gave Lacey two thumping pats on the ribs that had the dog's tail whipping cheerfully against his legs. "She was a little dehydrated by the time we finally knocked off, but it was nothing that some extra

TLC and a solid night's rest couldn't cure." He slid Meg a sideways glance, keeping his voice low. "Speaking of pushing too hard, did . . . uh . . . did you see today's *Post*?"

"I went out of my way to avoid all forms of news this morning. I saw enough yesterday; I don't need reporters rehashing it for me."

"Well, you might want to see this." He picked up the newspaper sitting on the empty seat next to him, unfolded it, and handed it to her. "Page two."

She stared at him quizzically, her stomach clenching at the tone in his voice that warned of something she wouldn't like. She took the paper, her gaze skimming over the front page above the fold and a picture of the Whitten Building, surrounded by emergency vehicles and spewing black smoke. She snapped the paper open to page two and froze.

Because she'd taken her helmet off before collapsing on the bench, the photo showed an unmistakable likeness of her and Hawk huddled together in front of the Freer Gallery. Embarrassment crawled through her like lava, the heat of it burning her face. It was a private moment of weakness, displayed for the entire world to see. She closed the paper, groaned, and dropped her forehead into her hand. "I hate reporters. . . ."

Brian slid the paper out from between her lax fingers. "Knew you wouldn't like it. If it makes you feel any better, you're not named, but instead are described as a member of the FBI's K-9 team."

Her head snapped up. "Who else could it be? It's clearly not any of the guys. And there's not enough blond hair and gorgeous curves for that to be Lauren—"

Brian drew back a few inches at her sharp tone. "Hey, that's enough. You have curves."

She fixed him with a flat look from under her eyebrows. "Like you'd notice."

"Just because I'm happily married"—he raised his left hand, wiggling his fingers so the light glinted off the plain gold band he wore—"to the most gorgeous man in DC doesn't mean I can't appreciate the female form." He let his gaze run over her with an exaggerated assessing gleam. "And, honey, yours is fine."

One eyebrow cocked in disbelief. "Laying it on a little thick, aren't you? You had me up until 'honey.' "

Brian laughed and relaxed back in his seat with an easy grace. "I thought that might be pushing it. But seriously, I knew you'd rather hear it from me than see it on TV."

"It's on the news?" Her voice rose, the words ending on a guttural groan.

"I caught it on the morning report before I even opened the paper." When her eyes shot daggers at him, Brian patted her hand. "Don't stress about it."

"Don't stress?" Meg dropped her head into her hands. "It makes me look weak," she mumbled through her fingers.

"It does not." The anger in Brian's voice caught her off guard, and she looked up into green eyes snapping with temper. "It makes you look human. You held in there when you needed to, ignoring the horror while you did what was necessary. How you deal off-site and off the clock with the stress and grief is up to you. And there are no wrong ways. Personally, I went home and split a bottle of red wine with Ryan and got comfortably tipsy." He tapped the paper sharply with an index finger. "What I don't like is this was a private moment and someone intruded on it."

Her arms dropped to dangle loosely from the armrest as if too exhausted for any more effort. "I'm afraid to see the caption."

"Actually, it's not bad. Heroic, exhausted rescue worker and her heroic, exhausted dog yada yada. Hawk couldn't have been a better ambassador for us, though. No mistaking the FBI vest."

"That's not going to make the bomber happy. This kind of guy wants the attention on him. Not on the vics, not on the rescuers, and not on a dog. So what's he going to do to get our attention back?"

"I'm sure the Powers That Be have seen this and are already wondering the same thing. If this briefing ever starts, they might even tell us."

Meg scanned the room. While they'd been talking the room had rapidly filled and now there were very few empty chairs.

She glanced back at Brian. "Have we heard anything from Greg yet?" Greg Patrick was the ex-army explosives expert who'd given up working with bombs to train and handle dogs that could find the tiniest trace of them.

"Not as far as I know. He and Ryder are over at the Whitten Building with Cheryl and Auria, but I don't think they've had enough time to report anything yet."

Meg glanced quickly at her watch. Two o'clock. "You're right. It's too early. They couldn't even get in until this morning when the rescue operation shut down. Sifting for bomb fragments in all that debris is going to take some serious time."

"Even when they find the fragments, there'll be all the residue testing, and you know they'll try for prints," Brian said. "It's unlikely, but they might pick something up. But serious time either way."

The side door opened again and Lauren and Rocco jogged through, followed by the last stragglers.

"Hey." Lauren dropped into the chair on the other side of Meg. "Thought I'd be late, but it looks like Director Clarkson isn't here yet."

Brian leaned around Meg. "You think Clarkson is going to show up?"

"I'd be surprised if he didn't. You watch, but with the secretary of Agriculture in the hospital, I bet the president is looking for answers and he's going to go straight for Clarkson. Which means Clarkson will be coming straight for *us*."

As if on cue, a door opened near the front of the briefing room and a tall man with neatly cut dark hair, wearing a navy suit, entered the room. He didn't call for order, but his very presence settled the buzz of conversation into an attentive hush as he moved directly to the podium. "Thank you all for attending on short notice. I know some of you have been called in from out of town and some have been working all night. We'll try to keep this as succinct and to the point as possible.

"As you all know, the Jamie L. Whitten Building was bombed just before three PM yesterday, resulting in eleven deaths and forty-six casualties, twenty-three of which were serious and required hospitalization. As of twelve-forty this afternoon, one of the fatalities was secretary of Agriculture, Thomas Ketteridge." A murmur rose from the crowd. Secretary Ketteridge had been recovered from the rubble late the previous night, and while his injuries were serious, it was widely believed he would survive. The fact that he had succumbed to his injuries was a shock to the whole room.

Clarkson put word to the thought shared throughout the room. "The president is intensely committed to finding the person responsible. He called me personally ten minutes ago and I was able to share some of the preliminary investigation results with him. He would like to be briefed daily with new updates." The cold steel in Clarkson's eyes and the grim set to his mouth clearly spoke of the pressure he was under. "We will not disappoint him."

Brian leaned in to whisper in Meg's ear. "Clarkson is *pissed*. He looks calm and collected, but underneath you can see the anger."

"Unless there is a crucial need," Clarkson continued, "or a life in the balance, as of right now, all other cases for this task force are on hold. We have reason to believe this is only the first incident in a series of intended incidents, so we must catch the person or persons responsible immediately. So let's get the room up to speed. EAD Peters?"

A balding man of medium build stepped up to the mic, adjusting wire-framed glasses on a slightly bulbous nose. Executive Assistant Director Peters was so average looking he tended to meld into the people around him, taking on a cloak of anonymity, and it made his skill in the field legendary. Because he was never seen, he could slip in and out of locations and no one ever remembered him or was ever able to identify him with certainty. Smart, quick on his feet in a crisis, and willing to use his looks to the Bureau's advantage, he was a brilliant undercover investigator and moved up quickly through the ranks. By the age of forty-five he was already the EAD for the Criminal, Cyber, Response, and Services Branch, including the Critical Incident Response Group and the Criminal Investigative Division. Everyone in the room knew Clarkson answered to the president, but the man really running the show was Peters. Never a micromanager, he gave his special-agents-in-charge the room they needed to work, but was always in the background to encourage, advise, or offer his considerable knowledge if needed.

"As you all know, we're only in the beginning stages of this investigation, but we've already made significant headway. I'm going to call up each of my relevant division heads to brief the room." He turned to a woman standing slightly off to the side. "SAC Maloney?"

Maloney stepped up to the podium with the confidence of someone comfortable in her own skin. In an organization overwhelmingly composed of men, Maloney never felt the need to compete or be "one of the guys." She simply put aside all the politicking and concentrated on doing the job right the first time. While it may have taken her longer than Peters to rise through the ranks, she showed great promise and many thought she might one day be the first female director of the FBI. But, for today, she was in charge of the Criminal Investigative Division.

"The bomb was delivered to the Whitten Building by a drone. Detonation was at fourteen fifty-seven yesterday afternoon. The first eyewitnesses report seeing it at approximately fourteen fifty-two flying over Pennsylvania Avenue by the Grant Memorial. It was then tracked by multiple witnesses flying over the National Mall, on a direct trajectory for the Whitten Building. We have several bits of video footage as evidence, from eyewitnesses and local security cameras, but this is the best of them." She picked up the remote from the podium and turned to the screen at the front of the room.

Video footage instantly appeared on the screen. Taken on a cell phone, it showed a drone, inky black against the cloudless blue sky, as it flew about thirty or forty feet overhead. In the background, two male voices could be heard.

"I thought drones were banned this close to the White House and the Capitol."

"They are. Probably just some joker out on a lark, but they're going to fry his ass when they catch him."

The videographer looked like he must have been standing in the middle of the Mall opposite the Air and Space Museum as he followed the dark shape of the drone past the hexagonal Norman tower of the Smithsonian Castle and out of sight before the video ended.

"Agents in the Cyber Division were able to isolate this image of the drone." A still picture flashed up on screen. It was blurry and over-pixelated, but aspects of the drone were clearly visible. "This is the drone itself. It has been identified as a handmade specialized octocopter, as opposed to an off-the-shelf model from a hobby shop. This means there won't be any built-in kill switch and it's likely been customized to carry the maximum amount of weight. As you can see at the front, it has a high-res forward-facing camera to allow the operator detailed visuals along its flight path. As for the operator, he or she would have been using a radio transmitter with some sort of view screen to pilot the craft."

A hand was raised in the front part of the room. SAC Maloney pointed to it. "Yes."

"Based on the range you've outlined, the drone was likely too far away to have been piloted from a position close to the target."

"It was. So our working theory is this." She pulled up a map of the National Mall, running from the Lincoln Memorial in the west to the Capitol in the east. "The suspect doesn't want to be seen with the drone when it's in the air, so he hides it somewhere near the Capitol. A location where it would be clear for takeoff, but not where someone might pick it up and inadvertently set off the bomb early. Perhaps it was placed in an alley between buildings where it could have a vertical liftoff. Or perhaps it was on the rooftop of an office building surrounding the Mall. Go in looking like a delivery guy with a big box, go up to the roof, unload the drone, exit the building like a delivery guy, except your box is actually empty at that point. No one would look at you twice."

Walking over to the map, she circled a number of buildings northeast of the Capitol. "We're going to search the area to confirm, but we hypothesize the drone was left in this area. We think the suspect then moved to a much more central location." She circled the center of the Mall. "Possibly somewhere in this area. More chance of being spotted in the open, so he probably was near one of the buildings away from an entrance, or maybe in one of the sculpture gardens. This would make the one-mile radius for the drone to fly anywhere from this centralized position. It could come in from one side and fly to the target on the other, giving it a much longer range to avoid detection of the suspect. Witnesses confirm the drone entered the Mall from the east, flew west down the Mall on a direct line for the Whitten Building at approximately sixty feet off the ground, matching the height of the building. Witnesses reported it didn't have to fly up over the building, but moved right into place and then dropped out of sight as it lowered into the courtyard. The camera would have given the suspect full visuals to guide it exactly into position. We have no witness reports of anyone suspicious who might be responsible. Anyone who noticed the drone was looking up at it, not around for who was controlling it, but we haven't closed that avenue of investigation yet." With a nod to Peters, Maloney moved back from the podium.

Peters quickly stepped back in front of the crowd. "Now, on to what many of you are really waiting to hear about—who is responsible. As of an hour ago, we have a considerably better idea of that. I'm going to turn the floor over to SAC Williams."

Special-Agent-in-Charge Williams, head of the Behavioral Analysis Unit for counterterrorism, arson, and bombing matters, was in his late thirties. He wore a stylish suit with quietly expensive Italian leather shoes and had a surprisingly athletic build for what many considered the "egghead brigade"—agents who spent more time studying suspects than actually confronting them in the field. "Good afternoon. Late this morning, reporter Clay McCord of the *Washington Post*"—a collective groan filled the room at the mention of the *Post*, but Williams ignored it—"received an anonymous message through their SecureDrop system from someone claiming to be the bomber. Accompanying the message was a digital image so we'd know it's legitimate." He brought up the image on screen. A murmur rippled through the crowd.

Meg stifled a small gasp. She'd seen that gridwork of the courtyard skylight from below just yesterday, and had no doubt she was now looking at a bird's-eye—or drone's-eye—view only a matter of seconds before the drone dropped into the courtyard and exploded. Sensing her disquiet, Hawk raised his head from his paws and nudged her calf. She reached down to stroke him, both quieting him and trying to reinforce her own sense of calm. He was too smart for her to fool him, but he put his head back down anyway.

"It's been confirmed this is the roof of the Whitten Building," Williams continued, "directly above the skylight over the courtyard. This picture is likely a still from the video feed that the bomber was using to remotely control the drone. Cyber Division has already had a quick go at the file, but the image has been scrubbed of all meta data. And this is the message he sent." He put the bomber's message up on screen and then stepped back for a moment to allow the agents in the room time to read it for themselves.

Leaning forward, Meg skimmed the message, her hands going clammy with each new line. "Tyranical government."

"A man who's been crushed too long under its jackboot heal." "His first Goliath."

"Holy Mother of God," Lauren breathed. "He's a spree bomber."

"A homegrown spree bomber," Brian agreed. "He's not an Islamic terrorist. He's one of us."

The low roar gradually started to build as heads turned to each other all over the room. Peters finally stepped forward again and tapped the mic twice for their attention. "Settle down. Williams, please continue."

"We've only had a short time to consider this note, but several things are immediately obvious. He outright states he's a man, and there's nothing in this note to contradict that. From the writing itself, it's someone with minimal education, who spells phonetically, and therefore makes substitution errors. He uses the term 'jackboot,' which many modern city dwellers won't even recognize, but was a well-known term during the Second World War and into the nineteen fifties. It's unlikely he himself was ever in the military, but considering the language, it's possible a male relative like a father or an uncle might have been. There's a famous quote by George Orwell of *1984* fame that a jackboot is what you put on when you want to act tyrannical. So we're getting overkill of the 'government as tyrant' message.

"This is a man who works alone and likely views himself as a patriot. He acts not only for himself, but also for anyone else who is oppressed by the government. Note the first line—he doesn't consider himself a terrorist. As far as he's concerned, no red-blooded American standing up for his rights could be considered a terrorist. That's a label strictly for foreigners. Clearly, we have a different view of the matter."

Williams contemplated the screen, his hands on his hips.

A full ten seconds of silence passed before he turned back to the room. "Our biggest concern is the statement that this is only his first salvo—'the first grenade,' 'taking down the first Goliath.' He plans to do this again. His only slight remorse is for the injured children, but it's clear he considers them collateral damage and martyrs to the cause. More than that, he's assuming any children in Washington could only be the children of those who work for the 'tyrannical government' he hates so much, and are therefore beneath his notice.

"As far as a profile, we're looking at a white male in his mid to late thirties, from the lower income brackets. Minimal education, likely not even finished high school. He's not necessarily geographically local to DC; he may have traveled here to make his point. Considering what he would have been carrying, he would only have traveled by car, not air. But that could put him anywhere on the eastern seaboard. We're checking every hotel register within a two-hundred-mile radius, but if he's close enough, he could be using his own home as a base. As more data come in, we'll be able to provide a more detailed profile."

Peters took charge again. "In light of the content of the message, all government buildings will remain on lockdown and extra Secret Service details have been assigned to the president. While there's been no direct threat against the president, there's been a threat against the government of which he's the head. We'll be reviewing his schedule with his staff and canceling any events deemed potentially dangerous.

"We've set up a public tip line to channel the incoming information." Behind him, a 1–888 number splashed onto the screen. "Anyone who saw anything suspicious yesterday, or overheard a conversation in their local bar, can call and give details. We're putting this number out on every TV and radio station, and it's already going viral online.

"As with any incident like this, there's going to be a lot of incoming information. We're going to need every pair of hands we can get. So we're pulling in everyone we can. If you work in my division and aren't called out into the field for this investigation, you're going to be sifting through data, researching leads, and getting that information out to our field agents for follow-up. Ninety-five percent of the information that comes in isn't going to be relevant, but we need to work through it all and weed out what's not useful to us. We only have so many agents to go out and do time-consuming legwork, so we need to minimize those efforts here in this building. It's going to be new work for many of you, but I have every confidence you'll apply your existing skills to this new task."

The screen flashed back to the bomber's message. "This kind of effort is going to be extremely important," Peters continued, "because we're giving the *Washington Post* the green light to publish this message. We want to know if anyone recognizes the writing or the mind-set behind it. Normally, we wouldn't do this so quickly, but considering the threat of continued attacks, in the name of public safety we won't hesitate. We expect a landslide of tips from that alone. It's going live online at fifteen-hundred hours today to give us enough time to get ready for the onslaught, and will go out in print format in tomorrow's edition. After this meeting, everyone is to meet with their direct supervisors for their assignments. Thank you." Peters moved back into the line of suits at the wall.

Clarkson stepped back up to the mic. "Thank you all for your time and attention. We have a lot of work ahead, and the country's eyes are fixed on us. Now is the time for your very best. Bring that to the table and we'll have the bomber in custody very quickly. Thank you very much." He turned and left the room without a backward glance.

The room instantly filled with chatter. But Meg only silently met Brian's grim gaze.

One angry David taking down his first Goliath . . .

They had their orders. Now it was simply a matter of waiting. But whether it would be for data or to be called out to the next bombing was anyone's guess.

Chapter 7

Staging Area: A designated area where nose work competitors who have not yet searched wait and prepare.

Thursday, April 13, 10:09 AM
Outside Moorefield, Hardy County, West Virginia

The man strode through the deserted barn, flanked by empty stalls, only a scattering of old, rancid straw marking the animals that once lived there. His boot heels echoed against warped and weathered boards, laid down over a century ago in an old-fashioned barn raising. The floor was scarred by decades of cloven hooves of goats and sheep and gouged by iron-shod hooves of horses, while the ceiling overhead was darkened with the smoke of a century of glowing lanterns.

He hardly noticed the stalls or the empty tack room. Instead his eyes trained upward, toward the ceiling and the dark gap that opened at the end of the aisle above the crude wooden ladder.

Grasping the rough-hewn rungs, he hauled himself up the ladder and into the dim space above. All around him, light snuck through cracks edging warped wall boards and around the rectangle of the loading door at the far end. Dust motes danced in the rays of sunlight that fell over the few bales of hay that still remained.

He didn't need the light. He could have made the trip in the dark if need be.

Partway along the length of the hayloft a short ladder rose to a small platform tucked under the roofline. He scaled the few steps easily.

Boxes were neatly stacked under the waterproof cover of a tarp. He flicked back the corner and pulled the closest box toward him. Elongated blocks wrapped in olive green Mylar stamped with CHARGE DEMOLITION M112 WITH TAGGANT (1-¼ LBS COMP C-4) filled the box.

He smiled down at death and destruction sleeping peacefully inside. But he knew just how to bring it to life.

He placed eight of the blocks in an empty box he'd left there for transferring materials and added a bag of blasting caps and a spool of detonation cord. With a flick of his wrist, he flipped the tarp back into place. He settled the box in the crook of one arm and then scaled backward down the ladder one-handed.

Back down on the hayloft floor, he allowed himself a moment to scan the space, seeing it as it had been when he was a boy—full of fragrant hay, row after row of bales stacked to the roof. Closing his eyes for a moment, he could hear his brother's shriek of laughter as he tumbled off the highest bale and fell spread-eagled into the embrace of a loose pile of fragrant strands. Back when they were boys, when snow covered the ground and drifted up against the barn walls, their best place to play had been the warm, dry hayloft.

Back before the fevers and the rash. Before the suffocating pressure of pneumonia. Before the pained wails of his little brother dwindled to wracking sobs and later to breathless gasps. Until even those stopped.

He closed his eyes, turning his back on the memories to face the present.

He returned to the ground floor, his gaze drawn to the open door at the far end of the stalls. Inside the room, the stacks of copper pots and stills that had once been his family's moonshine operation glinted dully in the light cascading in through the single grimy window.

He had a job to do. And he knew exactly who would pay next.

Chapter 8

Depraved Heart Murder: The deliberate commission of a knowingly dangerous act with reckless and wanton unconcern and indifference as to whether anyone is harmed or not. Common law considers such a state of mind just as blameworthy, just as antisocial, and therefore, just as truly murderous as the specific intent to kill or harm.

Friday, April 14, 10:34 AM
IRS Office
Cumberland, Maryland

The line snaked through the foyer and the air practically sparked with impatience and tension. A low hum of irritated muttering filled the room as people scuttled forward a few inches, then abruptly stopped, shifting their weight anxiously, necks craning toward the front of the line. Not a single person wanted to be there—including the employees—but the tax man cometh in just a matter of days, and Uncle Sam wanted his due.

Naomi shifted the squirming baby on her hip, patting his back with a damp palm and glancing for the fourth time in as many minutes at the slightly cockeyed analog clock on the wall that seemed to move with preternatural slowness. Joe started to fret in her arms, pushing clumsily against her shoulders. At nearly a year old, he'd been walking now for a full four weeks. Well, walking was an understatement. She swore he'd gone from crawling to running in only a matter of days. And he didn't like to be held, not now when he could walk.

Joe balled a fist and swiped at one eye, his lower lip starting to quiver.

She patted his back again and bounced him up and down a few times. "Hang on, Joey. Almost there." She glanced toward the front window where sunlight slanted in radiant beams onto the floor. It was the first day since the fall that had been mild enough to play outside without the suffocating bulk of winter jackets and she was just itching to take him out and simply bask in the warmth and the light.

"Next!" The voice was flat, dull, worn down by weeks of nearly there tax deadline hysteria.

The line shuffled forward again. Naomi nudged the diaper bag at her feet, pushing it ahead of them as they crept forward. Only three more people and then it was their turn.

Joe's whimper accompanied a whole body squirm. She clamped her arms around him, familiar with this move and how he'd nearly managed to slither free a few times before. The pressure of her hold only increased his distress and he started to whine. Heat rose in her face as sideways glances began to slide her way.

What kind of parent are you? Can't you control that child? Who's in charge—you or the kid? The crowd's unvoiced thoughts rang in her head.

"Ignore them. Ignoooooooore them . . ." she singsonged to herself, bouncing him again. It's too early, naysayers advised, but she knew the reason he'd been up half the night was his one-year molars coming in. Her normally placid baby was riding a razor's edge of exhaustion right now. And, as a result, so was she. Never a good combination.

An older woman on the opposite side of the cord divider caught her eye, giving her a smile and the universal nod every mother recognizes. *Been there, done that, survived to tell the tale. Know exactly how you feel.* The tangled knot in Naomi's belly loosened slightly as she returned the smile.

"Next!" A different voice. Moving along.

This time after they shuffled forward, she squatted down quickly, rooting around in one of the outer pockets of the diaper bag before finally finding the bag of teething biscuits. She pushed to her feet, staggering slightly as Joe shifted his weight reaching for the biscuit in her hand. Recovering just before slamming into the shoulder of the man beside her, she tried to throw him a bright, apologetic smile, but his narrowed eyes gave no forgiveness or understanding. Her shoulders slumping, she turned away, drawing Joe in, making them both smaller. *You're not a bad parent. You're not a bad parent.*

"Next!"

Suddenly the way before her was clear and the window at the front counter lay ahead. "So close, Joey. We'll talk to the nice man or lady and then we can go home. How about a walk by the duck pond? You love the duck pond. What does the ducky say?"

Joe looked up at her, all rosy cheeks and luminous blue eyes. Cookie paste was smeared around his mouth and over his fingers where he clutched the slobbery chunk of biscuit. "Gak!"

The laugh bubbled up from the pit of her stomach, a sound of joy and love. "That's right, baby. *Quack.*" She didn't even look at the restless crowd surrounding her. The love she had for this precious little man outweighed anything they could throw at her. She pressed a kiss to his cheek, coming away with a faint taste of vanilla. "That's my smart little man."

"Next!"

Oh, thank God . . .

Naomi stooped to grab the diaper bag and then moved to the open window. A young woman sat on the other side of the desk with a pinched expression that spoke of too many hours dealing with angry customers, not enough fresh air, and the stress headache that went along with tax time. "Hi, I'm filling out a final tax return for my father who passed away last year and I don't understand what I need to do with this form." Pulling out a Form 1041, Income Tax Return for Estates and Trusts, Naomi pushed it across the desk to the woman.

Ten minutes later and she was finally done. Forms all filled out, copied, and submitted. She couldn't get out of that stuffy room of cloying tension fast enough.

It was such a relief to finally step out into sunshine. Naomi let the door close behind her, shutting out the discontented buzz, and took a moment to just stand still, listening to birdsong and the sound of the wind blowing through the newly leafed trees surrounding the small strip mall. She took a deep breath, letting the fresh air soothe her.

An odd sound overhead caught her attention, a mechanical sound out of place among the natural sounds of the outdoors. It was a constant whine, deepening and growing louder by the second. A small dark object burst from over the trees to the east, just skimming the upper branches. She followed it with her eyes for a moment until it disappeared from view behind the stepped roofs of the building, the sound of the engine suddenly dropping away. *Odd.*

She shrugged and turned back to her boy. "Okay, Joey, my man. Let's go find those ducks."

She hiked him a little higher on her hip and turned toward her car. She'd only taken a few steps when a deafening blast came from behind her, lifting her off her feet as if an invisible hand picked her up by her collar and tossed her like a rag doll. She had a second of blinding panic and only enough time to clutch her son tighter. Then there was nothing.

Chapter 9

Afterdamp: An unbreathable mixture of carbon dioxide, carbon monoxide, and nitrogen left in a mine after an explosion of firedamp.

Friday, April 14, 12:07 PM
Highway 40
La Vale, Maryland

Meg laid her hand on the back of Hawk's neck, her fingers curving into his soft fur as the helicopter vibrated around them and rotors roared overhead. Hawk looked up from where he lay between her feet and Lacey's body, his tipped head clearly conveying his understanding at her show of nerves. The FBI K-9s were accustomed to air travel, since they were often deployed at a moment's notice for remote tracking incidents. They were used to the noise and sensations of both planes and choppers, and he knew her need to touch him wasn't concern for his welfare. He knew helicopters put Meg on edge in a way that planes didn't. Planes seemed so closed and secure. All it would take in a helicopter is an open door and there'd be nothing between her and the ground but thin air. It would be a long, long fall. . . .

She hadn't always been afraid of heights. In fact, it was that lack of fear that had prompted her six-year-old self to lead her more than willing four-year-old sister out onto the rickety widow's walk on the roof of their grandparents' ancient Nantucket cottage. She'd always wanted to go up there, to stand in the strong sea breeze and look out over the Atlantic Ocean, just like the elegant ladies in long dresses from the stories their grandmother told them. Hundreds of years ago, many of their relatives had spent many hours standing above the wave-battered rocks and wind-swept beaches, watching for the whaling ships that would bring home their husbands after months at sea. Or not.

Curiosity won out that day and the girls slipped away from under their grandparents' watchful eyes. Sneaking up to the rooftop platform wasn't hard, but the wood was frail and gave way the first time Meg leaned her elbows on it to gaze out into the distance. Her own weight sent her tumbling head first off the platform to slide over the roof; only lightning-fast reflexes left her clinging to the eaves, dangling from both arms.

Cara's frantic screams brought their grandparents, and her grandfather had climbed down and hauled her up. The girls had been so terrified that no lecture was required. Meg's lasting scar from the experience was a heart-stopping fear of heights and falling. Some nights, the nightmares came, leaving her dangling in the buffeting wind, certain death only seconds away on the jagged rocks below as her arms ached with the effort to hold on and her screams for help went unanswered.

Meg swallowed hard and blocked the memory from her mind. *Don't look down. Stare at the front cabin wall and just think of it as a really noisy bus ride.*

Meg glanced up and met Brian's somber eyes, staring unblinkingly from under his aviation helmet. They were both mic'd so they could talk during the flight, but no words were needed. He understood both her fear and her refusal to let it stop her from doing her job. On top of that, they'd stood in the same bomb site only four days earlier and she could read the same dread in his eyes that frosted her own blood. *So soon. We barely had time to mentally recover from the last one.* She thought about the brief overview they'd had, complete with fuzzy Google Maps photos of the plaza. *So small. Nothing to shield anyone inside from the full force of the blast. The fatality rate is going to be high.*

She tore her gaze away as the helicopter started to lose altitude, swaying gently from side to side as it lowered toward asphalt. Through the window, dark smoke filled the sky, fading to a lighter gray and then dissipating as it rose.

It had been a wild rush from DC. The call came in only about fifteen minutes after the bomb exploded; it had only taken a few eyewitness reports of a drone spotted flying over the building just before the explosion for the local police to connect this incident with the Whitten Building bombing and to contact the closest FBI field office in Baltimore. Agents were in the car trying to cover the two-hour drive in considerably less than that even as the Forensic Canine Unit was alerted back in DC.

Maryland State Police K-9s were also called in, but were similarly coming from locations spread across the state. The feds had the advantage of access to private flights when needed during an emergency; this was clearly one of those times. The bomber had crossed state lines, so the FBI had jurisdiction. Peters didn't even consider that the locals could and normally would handle it. His task force, his skilled teams—they were going in, no question.

The helicopter gave a small bump as it touched down at one end of a roped-off asphalt parking lot. The engine spooled down immediately, the rotor blades still spinning overhead, suddenly quieter.

Inside the chopper, Meg let out a long, pent-up breath,

the muscles across her shoulders relaxing slightly. Terra firma. She and Brian slipped off their helmets just as the copilot hopped out to open the side door for them.

"Stay low," he ordered from his own crouched position. "We had to land nearly a mile out. Couldn't get any closer." Over his shoulder, Meg could see the distant shops, a rural version of a big box complex. "A state trooper is here to transport you to the site."

The dogs rose as their handlers did, following them to the open helicopter doorway. Meg and Brian jumped out, hunching down to stay well below the rotor blades. A single glance back had the dogs following. Hawk and Lacey waited patiently as leads were clipped onto the top ring on their FBI vests, and then they were moving across the parking lot toward the trooper in beige and khaki standing beside a black SUV with the Maryland crest on the door.

He touched his flat-brimmed hat in greeting as they approached. "Hop in the back. I'll run you to the site."

Meg and Brian got into the SUV, their dogs settling at their feet before they slammed their doors in unison. "How bad is it?" Brian asked.

Steel gray eyes flicked toward the rearview mirror momentarily before turning forward again as the SUV pulled out of the parking lot. "The target was a small strip mall just down Highway 40. Six one-story units, built into a hill, so the units climb in steps up the incline. Looks to me that not being constructed as a single continuous block took away some stability, not that the contractors built the place to be bomb resistant. The IRS office was right in the middle and it collapsed like a house of cards, taking the units on either side of it down too. A taco and breakfast restaurant, and a methadone clinic, both with victims inside."

Meg winced. *Victims—it's not like you didn't see it*

coming. Up ahead, oily black smoke surged upward in huge clouds.

The SUV sped down Highway 40, but the trooper didn't bother with lights and siren. The road was deserted, closed to traffic in the wake of the explosion.

"The explosion ruptured a natural gas line going into the restaurant, which started a three-alarm fire. We got that under control. The firefighters tried to get in to rescue any victims, but in the end, they had to pull back and simply fight the fire from the outside." He paused, his lips flattening into a tight white line. "I'm afraid we brought you folks out here for nothing. I don't think there's anyone left to find alive now."

"We're here, we'll try anyway." Brian's words were flat, but Meg could hear the discouragement tucked under them.

The knot of dread in her belly wound tighter and she glanced down at Hawk, lying quietly with his dark head cushioned on his paws. Finding victims or tracking and finding someone—a suspect or a lost child—that was the most important part of the game for the dogs. They really did consider it a game, and they liked to win. It felt good to win. They also liked to be rewarded, but in many situations the praise from their handlers was enough.

However, when the only people to be found were already dead . . . That scenario was hard on the dogs and they often got discouraged. She'd had searches like that before. The best way to snap a dog out of that kind of funk was for one of the handlers or a law enforcement volunteer to go out and get "lost" so the dog could find them. As far as the dog was concerned, that was still a win.

The clump of police cars and fire trucks ahead told Meg they were nearly there. The trooper didn't even attempt to get close; he simply pulled to the side of the highway. "This is the closest I can get you. A command post is set up on the narrow stretch of grass between the highway and the parking lot. Captain Morrison is running the post until the feds get here to take over, since it's clearly a related case. Good luck."

"Thanks." Brian gave him a curt guy nod, then turned away to open the door and climb out.

They jogged down the road, quickly finding the command post and introducing themselves. Captain Morrison, in his early fifties with buzz cut salt-and-pepper hair, shook hands perfunctorily. "Glad you came. Hope we haven't wasted your time."

"The trooper who brought us in gave us the bare bones. The situation doesn't sound promising," Meg said.

"It's not. Whoever the bomb didn't take out, the fire likely did. We're just waiting for the green light to go in, but that should come any minute. When you go in, any of my men or the firefighters will give you whatever help you need. Ambulance crews are standing by."

Meg's gaze drifted over his shoulder to the back of an ambulance, its doors thrown wide open. A young woman with curly red hair cradling a wailing baby sat on the bumper, her legs dangling. The young mother looked up briefly, residual terror still reflected in her eyes and in the tear tracks that washed down her dirty cheeks. Bending her head, she pressed a kiss to her baby's head and rocked, trying to comfort them both.

"We have some survivors, I see."

Morrison glanced over his shoulder and nodded. "She was beyond lucky. She'd just left the tax office and was outside the door when she spotted the drone coming in. She didn't think much of it, and headed for her car, so she was a good ten or fifteen feet away when the bomb exploded. Knocked her clean off her feet. She managed to not only hold on to her baby, but cushion his fall. They both got banged up pretty good though and she's got a serious case of road rash from where she slid along the pavement from the force of the blast wave. But they're still better off than anyone inside. She says there must have been at least twenty people in there, all adults, maybe more depending on how many workers were in the back."

"The day before taxes are due?" Brian's eyes were fixed on the charred remains of the office. "As many as they could book in to work." He shifted back toward Meg. "This was totally planned for maximum effect. If he'd waited to hit this place next Tuesday, it would have been deserted."

"That's what we think," Morrison agreed. "It's no coincidence this was his next target."

A shout came from near the building and Meg turned to see a firefighter in a red helmet waving an arm in their direction. "And that's the signal. Good luck."

"Thanks." Meg swallowed back any misgivings and looked down to find Hawk's eyes already fixed on her. "Come, Hawk. Let's get to work."

Friday, April 14, 1:22 PM
Strip Mall, Highway 40
La Vale, Maryland

Meg followed one of the state police handlers and his Belgian Malinois through what was left of the breakfast bar's front door and back out into daylight. Hawk followed two steps behind her, dejection in every movement. His head drooped and his tail hung limply, his steps dragging. Meg's blue coveralls were coated in soot and she knew her face had to be as well, from the gritty air inside the restaurant. She paused, letting Hawk catch up to her, and ran a gloved hand down the black fur on the back of his neck. It came away smeared with soot.

She caught sight of Brian, between squad cars still in place with lights swirling and flashing. He sat on a concrete curb at the edge of the parking lot, Lacey sitting between his knees, her chin on his thigh as he rubbed his hands back and forth over her blackened fur.

"Come on, Hawk, let's go see Lacey."

Hawk's ears perked up at Lacey's name and his pace quickened for a second or two before slowing again.

She frowned down at him, but kept moving across the parking lot until they reached Brian.

He looked up at her. Soot coated his face, except for white lines radiating from his eyes and bracketing his mouth. "We struck out in the tax office. Any luck in the restaurant?"

Meg let out a long, discouraged breath as she sat down next to him on the curb, set down her helmet and heavy gloves, and coaxed her dog closer to pet and praise. "Not one. They didn't have a chance. There were a few who were closer to the door, like they were trying to get out, but some were under rubble from the explosion. And even if they'd survived the bomb, they didn't survive the fire from the gas line break. We found fifteen."

"Twenty-two for us. Don't know how many were in the methadone clinic; the staties are in there. I'm hoping no more than a few. Hopefully it was too early in the morning for addicts to get out of bed and go for treatment." He dropped his head to rest his forehead between Lacey's ears. "Who the fuck is doing this?"

Meg's eyebrows shot upward. It was unusual for Brian to swear. Normally, he was the happy-go-lucky one in the unit, always with a quick grin or a stupid joke to raise the spirits. For him to get sucked in to the abyss normally reserved for others said something about what he and Lacey had just gone through. She laid a hand over his forearm and squeezed gently. "Bad?"

He only turned his head far enough to fix her with a sidelong gaze. "Bad doesn't cover it. Most of what we found was in pieces. Not that what you had must have been any better. Most of what you found had to be burned to a crisp."

"Not most. All." Her gaze rose to the remains of the building. Now only wisps of gray spiraled from the depths of the wreckage, but the nightmare remained contained inside. "I want to hurt him for doing this."

"Get in line. And I guarantee we're not the only ones who want that. Jesus H. Christ, Meg, I understand having a grudge against the government, but this isn't how you solve it. You don't fix your issue by killing innocent civilians." His hand curled into a fist, the muscles under her hand tightening to rock. "He can't be right in the head."

The anger rose so violently in Meg it caught her off guard and left her shaking. "Don't you go making excuses for him," she spat. "He is one hundred percent responsible for this carnage."

Brian turned his arm under her hand and caught her fingers in his, held on in solidarity. "Hold up, that's not what I meant. And I agree he's responsible. I didn't mean he was insane, just twisted. He sees his actions as justified because his almighty cause is important. Everyone else is just collateral damage. And now he's hit the IRS and the Department of Agriculture. Who's next? The Treasury? Health and Human Services? Veterans Affairs? The DoD?"

"Any of them." Meg pulled her fingers free to scrub both her hands over her face. She pulled them away to find the soot smeared over her palms. "All of them. Hell, Brian, who knows?"

"Maybe we'll be lucky and he'll feel free to talk to that *Post* reporter again."

Meg turned to look at Brian with speculation. "You think that guy knows something?"

"McCord? The thought had crossed my mind. Why did

the bomber pick him? Does he know him personally? Professionally? Did he pick his name out of a hat?" His eyes narrowed to slits. "Or is McCord really the bomber?"

"You mean he sent himself that letter because he knew it would be untraceable through that system?"

"It would be pretty smart."

"I don't know much about him," Meg said. "But I've read some of his articles. He's clearly got a lot more education than the bomber seems to have."

"Or he's faking that lack of refinement. But I'm just tossing out ideas. What I can tell you is that I've seen him in a dog park not far from my place. He must live nearby and he brings his golden to the park. A young one, so they come often to burn off energy. I recognized him from his byline picture."

"Really . . ." Meg drew the word out, her eyes narrowed on the asphalt in front of her, but seeing nothing.

"Feel like doing a little off the books investigation?"

"Actually, yes, I do." She turned and met Brian's eyes, some of the weight of their nightmare search through the restaurant finally starting to slide from her shoulders. "Look out, Mr. McCord. You're not going to know what hit you until it's already run you down."

Chapter 10

Schutzhund: A dog sport developed in the early 1900s emphasizing athleticism and excellence in tracking, obedience, and protection. The dog must never bite unless it or the handler is attacked, and it must always stop biting on command.

Friday, April 14, 7:14 PM
S Street Dog Park
Washington, DC

Meg pushed through the wrought iron gate into one of the two park entry and exit vestibules. Double-gated to ensure no dog could escape, it was only big enough to hold one dog-owner pair at a time.

"Ready, Saki?"

Saki raised her wide head, gazing up at Meg with vibrant blue eyes. The excited tongue lolling out of her mouth and the quiver running through her body pretty much answered Meg's question.

"In we go then." Meg bent and unclipped the leash from Saki's pink leather collar before giving her lower back a rub. Then she unlatched the gate and held it open. "Okay, Saki, play!" Saki was off like a bullet toward the pack of dogs on the far side of the park. Meg watched her go—a small American bully, she was a "stubby" dog standing only about eighteen inches at the shoulder, but she could run surprisingly fast for such short legs. While pit bulls weren't outlawed in DC, many people still believed the "breed" was dangerous. Meg wanted to sit each of them down and explain which end of the leash was the problem. It wasn't any breed that should be legislated; it was the people who owned them. Saki was living proof of the gentle nature of many pit bulls. Her cleft upper palate—revealing an underbite of lower teeth and incisors—softened her look and made people naturally less afraid of her. A lovely soft smoky-gray with a white chest and belly and those brilliant blue eyes, she was short of leg with wide shoulders and a deep chest. Her diminutive size made her less threatening, and once people got to know her, they realized what a gentle girl she was. Saki was hands down the best therapy dog she and her sister had ever trained, and was a living testament to her breed.

Watching Saki safely integrating into the pack racing around the park, Meg surveyed the space around her. The park was triangular, fitting neatly into the plot formed by the intersection of S Street, New Hampshire Avenue NW, and 17th Street NW. Encircled by a waist-high wrought iron fence, the park enclosed facilities for both canine and human. The largest part of the park was the huge open space where the dogs now ran. Carpeted with K9Grass it was a tough, long-lasting, maintenance-free surface for the dogs to romp on.

Flowering cherry trees were planted at the edge of the turf bordering 17th Street. Each was encircled with an iron bench for owners to sit and watch while their dogs played only feet away. Overlooked by historic brownstones on the west, it was a lovely, peaceful oasis in the middle of a bustling metropolitan city.

Meg took a deep breath of fresh air. Hours away from the bomb site this morning and even after a very long shower, she could still smell char in her nostrils, so the sweet smell of cherry blossoms was a welcome relief.

She scanned the owners around her. There were about twelve dogs using the park right now and each one of them had at least one owner present. She knew what Mc-Cord looked like from his byline picture, but didn't see anyone even remotely resembling him. As a dog person, she automatically looked over the dogs; if you saw one you recognized, then you knew the owner was also present. She remembered Brian's statement that McCord had a golden retriever, so she scanned the dogs with that in mind—not a golden among them. Well, there was never any guarantee he'd come tonight. Or maybe he'd already come and gone. She'd tried to gauge when he might visit based on a standard workday, but he was a reporter and they often worked weird hours. So she might have to try again tomorrow. Or the next day.

Saki was part of her camouflage. Extremely aware of the picture in the *Washington Post*, Meg wanted to stay under the radar. There was less chance she'd be recognized with a different dog, so she had left Hawk at home after his hard day to rest with Blink and brought Saki out to play. For nothing, as it turned out, but she couldn't regret the outing as she watched Saki race a beagle to the far end of the park with a happy bark.

Still keeping an eye on Saki as she played, Meg strolled along the line of cherry trees, stopping every once in a while to simply breathe in the freshness of spring. She loved DC in April. After a long hard winter, the city came alive again in young, tender grass, bright green leaves, and blossoms bursting from every—

Meg stopped dead in her tracks at the sight of a tall man standing on the corner of New Hampshire Avenue NW and S Street, a golden retriever at his knee. A young, very bouncy golden retriever. Sitting down on a bench under a cherry tree, her gaze stayed locked on him as the light changed and he and the dog crossed and quickly traversed S Street. Circling onto 17th, he entered the park through the same gate she and Saki had just come through minutes before.

She'd taken the time before leaving home to Google McCord. She already knew a little about him—he'd become a household name for a short time when the tragedy in Haditha, Iraq, and his part in blowing it wide open came to light—but wanted to know more. He carried the general reputation of a hotshot, but that didn't surprise her. That was exactly the type of personality that tended to go to war zones to get the story. Danger probably gave him a thrill.

But what she'd read surprised her. In interviews he was more thoughtful than expected, and showed honest emotion when talking about his experiences in Iraq. But he'd been ruthless when he talked about the investigation into the American marines who killed twenty-four civilian men, women, and children in Haditha. War was one thing, as was protecting yourself against an armed combatant, but killing innocent children and harmless, unarmed elders was inexcusable. He was clearly at peace with his part in revealing the cruelties done by his own countrymen.

As part of the FBI and as an ex-cop, Meg's distrust of the media was bone deep, but she grudgingly respected what he'd done. When he'd finally come home, instead of using that notoriety to pave the way to high profile stories, he'd nearly gone underground. He still wrote for the *Post*, and his stories often graced the front page, but it was done quietly. There were no rounds of media interviews, and no best-selling tell-all about his experiences. For all intents and purposes, he'd closed the door on that part of his life and moved on.

Inside the vestibule, McCord released the retriever and then pulled open the gate into the park. He stood for a moment just inside the fence watching the dog run toward the constantly shifting pack. He coiled the leash and stuffed it away, and then jammed his hands in his pockets, his stance stiff, and his shoulders riding high toward his ears, a picture of stress.

Not sure how long he'd stay at the park, Meg pushed up from the bench and strolled casually toward him. She'd learned long ago that nothing made conversation with a stranger easier than dog talk. She pulled Saki's leash out of her pocket, casually and unmistakably marking herself as a pet owner. She stopped just a few feet from him, watching the dogs in companionable silence for a moment. "Is that your golden?" she asked, turning slightly toward him.

He turned to look at her. Dressed casually in blue jeans and a denim shirt with the cuffs rolled up his forearms, he had dark blond hair left slightly shaggy and clear blue eyes shielded by wire-rimmed glasses. It gave him an attractive yet studious appearance. The lines around his eyes only magnified that look and gave him character. *Eye on the prize, Meg. He's not a man, he's a reporter.* Even in her mind, the descriptor dripped acid.

"Yeah, he's mine." Suspicion laced McCord's words. "Did he do something?"

Meg stopped coiling and uncoiling the leash in surprise at his tone. "Do something? No. He's just a beautiful dog."

"Good." He let out a long sigh. "Sorry, he's been driving me crazy lately. Gets into everything, never seems to sit still."

"How old is he?"

"Ten months."

"Ah . . ."

He sent her a sidelong look. "What does 'Ah . . .' mean?"

"I've seen more than a few puppies in my time, quite a

few goldens among them. They tend to be high energy and rambunctious. Is he neutered yet?"

He turned and faced her full-on now, hands on his hips. "Are you one of those militant dog types?"

In her surprise at his sudden change in attitude, the fact that he was a reporter totally slipped Meg's mind, and she didn't know whether to laugh or step back a pace in alarm. Someone was riding a fine edge tonight. So she went with laughter. "No, although I'm in favor of spaying and neutering. We have enough animals out on the streets as it is. Why I asked is because a lot of goldens really settle down after the procedure and become much calmer. Most owners do it around eight to ten months of age for bigger dogs, so he's old enough if you wanted to take that step. Or were you planning on breeding him?"

He continued to stare at her. "You know, this is kind of a pushy conversation. I don't even know your name."

She pasted on a sunny smile—hoping it was convincing—and held out her hand. "Meg. See that stubby gray pittie out there? That's Saki. She's a certified therapy dog. My sister and I train dogs and she runs an obedience school."

"So not pushy, just informed." His smile was sheepish as he shook her hand. "Clay. So it's something that could calm Cody down?"

"Can't promise it, but most of the time, yes. Some obedience lessons might go a long way too, if you're interested."

"I've been thinking about it. But I don't know where to start."

Meg pulled a card out of her pocket; she always carried a few on her for just this scenario. "You could start here; this is my sister's card." She handed it to him and then made a show of staring at him as if puzzled. "You seem familiar to me somehow. Are you on TV?"

"Close. I'm an investigative reporter at the *Washington Post*. You've maybe seen my picture with my byline."

"That's it. Clay . . . Clay McCord, right? The one named after the cowboy."

He drew back in surprise. "You know who Clay McCord is? Not me, I mean, the 'real' one."

"My dad has a thing for old TV westerns. As soon as anything was released on video, it went right onto his Christmas list. I grew up on *Rawhide* and *Gunsmoke*. Or, in your case, *The Deputy*."

"It's not one of the better known shows. Most people don't connect the name."

"Did your parents do it on purpose?"

"Name me that?" He rolled his eyes, giving his head an exasperated shake. "My dad grew up with the show when it aired. He was just the right age to be influenced by it. There was this deputy, who always got his man, who just happened to have the same last name as him. I think he thought about him for a long time as an older brother to look up to. So when I was born, he pushed for the name. My mother only found out later who I was named after because she'd never heard of the show or the character. She was not amused that her son was named after a cowboy."

"Hold on . . . Clay McCord. Aren't you the reporter the bomber contacted? That was your name attached to the story?"

"That's me."

Meg leaned in as if they were sharing confidences. "And the FBI let you publish it?"

"Look, Meg, you seem really nice, but I came to get away from the job and to get some fresh air. Not to talk shop and rehash my family history." He started to turn away from her. "Enjoy your night."

She reached out a hand to stop him, pulling him back

around. By the time he'd turned around, temper sparking in his eyes, her FBI identification was in her other hand, flipped open and in his face. "Some of us can't get away from the job. Some of us had to deal with the second bombing just a few hours ago." She flipped the ID shut and slid it back into her pocket. "Meg Jennings, Forensic Canine Unit, FBI."

Temper died away and a mixture of compassion and caution filled his face. "Agent Jennings—"

"Handlers aren't agents. We're highly trained canine experts."

"So you're not really law enforcement."

Part of her knew her own spike of irritation at his misunderstanding wasn't really reasonable, but she stepped up and into him anyway, her voice low. "We're as law enforcement as it gets. On top of that, I was Richmond PD K-9 patrol for six years before I took a step sideways into the FBI. We're not bumbling animal lovers. We're K-9."

McCord took a step backward, his hands raised in mock surrender. "Okay, sorry. Didn't mean any offense." He stared at her for a moment. "You were at the other bomb site this morning, the one in Maryland?"

"Yes." The word was short and tight.

"Bad?"

"Never seen worse."

"I'm sorry." His face went feral with sharp eyes and bared teeth. "I'd like to get this son of a bitch, to show he can't get away with this."

"Trust me, after this week my whole team is in complete agreement." Meg blew out a long breath and forced herself to relax. She knew the stress of the day was catching up with her, putting her on the same razor's edge as McCord. "So give a girl who's had a horrific day a break and help me out here. Why do you think he picked you? And why the *Washington Post*? Why not the *New York Times,* which sells way more papers?"

McCord winced. "Thanks for that little reminder." Cody raced over to him with a bright green tennis ball locked in his jaws. He dropped it at McCord's feet and looked up at him with eyes full of hope. "Where on earth did you get this?" Cody just gave a whine in response. "Okay, bud, you got it." Picking up the ball, he lobbed it across the green space, grinning like a kid when Cody took off after it, six other dogs, including Saki, joining in. "Truthfully, we actually wondered the same thing, especially when it became clear we were the only paper with his message."

Meg appreciated his ability to quickly change gears. "And what conclusion did you come to?"

"We had a picture no one else had. An FBI K-9 handler . . ." His words petered off and he stepped back a pace to stare at her, hard. Then his head whipped toward the pack of dogs. "Which one did you say is yours?"

"The blue American bully," she said. She waited for him to face her before she finished. "I left Hawk, my search and rescue black Lab, at home. Yes, that was us."

"Christ almighty."

"You didn't like that picture either?" Meg asked sweetly. Too sweetly. "It didn't win my appreciation to be caught at that moment."

"No, I'm thinking about what you've been through in the past four days. What your dog's been through. That must have been hell. I'm sorry."

Meg blinked at him, at a complete loss of words. Not only was he not pumping her for information, he was being sympathetic. Silence weighed heavily until she finally found words to fill it. "You have nothing to be sorry for."

"Not me personally, but anyone with an ounce of compassion would be sorry about what you must have seen on Tuesday. And today had to be worse."

"It was. Not a single survivor inside those walls."

"It sounds like some war zones I've been in, so I won't ask you for details. I know you can't give me any and your job doesn't set you up for them anyway. You try to find the survivors. When it comes to details on the perp, that's not your wheelhouse."

"No, it's not. Although I can tell you a thing or two about him from the destruction he leaves."

"You don't need to tell me. He's a cold son of a bitch. Look, I can promise you this. If I hear anything, *anything at all,* I'll make sure your superiors are in the loop immediately."

"No matter what? Or only on the grounds that they'll let you publish it?"

McCord's jaw locked, as if he was struggling to keep calm in the face of her continued disbelief. "No matter what. Look, this is bigger than me or my paper. Yes, my editor and I made a case for publishing it based on how that worked for the FBI in the Unabomber case. And after some discussion, the FBI agreed it would be best to let the public read it and see if it rang bells with anyone. But it was theirs no matter what. Here, let's make a deal." He pulled out his wallet, drawing a business card from it, and held it out to Meg. "If I hear anything, I promise to pass it up the line. If you hear anything, you let me know. Maybe we can do a little off the books research if needed."

Meg fought back the tide of suspicion that rose at his words long enough to take his card, only to hold it by the edge as if it was soaked in a corrosive chemical. "You're seriously proposing a partnership? Between the FBI and a reporter? I can see what's in it for you, if you can pump the FBI for info, but what's in it for me?"

"I'm thinking a little cooperation might not be amiss. Our end goal is the same, isn't it? I'm a conduit; you're the long arm of the law. You keep me in the loop, I can make sure any message you want gets out there, either quietly or as a sixty-point headline. And I have contacts. Contacts who would never talk to law enforcement of any kind, but with information the FBI would find useful. So maybe if we work together, we can make a little magic."

"My version of magic has that bastard locked in a cage on forty-eight counts of murder one," Meg said. She studied Clay for a moment, weighing her options. *Did she dare trust him? Maybe not, but considering what was at stake, an uneasy partnership for the greater good might be the only way. But the moment he dropped the ball....* She jammed his card in her pocket and then handed him one of her own cards. "My cell is on there. That's the best way to reach me because we're so often on the move."

"Thanks. And I like the way you think, because right now, I have a bad feeling that we're not done at forty-eight. I'm not sure how many more he'll get in before you nail his ass to the wall. I just pray to God you nail him soon."

Meg hoped so too. And hoped she hadn't just made a deal with the devil to make it happen.

Chapter 11

Hasty Search: A search designed to cover the most likely places a subject might be located in the least possible time. It is usually the first search tactic used.

Saturday, April 15, 7:11 AM
McCord residence
Washington, DC

"All right, all right. Just hold on a minute." McCord nearly stumbled over Cody dancing around his legs at the bedroom door as he clumsily pushed his glasses up his nose. Pushing past the excited retriever, he shuffled toward the kitchen with only one thought in his head.

Coffee.

Blessedly, the coffeemaker was ready with a full pot of manna-from-heaven waiting for him. He poured a cup and braved the heat for two large swallows, then leaned back against the counter to let the caffeine start to make its way into his bloodstream. He had less than a second though, before a cool, wet nose pushed against his hand and silky fur brushed over his knees. He cracked open one eye and stared down into wide brown eyes above a smiling mouth and lolling tongue. "Okay, I get it. Give me a second. And the coffee's coming with us."

Stumbling back into the bedroom, he snagged yesterday's jeans off the armchair in the corner and pulled them on over his boxers. He leashed the dog, grabbed his coffee, keys, a jacket, made sure he had enough poop bags, and then they were heading down the stairs.

Once again he questioned his sanity over getting a dog when he lived in a converted third-floor apartment in an old Victorian brownstone. *You couldn't have been that lonely*, he chided himself as Cody pulled hard on the leash when they burst through the front doors and out into cool spring sunshine. He barely had time to pluck his copy of the *Washington Post* off the front step before Cody was yanking him down the street.

Fifteen minutes later they were back inside, Cody having done his business and now tucking into his bowl of kibble. McCord threw himself—carefully, coffee was liquid gold at this hour of the morning—down onto his leather sofa. Wrapping both hands around his second cup, he drank deeply and then let his head fall back against the cushions.

He'd been unsettled when he came back from the park last night and was restless well into the wee hours of the morning. He wasn't sure if it was the nonstop news coverage of the second bombing attack, or remembering the haunted look in Meg Jennings's eyes when she talked about not being able to get away from the job. He'd seen pictures from the bombing, but only from helicopter flybys; the FBI and the Maryland State Police weren't letting anyone into that site, let alone reporters looking for a hot story. She'd been on site, had gone into that building, seen the victims. And worse. Early in his career, he'd covered an arson spree that had taken out a number of empty warehouses back home in Portland. Except one of the fires had taken out a drunk, homeless man. He'd never forget the sight and smell of the body being removed from the burntout skeleton of the warehouse.

But thirty-seven people died in that attack alone.

He reached for the remote control sitting on the old, battered sea trunk that served as his coffee table. His hand hovered for a moment—did he really want to immerse himself back in the tidal pool of pundits and political theories? Right-wing activists, paramilitary groups, homegrown terrorists. Reporting the news was one thing; seriously analyzing it was something else. But the unending drive to fill the airwaves and get higher and higher ratings by constantly keeping the nation petrified and off balance wasn't right. It made him second-guess his choice of career.

"Thirty-five and you're already too old and jaded to play the game, McCord. This is when you're supposed to be coming into your prime."

He snatched up the remote, flipping on the top national cable news channel. As usual, two commentators were rehashing yesterday's bombing. Thirty seconds told him nothing new had surfaced in the case.

Setting his coffee down on the trunk, he picked up the *Post* and started to leaf through it quickly. Nothing new there either, at least not that he hadn't already known or written himself. His article on the second bombing was front page, above the fold with a screaming headline: HOMEGROWN BOMBER STRIKES AGAIN—37 DEAD IN SECOND ATTACK.

McCord swore under his breath when he saw the smiling, lively pictures of some of the victims clustered below the fold almost like an afterthought. He'd lost that argument in spades: He'd wanted the pictures of the victims front and center—they were the story, not the bomber. But the Powers That Be didn't agree and put them below the fold. The sensationalism of print media wasn't that different from the TV stations.

What was missing from his story, and everyone else's, was the single eyewitness the FBI had under wraps. By the time the story leaked to the media that one person just narrowly escaped the bombing, the FBI had him or her safely hidden away. That eyewitness was their best informant, and they wanted to keep that witness out of the hands of the media. They didn't think the bomber would go after the witness—his job was done with the actual bombing—but they knew his or her life would be hell if the media ever caught on.

McCord's attention was caught by the sound of singing and he looked up to the video footage of a mass of candles filling the darkness and the strains of "Amazing Grace." The title "National Mall Candlelight Vigil" stretched across the bottom of the screen. The footage showed the people of America mourning their dead, leaving flowers and cards outside the Whitten Building and at the side of the road near the police roadblock on Highway 40 in La Vale.

How many more dead before they caught this sicko who saw his own needs as more important than anyone else's? An idea sparked in McCord's head for a piece—the bomber versus the dedicated personnel that tracked him. He'd never get near the FBI's Behavioral Analysis Unit until they made themselves available for a profile, but he could talk to some of the best psychological experts in DC, then compare and contrast the mind of such a twisted killer to those who swore to get him, people like Meg. People who were affected and invested, who needed to catch him to put themselves at peace. Who wouldn't—who *couldn't*—rest until he was caught. It was a great way to highlight those who tried to stay out of the limelight. Sometimes in the media, evil trumped good simply because of the amount of time spent focused on it. Time to highlight the good, to bring it out of the shadows.

He reached for his laptop to make a few notes before the idea fizzled. He quickly booted up, started a new document with his notes, and saved it for future reference.

Seeing as he was already online, even this early in the morning, he flipped over to his e-mail to see if there was anything new since he last checked at three in the morning.

His breath caught at the sight of the only new e-mail: *SecureDrop message for C. McCord.*

It doesn't necessarily have to be him. It could be about anything else, or it could be a tip to his identity.

Or it could be him. Find. Out.

He logged on to the web site, cursing the mere seconds it took to authenticate him and take him to the SecureDrop site. There was a single message listed for his access. He took a deep breath and opened it.

Mr. McCord,

You DISRESPECT ME sir. I gave you a great story and when I looked at your paper in the library I couldn't even see it on the rack because it was so low down on the page. Even worst, I give you a great picture and then you didn't print it. I spent good money on a camera so youd know I ment bisness, and I had to reduce payload too. Should I take my bisness to the New York Times?

Did you like the cumotion at the Infernal Revenue Service? I have pictures of that to but maybe Ill send em somewhere else. The IRS targeting of Conservative and religious groups was more than a scandal, it is an outright terrorist attack against the American people! IRS can seize anything it wants, and take away any money a man can make. Nothing is safe. Nothing is sacred. Even what's past down. The U.S. government has set itself above the people and exercised its global influences unlawfully against the Constitution. And they publish shit like "Public education is the cornerstone of conflict management efforts." Or "application of aversive conditioning techniques may provide immediate

relief for agricultural damage and provide public satisfaction that a problem is being addressed". When any
fool knows the best answer is a bullet. Shouldn't need
no dammed permit either.

   If you want my pictures from yesterday you need to
ask me nicely.

   Sincerely,

   ~ This Angry David has taken down two Goliaths.
Stay tuned.

McCord took the time to pick up his coffee and guzzle
half of it in hopes of instant clarity. He glanced at his cell,
knowing he should already be calling his editor. But he
gave himself a moment to study the message first, before
any arguments with the offices upstairs and discussions
with the FBI. Just to study it and learn its secrets.

The arrogant yet condescending tone of the first message was mostly gone. In its place was anger, pure and simple. *You're not getting the attention you want and it's
pissing you off. Meg and the rescuers were highlighted, the
victims were highlighted, you were not.* The call not to
print the photo of the Whitten Building could be laid at
the feet of the FBI. Printing the message had a purpose—to
get public input into the killer's identity—but they didn't
want to give out details about how the crimes were being
committed. In this day and age of Internet searches, excess
information could spawn copycats, and that was the last
thing they wanted. Not to mention they didn't want to
sensationalize some of the victims' last seconds as they
stood in the windows, staring up at the drone. Publishing
the message served a purpose; publishing the picture did
not. McCord didn't disagree.

He considered the comment about agricultural damage
and weighed the possibilities he was referring to his first
target. "The best answer is a bullet"? That didn't make

any sense. He'd used a bomb, much more heavy handed than a bullet.

It was the last line that filled his stomach with dread. "This Angry David has taken down two Goliaths. Stay tuned." He wasn't finished. Not even close. Time to call in the cavalry.

He picked up his cell phone and speed-dialed the call, waiting impatiently while it was picked up. "Sykes, it's McCord." He paused as a sleepy, irritated voice filled his ear. "Yes, I know it's not even eight yet. I need you to meet me at the office. He's contacted me again. I'll be there in twenty." He ended the call before Sykes could pepper him with questions. Better to just deal with the whole thing in one shot. And if he knew Sykes—and after five years working under him, he thought he did—he could bet money on the fact Sykes was on the phone with the brass at that second and they were all going to meet in twenty minutes at the *Post*.

Cody dropped his favorite stuffed toy—a comical raccoon with ridiculously oversized eyes—at McCord's feet. McCord ruffled his ears and gave him a thumping pat on the side. "Sorry, buddy, not this morning, but maybe you can sweet-talk Pattie into some extra play time." He made a mental note to call his dog walker from the car, telling her he had to head into the office unexpectedly and would need her again today. Luckily for him, she was extremely flexible, and had a soft spot for both him and Cody. "If not, when I get home again." He stood. "Whenever that will be," he mumbled under his breath, as if his dog could understand him.

He quickly pulled on clean clothes and grabbed his phone, laptop, and car keys. "Okay, bud, see you later. Be back as soon as I can." He tried to ignore what he thought was a look of sadness from where the dog curled up in

McCord's old recliner. He turned to the door, but stopped with his fingers on the handle. *Why not?*

Then he dug a card out of his wallet and quickly keyed the number and a short text into his phone: **He contacted me again. Heading to the office now to discuss with the brass. Will likely be reporting it within the hour. Keep it under your hat, but will let you know more when I can.**

Chapter 12

Distractors: Items like food or favorite toys placed in search areas to confuse or distract working scent dogs.

Saturday, April 15, 9:34 AM
Forensic Canine Unit; J. Edgar Hoover Building
Washington, DC

"Greg, got a second?"

Greg Patrick looked up from digging through a desk drawer on the far side of the office. "Sure. What's up?"

Meg crossed the office to him, Hawk ambling along behind. "Can I pick your brain for a minute?"

Greg gave up the drawer search and dropped into his chair on an exhausted exhale. "Sure. What do you need?"

Meg pulled up a chair and rolled close so she could keep her voice low. "Were you out at Cumberland yesterday?"

"Just back from it. We haven't even made it home yet. Worked all night."

"That explains why you look so beat." Meg glanced down at the German shepherd at Greg's feet, who was cheerfully greeting Hawk with sniffs and enthusiastic wagging. "How's Ryder?"

"He's the Energizer bunny. He'll grab a catnap while we travel and be good for hours. I wish I could sleep on planes like he does. Twenty seconds in the air and he's out like a

light. Meanwhile I feel like something the cat dragged in."
He stifled an enormous yawn behind his hand. "Sorry."

"No need to apologize. You know I get it. Now . . . I
know it's too soon for any of the evidence from yesterday's
attack, but what about Tuesday's? I heard you and Ryder
had some good finds at the Whitten Building."

Greg glanced across the room to where Brian and Lauren sat, their dogs under their desks, as they combed
through teetering stacks of files. "What makes you think I
have information on that?"

While the different arms of the FBI's canine program—
criminal apprehension, explosives detection, and forensic
applications, which included both their own Human Scent
Evidence Team and the Victim Recovery Team for human
remains—had only minimal interaction because of the significant differences in their work, Meg, as a former police
officer, had the strongest connection to the FBI Police officers who made up the other two sections of the program.
She and Greg often stopped to touch base about each
other's cases or to discuss law enforcement issues outside
the Bureau.

"Because I know you," Meg said. "You're like me—you
don't like to leave a case unfinished. Finding evidence is
only part of the job. You want the whole story and want
to know what the evidence tells us." She scooted forward
another few inches, letting her own intensity rise to the
surface for him to see. "I was in there with the victims,
Greg. I helped the live ones and had to turn away from the
dead. I need to know too."

He met her gaze for a few seconds, his lips drawn into a
thin downward curve. "All right. But this is between you
and me until the data is officially released. I wheedled the
results out of a tech downstairs, and I don't want to get
her in trouble."

"Deal. Now spill."

Greg turned his chair so his voice wouldn't carry toward the far side of the room. "The bomb was pretty standard, but effective. C-4 with RDX boosters and PETN detonation cord."

Meg's brows snapped together in a frown. "I was expecting something more homegrown."

"The problem with homegrown bombs like Timothy McVeigh's is that they're big and heavy to get the kind of bang you want. It took a van with seven thousand pounds of explosives to tear apart the Alfred P. Murrah Building."

"Considering the bomb was delivered by drone, fifty pounds probably wasn't doable, let alone seven thousand."

"Not even kind of. The max carrying capacity of the drone was likely ten or fifteen pounds. Thus something lighter, yet still effective."

"But C-4 doesn't just grow on trees. How did he get his hands on it? Commercial use?"

"Actually, we know exactly where he got it from. They found enough of the chemical tag added to the C-4 to make it traceable." Greg's gaze shot over her shoulder to check the room before returning to her face. "This particular taggant marks it as military grade C-4."

Meg stifled a sound of surprise. "Military? How on earth did—" She cut herself off as a memory crystallized. "Wait a minute. That theft in West Virginia late last fall, the one at the army reserve in . . . where was it?"

"Wheeling?"

"That's it. Wasn't explosive material stolen from there?"

"That's what I heard. But the army, or CID, as the case may be, was very hush-hush about the whole thing. After the initial reports, which the media jumped all over, I never heard anything more about it. But now you have to wonder."

"You certainly do. Okay, so the taggant tracks the C-4. Any way to track the other materials?"

"The detonator cord and primer and blasting caps are all pretty generic, but with further testing they might be able to find a signature. But my money's on the C-4 as the biggest lead."

"Where are they going with that?"

"I'm not sure. I don't even know if anyone has connected the dots yet with Wheeling. Remember, I'm not on the inside track on that part of the investigation. As far as the agents are concerned, we've done our bit."

"I really wish they'd let us help more. And not keep us so compartmentalized because . . ." She trailed off as a thought occurred to her.

Greg's eyes narrowed on her face. "What?"

"I might have an inside angle on some info."

Greg leaned back in his chair, suspicion carved deeply into his haggard face. "How?"

"My old sergeant back at Richmond PD. He's ex-army."

"*I'm* ex-army. That's not going to help us."

"He's ex-CID."

"Now that puts a new spin on it."

"I haven't seen Sarge for a while. Maybe it's time for a visit. You know someone will make the Wheeling connection at some point, but it might not be for a day or two, especially if they are waiting on other evidence." Meg glanced back toward Brian and Lauren, heads down, paging laboriously through files. "You remember what Peters said about everyone in the division being put to work scouring tip line info and back files. I'm chained to a desk and it's killing me. I need to be out there doing something." She braced her hands on the arms of the chair. "So that's what I'm going to do." She pushed to her feet before pointing a single finger at Greg. "Not one word of this."

Greg held up both hands as if in surrender. "Hey, I'm so tired, I'm pretty sure we never had this conversation." He pinned her with a steely look. "I'm pretty sure I never passed on any results either."

"I certainly don't have any recollection of it." She grinned at him. "Thanks, Greg. Appreciate it. Now go home and get some sleep."

"Don't have to tell me twice."

Meg watched Greg trudge out of the office, Ryder at his side, before returning to her desk and the depressingly high pile of paperwork. She glanced at the cell phone sitting beside her keyboard, hoping that in the few minutes she'd been talking to Greg a new text had come through, but it remained frustratingly silent and dark.

She'd left it lying screen-up and had been surreptitiously keeping an eye on it since coming into the office an hour ago. Too restless to sleep well last night, she figured she'd do better coming in to help with the ongoing task force efforts. The tip line was swamped, and it took significant manpower to sift through all the tips, separating the wheat from the chaff, the crazies from the legitimate tippers. And then there were the thousands of files on people who sent threatening or furious notes to the various government departments, any of who could be the bomber before he started killing to get attention. Doing something was better than doing nothing, but within thirty minutes she was getting restless with the feeling that she wasn't actually accomplishing anything.

Welcome to investigative work. Sifting through data isn't sexy, but sometimes it's the way to find the bad guy.

She'd been given stacks of files to comb through, filled

with people with grudges against the two departments already hit.

> *George Stanworth, Las Cruces, New Mexico.*
> *To: Department of Agriculture . . . Your require-*
> *ment to file quarterly is entirely unreasonable*
> *and untenable. And the fines levied against hard-*
> *working, honest folk are crippling. . . .*

> *Debbie Pickering, Timber Lake, South Dakota.*
> *To: Internal Revenue Service . . . Paying taxes is*
> *like paying you off. When you pay someone off it*
> *should be for something, but we get nothing in*
> *return. We're not even free individuals. Our lib-*
> *erties are at the whims of a government that*
> *makes its own rules and then enforces them only*
> *when and on who they want. . . .*

> *Ambrose Watkins, Abilene, Texas. To: Inter-*
> *nal Revenue Service . . . When we take Texas*
> *back, there'll be no more dealing with your un-*
> *derstaffed offices and ludicrous tax laws that no*
> *one can keep up with. I recently visited one of*
> *your offices, complete with a four-hour wait to*
> *finally see someone. Just how many changes can*
> *one government make in a single year? You've*
> *proved it's too many, and chaos is the result. . . .*

It went on and on and on. Hundreds of messages from Americans. Some irritated, some livid, some way past the red zone and straight into insane rage. Some with the barest hint of a threat, some anonymous messages with blatant descriptions of violence. Detailed enough to make an ex-cop wince at the mental pictures they conjured up. The things humans could threaten to do to their fellow man . . .

She'd thought when she came in that morning that she and Hawk would have the Forensic Canine Unit office to themselves. But Lauren was already there with her own pile of paperwork, Rocco snoozing contentedly under her desk.

After filling the largest coffee mug she could scrounge from her bottom drawer, Meg settled at her desk with Hawk lying at her feet. Fifteen minutes later, Brian and Lacey appeared. Brian had dark smudges under his eyes and was uncharacteristically unshaven. She didn't comment on his look and she was thankful he didn't comment on her lack of even minimal makeup and similar state of exhaustion. Coffee could only take a girl so far, after all.

Now if only McCord would follow up on his previous text with more info . . .

"You waiting for Prince Charming to call?" Brian's voice broke into her thoughts.

"Ryan's going to call me?" She blinked innocently at him. "Isn't that nice. It's been too long since we had a chance to catch up."

"Not *my* Prince Charming. Yours."

"I didn't know you had one," Lauren cut in from her desk, not even raising her head as she laid one document face down on a pile and picked up a second from another.

"Funny. Me either," Meg retorted.

"Well, the way you've been glancing at your phone all morning, it makes me think you're expecting a call," Brian continued.

"Not . . . exactly."

"Then what, exactly?" Lauren set down the report she was reading and rolled her chair closer, carefully ensuring no paws or tails got crushed under the wheels. She leaned forward, and Meg nearly pulled back under the intensity of her stare. "You always were a terrible liar. What are you trying to hide?"

"It's just . . ." She turned to Brian, who sat in the desk opposite her. "You remember what we talked about yesterday?"

His expression went comically blank for several seconds before his eyes suddenly went sharp. "You did it? You really did it?"

"And hit the jackpot."

Brian slapped a hand down on the desk and let out a hoot. And then apologized to the dogs when they jumped to attention. He ran his hand over Lacey's head. "Sorry, girl, sorry."

"Will someone *please* fill me in?" Lauren scowled at both of them. "Clearly, I'm the only one in the dark."

Glancing at the officers across the room, Meg scooted her chair a little closer and dropped her voice. "You know that *Washington Post* reporter who got the e-mail from the bomber?"

"Yes."

"I met him last night. Ran into him at the S Street Dog Park."

"Ran into him, my ass." Lauren leaned in conspiratorially. "What did he say?"

"He's as pissed as we are. More than that, he seemed . . . tired."

"Tired?" Brian braced his elbows on the desk and rested his chin on his clasped hands. "How could he be tired? This is the story of his career."

"Which is saying something, considering his career so far. I bet it's not the workload burning him out, it's the work. Even if doom and gloom is your lifestyle, it must wear on you after a while. So much dark has to grind down the soul."

Brian dropped a hand down to touch his dog. "That part I get."

"We see enough of it to get it. And we have our dogs to

keep us sane. He's essentially on his own, because his overexcitable puppy is nothing but a stressor. At least for now. Anyway, he and I exchanged contact info and we made a deal to keep each other in the loop . . . off the books, so to speak."

"Can you trust him not to just run with whatever you give him?" Lauren asked. "Reporters are known to be somewhat unscrupulous when they're after a hot story. If Craig found out, or worse, Peters, you'd be in some pretty hot water."

"Trust me, I know." Meg sat back in her chair and looked down thoughtfully at Hawk, patiently sitting beside her desk, eyes fixed on her as if waiting for her next command. "I don't have a great handle on him yet, haven't had enough time for that, and God knows I don't trust reporters for a second, but he seemed genuine. Kind of a straight shooter. So far I haven't given him anything. He, however, texted me over an hour ago to say the bomber had contacted him a second time."

Brian gave a small jerk of surprise, his head shooting up. "Whoa. Why haven't we heard about this yet? Why didn't you report it?"

"Because he asked me to keep it quiet. If I'm going to expect that of him, he should expect it of me. A little mutual back scratching. He said he was heading into the office to discuss it with his bosses and then they'd officially report it after that."

"Any chance they won't and you'll have to let the cat out of the bag?"

"He said this was bigger than him or his paper and that anything incoming would go straight to the FBI, no matter what. But once it gets here, then the news has to trickle down to us. When Craig hears, he'll let us know." She looked back at the towering pile on her desk, torn between wanting to make a trip to Richmond that second and being on hand when the bomber's next message broke. Patience finally won out. "We'd better get back to this. I heard they had over ten thousand tips come through in four days."

"Impossible to follow up on all of them," Lauren said. "Thus, the weeding."

"Anything look like a possibility?"

"A couple. I have a few piles going—strong possibles, weak possibles, unlikelies, and crackpots."

"I've had a few of the crackpots." Brian picked up the top sheet from one of several piles. "This old gal thinks her neighbor is responsible because he's a space alien. It's the first step in his plan of terror to take over the planet, she says." He laid it down on the pile. "I'm thinking . . . no."

"Hey, guys." Every head in the room spun toward the door as Craig leaned in to the office. The gleam in his eye told Meg something was on the move—either the *Post* had made contact or there was a break in the case. "We need everyone in the conference room." Craig was slightly out of the breath and paused to suck in air.

Brian flicked a glance at Meg before rising from his chair. "What's going on?"

"The bomber has contacted us again. More than that, we may have him. One of the analysts thinks they have a connection. We're getting briefed and then they're sending in SWAT. Let's go." He drew back and disappeared into the hallway.

Meg and Brian stared at each other, yesterday's despair falling away under the light of hope. Calling their dogs, the team jogged out the door. There was a perp to catch and no time to waste.

Chapter 13

Bastard Search: A search in which, for some reason unknown to the searchers, the subject is not within the search area.

Saturday, April 15, 5:14 PM
Forensic Canine Unit; J. Edgar Hoover Building
Washington, DC

They huddled around the big flat-screen panel attached to the wall, the dogs milling restlessly around their legs, clearly picking up on the building tension in the room.

"This shouldn't be happening," Craig muttered from where he leaned against a desk. "The public is going to lose it." His hand closed over the edge of the desktop and squeezed, his knuckles going bloodless. "They're going to call Ruby Ridge on us."

"This shouldn't be Ruby Ridge. How did it get out of hand so fast?" Brian ran a hand through his hair, making it stand on end. "It was supposed to be a simple follow-up interview. And now, six hours later, it's all gone to hell."

This morning's task force briefing had indeed show-cased the bomber's newest communication, but then took an unexpected twist when EAD Peters took the mic to share the news of their first concrete suspect. A farmer named Skinner, ninety minutes away in Sperryville, Virginia, had made multiple veiled threats against both the

Department of Agriculture and the IRS. One of the FBI's linguistic experts had evaluated the style and spelling of the letters and declared a very strong possibility the writer of both the letters and the bomber's messages could be the same person. At that time, agents were dispatched to Sperryville to interview the suspect and convey him back to FBI headquarters if warranted.

But the op had gone wrong right from the start. The agents were greeted at the farm by locked double wooden gates, an intercom, and an irate farmer who had no intention of cooperating with any government agent or law enforcement personnel. When the agents couldn't produce a search warrant to legally enter, they were told to vacate the premises. When the agents opted to remain outside the gates, angry words were exchanged. When the agents were still there several hours later, shots were fired and the whole situation quickly went to hell.

After that, it was a blur of swarming law enforcement from municipal, state, and federal agencies, immediately followed by a gathering crowd of reporters with cameras and microphones. One of the scores of arriving FBI agents set up a live video feed and now they were also patched in to audio. Meg knew this feed was being watched by every task force member wherever they could gather. And probably some not officially on the task force but with a vested interest in the FBI's image.

It was a bad situation everyone was frantically hoping wouldn't get worse.

The pictures before them told the tale. Heavy double gates closed off a short driveway that led to a two-story white clapboard farmhouse with a broad wraparound porch. Fences completely surrounded the property, containing the few cows visible in the pasture. But where the livestock couldn't get out, the agents couldn't just stroll in. Outside the gates, cars, SUVs, and trucks lined the driveway. Behind them, an ever-growing mass of media types stood at the public road, struggling to get closer to the action, damn the risk if there was a possible Pulitzer up for grabs. Local law enforcement was apparently in charge of keeping them back, but was clearly having trouble considering the growing crowd and the constantly shouted questions and pleas for interviews.

Near the gates but behind the cover of a hulking SUV, a crowd of agents in blue windbreakers with block yellow letters spelling out "FBI" huddled together, conferring.

"They have to get this under control," Craig growled. "They're doing everything in the public eye. Hell, Skinner is likely watching what's going on from both sides—out his window and then from our side on CNN and every other network there that has a live feed direct to TVs across the nation."

"They need to do something," Lauren said, her eyes locked on the screen. "Our hesitation makes us look weak."

"No, it makes us look careful," Meg said. "You heard what someone said. The negotiator is on his way up. He's the best we have and they have to get him there, which takes time. That's the only thing they're waiting for. What you can't see are the snipers they've lined up in trees or on hillsides surrounding the property. Right now they're trying to determine who's on the property and what the threat level is. And those snipers are their eyes inside that house."

She knew what it was like to perch on the top of a building or in a bush. To see your entire world through the circle of your scope, to concentrate with every cell in your body on that one tiny view with the voice of your orders in your ear. To trust that voice implicitly, knowing your line of sight was incomplete and someone else with a wider worldview needed to make the call. To obey without question, even when someone's life might be on the line.

She'd done sniper training as part of her work with the Richmond PD. She was good with a gun, but better with dogs, so in the end, that was the road she took. But she remembered what it was like as if it was yesterday.

"At Ruby Ridge, a fourteen-year-old boy was shot in the back as he tried to run away, and a woman holding an infant was shot and killed when a sniper shot missed his target," Meg continued. "These aren't mistakes they're going to make again."

"Especially right in front of the media," Brian said. "So I guess we're on hold until they figure out how to deal with this."

"Some of the news agencies are still going to spin it to make us look weak," Lauren insisted.

"Then they'll just have to correct themselves later. We're big boys and girls, we can take the heat." Impatient and feeling like an overwound watch spring, Meg turned back to her desk, pushing through papers on the surface to look busy while she calmed herself. She understood everyone else's stress—they were reacting to the pressure of not just today but of the past week. However, she needed to dial it down for her own sake, and even more for Hawk. All the dogs were sensing the tension in the room, and it showed in their restlessness. They couldn't settle either.

"Hawk, here boy." She held out her hand and the black lab trotted over to her. She bent down, ruffling his fur and murmuring to him. His coat still smelled of the vanilla and almond shampoo she'd used on him after the second bombing's fire scene. The familiar scent felt like home, and partially calmed her jangling nerves.

Hawk nuzzled his damp nose against her throat and exhaled, blowing warm air over her skin and tugging a small smile from her lips. "Good boy. Now, down." He dropped down at her feet, comfortably crossing his front paws and resting his head on them. She ran her hand over his shiny coat one more time and then straightened.

A glance at the screen showed her the negotiator had yet to arrive, so she picked up her cell phone, glanced up to see if anyone was watching. As everyone was focused on the screen, she typed out a quick text. McCord had let her know he'd received the message and, in return, it only seemed fair to let him know it was now official FBI news.

Saw the message. Task force briefing.

She hit send. The pause that followed her text went on long enough that she was about to slip the phone into her pocket, but then it vibrated in her hand.

Figured you'd see it sooner rather than later.

Meg glanced up again. Still no action in the standoff. She turned back to her phone.

He sounds pissed.

He sounds unstable, McCord responded.

We knew that already. He's killed forty-eight people, Meg texted back.

"Look at those vultures."

Meg's eyes rose back to the screen at Brian's words. The milling crowd of reporters filled the field of view, most of them jostling with each other for a spot closest to the line of cops who held them back. Her eyes narrowed on the screen, to the dark blond head toward the back of the crowd, the face angled down instead of staring at the house and the FBI around him. Suspicion dawned and she turned back to her phone to type out a short text.

Where are you?

Can't you guess?

She glared down at the screen. This was *not* the time to play games. Her tolerance for it this week was already buried in the basement.

Humor me. Where?
With your buddies in Virginia.

Her head snapped up to stare at the screen, but the camera was now focused on the road. In the distance, a dust plume rose as a vehicle approached the group.

"That has to be the negotiator," Craig said. "Finally."

Meg slid her phone into her pocket and rejoined the group. A dark SUV threaded its way through the parted crowd of reporters, down the drive and then up between the cars to pull in directly in front of the gates. An older man with a lined face and a neatly trimmed Vandyke climbed out and shook hands with one of the FBI agents. There was a brief conversation—bringing him up to speed—and then he was handed a bullhorn.

The negotiator walked around the SUVs to stand exposed by the gate in full view of the house. In full view of a gunman's sights. He raised the bullhorn. "Mr. Skinner, my name is Senior Special Agent Phillips and I'm a negotiator with the FBI. I'd like to speak with you."

One of the front windows slid up a scant inch, and a voice with a thick Appalachian accent boomed through. "Don't want to talk."

"We know you're in there with your wife and children, Mr. Skinner. Let's keep this from getting out of hand, because we don't want anyone to get hurt. Come out and they'll remain unharmed. Right now we just have some questions for you. We don't want to make this bigger than it already is."

"Too late. You Feebs will do anything to bury a hardworking, honest American who just wants to be left alone. Gun charges are the least of my worries."

"Not true. But you've turned this into something bigger by firing at federal agents. Come out peacefully with your hands up. You know this can't end well otherwise. We have the property surrounded. There's nowhere for you to go."

"You take me, I'll just disappear into one of your jails, never to be seen again."

"This isn't Russia, Mr. Skinner. That's not how our system works. Our system is innocent until proven guilty. And your family will know where you are at all times. Think about this carefully. The decision you make now could affect you and your family forever."

Seconds ticked by with no response, stretching out into glacial minutes.

"Christ, this is taking way too long." Lauren tapped a pen against her left palm to relieve the tension.

"He has to give him time to make up his mind," Meg said. "He's trying to avoid a bloodbath. But this can only go on so long. Phillips has to know that he's got some very twitchy agents surrounding the house and—"

She was cut off by an indistinct shout overlaid with a heavy layer of static. Nevertheless, the sniper's words were clear enough. "He's going for his rifle."

Phillips snapped to attention. "No, *wait!*"

The unmistakable sound of a shot ripped through the air. Even through the muffled mono of low fidelity audio, Meg recognized the sound of a sniper's high-powered rifle.

All hell instantly broke loose. Gunfire blew out the front window of the house, glass arcing in an outward spray to land in glittering fragments all over the front grass. The brutal slice of bullets into the metal of the FBI vehicles reverberated through the air only a millisecond before every agent had his or her gun out and was firing at the house.

In the office, the reaction was immediate but downplayed for the sake of the animals. Craig hissed epithets while Brian paced back and forth, his eyes never leaving the video feed. Meg automatically dropped a hand down onto Hawk's back, wanting the connection for both of them, but her attention stayed locked on the negotiator. He was crouched down in the lower left corner of the screen, his face white with fury as he screamed at the agents around him, his words lost in the sound of gunfire. His gaze dropped and then fixed on something off screen. Ducking, he scrambled out of the frame before popping back up, the bullhorn held in a death grip.

"Stand down! I repeat, stand down!" Phillips roared, his voice magnified to be heard over the din. As the nearby agents complied, lowering their guns and sinking back down under cover, Phillips dropped the megaphone, whipped around and glared at the lead FBI agent. "Tell your men to stand down," he snarled. "Before they get one of us or the suspect killed. No one dies on my watch. And someone report in—does anyone have eyes on the suspect?"

There was a crackle of static, then, "I have eyes. Suspect is down, lying under the living room window. Family members are still in the back of the house."

Meg didn't need audio to understand the full brunt of Phillips's anger, but she got it anyway. Just as he was unleashing every iota of fury on the unfortunate sniper who fired the first shot, a voice interrupted. "Wait! He's moving. Crawling toward the back of the house, dragging his rifle behind him."

Phillips apparently didn't need any more reason to proceed. Dragging open the door of his now riddled SUV, he wedged himself between the body of the car and the open door, propping his megaphone in the V. "Mr. Skinner, please step away from your weapon and let's avoid another episode like that. Your wife and children are safe. Let's keep it that way."

The voice that floated through the now shattered window was dripping with scorn. "What're you gonna do with them when I'm in custody?"

"Nothing, Mr. Skinner. We'd like to talk to your wife, but there is no suspicion pointed at her. She and your children are safe to remain at home."

What's left of your home, Meg thought ruefully.

As the silence stretched longer, tension curled tight knots through Meg's shoulders. *Come on, come on. End this now. You know you can't win this, and the longer you wait, the higher the odds you'll die today.*

"All right. I'm coming out. I'll be unarmed. Don't shoot."

The cool wash of relief surged through Meg. *Thank God. . . .*

With a buzz, the front gates swung open. Seconds later, a man appeared at the door of the house. In his midforties and of medium build, he wore dirty blue jeans and a ragged T-shirt. A furious scowl cut through the wiry beard covering his jaw and cheeks. Big, rough hands were held out on either side of his head, fingers splayed.

Agents streamed through the still widening gates and sprinted up the walk. Spinning Skinner around, they jerked his hands behind his back and cuffed them before hustling him down the front walk. They marched him to an SUV farther down the driveway—one that likely had avoided any bullets—and closed him in, leaving two agents standing outside the vehicle, watching him.

The sound of reporters screaming questions jerked Meg back to the fact that McCord and any of a multitude of other media types could have been hit. The agents were trained and prepared for gunplay, but a bunch of journalism majors were not. She pulled out her phone and typed quickly.

You okay?

Her question was followed by dead air for more than a minute. Just as she was starting to think more had gone wrong at the scene than they were aware of, and she was forming the mental picture of scattered reporters laid out bloody on the ground, he finally answered.

Yes. Minus a year or two shaved off my life.
Anyone else hurt?

Not that I can see. We all hit the dirt pretty fast when the first shot was fired.

Send the trigger happy sniper your dry cleaning bill. I guarantee that wasn't how the negotiator wanted that to go down, Meg texted back.

From his reaction, I think you're right. Coming back to town now. Any tips for a guy who just got shot at?

She couldn't help the smile. So far, he was the one providing all the information. She couldn't give him anything yet, but she had to give him marks for making the attempt.

Try to stay away from angry farmers with guns.

Thanks, that's really helpful. Over and out.

Meg looked back to the screen. FBI agents swarmed all over the property now, and a woman and two school-aged children were being led out of the house. Meg glanced at the clock on the wall. It would be hours before the agents got back with Skinner, and hours more still to interrogate him.

She could only hope this was truly the end.

Chapter 14

Refind: Search dogs alert their handlers in two ways—
they can stay with the subject and bark, waiting for the
handler to come to them, or they can return to the
handler and give some indication (jumping, tugging,
circling, etc.) that they have made a find. The handler
then follows the dog as it returns to the find.

Saturday, April 15, 9:12 PM
J. Edgar Hoover Building
Washington, DC

Meg moved silently through the empty hallways, past
darkened offices and conference rooms. At this time
of night, the Criminal Investigative Division was mostly
deserted. The main bull pen was still active—an organization like the FBI was never truly closed—but the peripheral
offices, especially those of the brass, were all dark.

But the division offices were not her goal. She was
headed for the interrogation rooms.

She'd gone home earlier, shared a late meal with her sister, and then had tried to settle in for the evening. Cara sat
hunched at her desk in the corner of the living room doing
the financials for her training school on her laptop, a task
she hated, which meant she was forever behind on them.
Meg sprawled in the recliner.

She was too tired to do anything productive, but too wired to sit still, so she settled for flipping through TV stations. Blink drew her attention as he jumped up onto the sofa across from her, nosing at Hawk to make room and then shoehorning his skinny body between Hawk and Saki where they dozed companionably together.

Meg found herself smiling at the contented pile of dogs. Some days she wished she could live as simple a life as Blink's. While Hawk and Saki were working dogs, Blink lived a life of leisure. After unspeakable horrors at the racetrack, he deserved nothing less. She turned back to the TV and her smile slipped away as she passed station after station of reality TV or political pundits, both of which she hated with an unbounded passion.

"Three hundred channels and nothing's on," she muttered.

Cara glanced sideways at her, one eyebrow cocked as her hands froze over the keyboard. "Why don't you just go back? You know you want to."

"What makes you say that?"

"I didn't just fall off the turnip truck, as Maimeó would say," Cara deadpanned, referring to their beloved Irish grandmother. "You're practically crawling out of your skin. *Just go.*"

"It's not really my place."

Cara pushed back from the desk, rising from her chair to sit on the arm of the couch, absently running her hand over Saki's smoky fur. "That's BS and you know it. You're part of the task force and no one on the team has been more affected by the victims than the Human Scent Evidence Teams. You've been hands-on with those victims, both those who made it and those who didn't. No one knows more about what they suffered than you. Not to mention that you're already making inquiries on the down low. So if you want to see this through to the end, why shouldn't you?"

"Okay, maybe you have a point. But either way, I'm here and the suspect is probably just arriving now."

Cara glanced across the room to the antique captain's clock over the mantel. "Which means you can be there in about twenty minutes. You'll have hardly missed anything."

Blue eyes met blue for the space of a few heartbeats, and then Meg was out of the chair and tossing the strap of her shoulder bag over her head to lie across her body and grabbing her keys. "Don't wait up."

"I wouldn't dream of it," her sister called after her, a smile in her voice.

Here she was twenty-five minutes later, hurrying down the corridor to the suite of interrogation rooms within the Criminal Investigative Division. As she got closer, a buzz of voices could be heard down the hallway. When she stepped into observation, she could see why—the room was packed. She scanned the faces, seeing a number of SACs, SSAs, and ADs as well as other task force members. Then her gaze fell on Craig. He was near the window, looking into the interrogation room, so she sidled over to him, slipping through the groups of people huddled in twos and threes.

"Fancy meeting you here," she said in an undertone to him.

"Couldn't stay away either?" The strain was starting to wear on Craig; his skin had lost some of its usual ruddy warmth and harsh lines carved deep around his eyes.

"Not even kind of. You either obviously."

"I never even went home."

"Maureen must not be happy about all the extra hours you're putting in."

He met her gaze, his tone going defensive. "Maureen gets it. She knows what's at stake."

"Of course she does. Sorry, sometimes I forget she's one of the rare ones who really do understand what we do." Meg turned and glanced into the empty interrogation room. "They haven't started yet?"

"No. They're making sure every *t* is crossed so there are no technical loopholes for this guy. They'll be starting shortly." On the other side of the two-way glass, a door opened. "Or right now, as the case may be," Craig finished.

The observation room went instantly quiet as two agents escorted Skinner into the room and seated him at the table. He rested his hands against the edge of the table in a gesture meant to showcase his confidence, but the white knuckles of his fists spoke of his actual mind-set. His head stayed down, his eyes downcast on the tabletop.

The door opened again and EAD Peters and SAC Maloney of the Criminal Investigative Division came in. Peters nodded to the other two agents, silently dismissing them. Maloney carried a file folder and set it down on the table at her elbow.

Craig whistled low under his breath. "Pulling out the big guns for this one."

"You think it's a mistake?"

"I think it's exactly right. Peters is climbing the ranks so quickly because he's such a good agent. He's got a good eye and can read people like he's known them for years. And Maloney was always known as a good interrogator. They want to do this one right. My bet is that Peters sits back and lets Maloney take the lead so he can observe without distraction. He'll want to know in his bones this is the responsible party. They can't afford to make an error at this point. Not with the president—hell, the whole world—watching. Here we go."

As the door closed behind the exiting agents, SAC Maloney fixed a steady gaze on Skinner. "Mr. Skinner, I know you were read your rights in the field, but I'd like to reiterate." She smoothly recited the Miranda warning. "Do you understand your rights as they have been explained to you?"

Skinner's gaze didn't rise from the table. "Yeah."

"And you understand you're entitled to a lawyer?"

Sullen eyes shifted upward briefly. "You don't leave me any choice there. Can't afford my own and I'm damned if I'm going to take one of yours. How stupid do you think I am? Your lawyer would never be on my side."

"That's not how the system works, Mr. Skinner, but as you wish." Maloney pulled several pieces of paper from the file folder and spread them out on the table in front of Skinner, sliding them directly into his field of vision. "Mr. Skinner, these are copies of your communications to the Internal Revenue Service. Do you remember sending them?"

Skinner stared at the documents for a moment, then simply shrugged.

She spread more paper before him. "And these are your communications to the US Department of Agriculture. You've been quite prolific, Mr. Skinner. Now, do you remember composing these documents?"

Skinner didn't bother to grace them with even a shrug this time.

"Mr. Skinner, can you tell us your whereabouts on Tuesday, April eleventh, at three PM?"

Skinner was in profile to the group behind the double-sided glass, so Meg could just see Skinner's eyebrows snap together in confusion, something she doubted Maloney herself caught. *He's not connecting the date.*

"Dunno," Skinner mumbled.

"What about Friday, April fourteenth, at ten forty-five AM?"

Meg studied Skinner's face keenly, but this time there was no change in expression.

"Dunno."

"That was yesterday morning, Mr. Skinner. You can't tell us where you were yesterday morning?"

"I'd have to check my social calendar. I can get back to you." Surliness rolled off his words in waves.

Meg glanced at Craig, who simply raised an eyebrow at her. She turned back to the glass. *He has no idea what they're really asking him here, or he'd put more effort into saying where he was or making something up to cover his ass.*

Maloney remained outwardly calm, her hands neatly folded on the table, her face unlined and serene. Meg was impressed. If it had been her, she'd have been tempted to reach out and shake Skinner. But Maloney's voice continued on with utmost calm, although there was a core of steel behind it. "Mr. Skinner, I suggest you answer our questions. You're here on a number of charges. The state of Virginia dictates several, including weapons charges and aggravated assault." She sat back in her chair and crossed her arms over her chest, seemingly at ease. "But the federal charges in play are somewhat more significant. We're looking at the use of weapons of mass destruction, destruction by explosives, and involuntary manslaughter of thirty federal employees." Skinner's head snapped up, his eyes suddenly alarmed, but Maloney simply rolled over anything he might have said. "Oh, yes, and the state of Virginia and the District of Columbia want a total of forty-eight counts of first degree murder. I guess I forgot to mention that one." She leaned forward, slapping her palms down on the table with a crack that startled Meg. "You'll go to jail and you'll never come out again, Mr. Skinner. *Now* do you remember where you were yesterday morning?"

Skinner licked his lips and shifted his hands down with a *clink* of metal on wood to grasp the edge of the table in a death grip. "At home, out in the fields, working the farm."

"Doing what? When? With whom?" Maloney mercilessly shot questions at him. She had him off balance now and clearly wanted to keep it that way.

"My wife was there. And the farrier stopped by to shoe one of my horses." He looked from one agent to the other, trying to maintain his persona of cool indifference, but failing. "What is this about?"

Peters finally entered the conversation, coming in hard and heavy as the voice of authority. "This is about forty-eight innocent lives lost in two separate bombings, one at the Department of Agriculture, right here in DC, and the other at an IRS office, right there in your home state of Virginia."

Skinner actually pushed back from the table with a small screech of chair legs. "I didn't do that." He looked frantically from one agent to the other. "I didn't do that. I can prove my whereabouts. You can search my home."

Maloney took the reins again. "We're already doing that, Mr. Skinner. We have the legal right to search your property for evidence as you are suspected of a crime. Explosive detection dogs are going over the property right now to determine if there has ever been a trace of explosives."

Skinner's shoulders relaxed fractionally. "Then I want you off my land."

"Pushback already, Mr. Skinner? Don't you want to be exonerated before you start that?"

"I'm not responsible for those bombings." Fear was dissolving under the weight of surliness in his words.

The shock wore off fast, Meg thought. *He's moving back to his normal stance of resistance.*

"Did you see that?" Craig whispered in her ear.

"What?" she whispered back

"The attitude change. From alarm to relief."

"Because of the dogs?"

"That's what I think. They aren't going to find anything on his property and he knows it. He doesn't live in a big city, so he can't anonymously rent space to build the bombs off site. In a rural area like that, he'd have to borrow space from a neighbor, and risk someone snoopy figuring out what he's doing and turning him in. No, he'd do it on his own property or not at all."

"You think it's 'not at all' and we have the wrong guy?"

"Not sure, but I think it's going to be hard to prove."

They turned back to the window as Maloney continued. "Mr. Skinner, you've had numerous run-ins with federal and state agencies."

"Don't recognize them. They can't regulate me."

"I see from your file here that you consider yourself a Sovereign Citizen."

"Yup."

"So you don't believe federal or state agencies have any authority over you because you don't believe in the government of the United States."

"I don't."

For the first time, emotion colored Maloney's voice, disgust dripping heavily. "So you live in this country, farm our land, enjoy our freedoms, but don't recognize us, so you don't feel the need to pay taxes or contribute to society. Is that about right, Mr. Skinner?"

"It's my land."

"Pardon me?"

Real anger radiated from Skinner for the first time as his voice rose. "It's *my* land. It was my daddy's land before me, and his daddy's before him, going back generations. I filed the patent and have the allodial title. It doesn't belong to the state or the country; *it's mine*. So no property taxes or municipal fees because I own it outright. The US government has no right to me and mine or my land or anything that comes from it and can go straight to hell."

"You sound pretty angry, Mr. Skinner. Angry enough to feel the need to make a point?"

"And rain fire down on my head? Why would I be stupid enough to do that? Don't you get it? We just want to be left alone. To make our own way without anyone interfering. To feed our families without handing anything over to greedy officials to steal for their own needs."

"And what if you ever run into trouble? What then?"

"I'd call the sheriff."

That seemed to take Maloney back a step. "You don't believe in authority, but you'd call the sheriff?"

"I don't believe in the government. But the Constitution called for there to be sheriffs. I believe in the Constitution and the Declaration of Independence. In the right to bear arms, and in life, liberty, and the pursuit of happiness. I know our county sheriff. He's a good man. I have no quarrel with him."

Maloney referred to the file in front of her. "I see you've had trouble with the state police. Got pulled over for having a homemade license plate on your truck."

"Don't recognize the state. Don't need their laws."

"What about US currency, Mr. Skinner. Do you at least recognize that?"

"No, but sometimes it can't be avoided. We try to be self-sufficient, grow food in our own gardens and on our land, get milk from our cows and goats, grow our own hay for the livestock, keep a few beehives and make our own honey. Barter for what we don't have. We live simply and don't want to make trouble."

"And yet you sent these." Reaching out across the table, Maloney tapped on the papers.

"In response to agencies prying where they damned well didn't belong." He grabbed one of the papers and scanned it quickly. "They have no right to regulate my handful of cows." He tossed it to the floor and picked up another sheet. "I will not pay federal taxes to a government I don't recognize. The US government is unlawful and I will not be a part of it." A flick of his wrist sent that paper floating gently to the floor as well. "I have no intention of hurting anyone. I just want to be left alone."

"And when you talked about the 'fire and brimstone of justice falling on their heads,' that wasn't a reference to the bombs you were making?"

" 'The Lord tests the righteous and the wicked, and the one who loves violence His soul hates. Upon the wicked He will rain snares; fire and brimstone and burning wind will be the portion of their cup. For the Lord is righteous, He loves righteousness; the upright will behold His face.' I don't need to do anything. Those who persecute me, their time will come from a hand mightier than mine. The Lord hates a violent man."

"What exactly would you call shooting at federal officers, Mr. Skinner?"

Skinner leaned forward, a light in his eyes. "Righteousness. The Lord would never smite a man for protecting what is rightfully his."

"So the Lord will protect you from the tax collector?"

"The Lord doesn't believe I owe you anything. 'Then render to Caesar the things that are Caesar's, and to God the things that are God's.' I owe Caesar . . . you . . . nothing."

"That's not how it works in this country, Mr. Skinner. You live here as a citizen, you contribute. You do realize you can be jailed for tax evasion?"

"I have no problem standing for my beliefs. And I'd have to be convicted first."

"That remains to be seen." Maloney pulled out another sheet of paper. On it were several paragraphs of type. She pushed it toward him. "Did you write these messages, Mr. Skinner?"

Skinner pulled the sheet toward him, pushing the other papers out of his way. He scanned the type and shook his head. "No."

"Do you and your family own a computer?"

"No."

"That wouldn't be a problem. You could have done it from a local library or an Internet café."

"You'd have to prove it first. I didn't do this or your bombings."

A buzz sounded and Meg, along with several nearby agents, turned to look at Craig. He slipped his phone from his pocket and quickly read the incoming message. "That was Neil. He and Groucho are out with the explosives team at Skinner's farm. No evidence of any explosives past or present," he murmured quietly. "They're getting word through to Maloney as well."

"I'm not a profiler, but this just isn't reading for me," Meg murmured. "He's pissed, but at all the wrong things. Craig, I don't think this is our guy."

"Me either. And look at Peters. He's silent, but his stance has changed during this interview. He doesn't think so either, but until they can prove it definitively, they'll hold him at least on the assault of federal officers charges."

Meg turned back to the window where the interview continued, Maloney questioning Skinner again about his whereabouts during the first bombing and his motivation for killing innocent people. But to Meg's eye, the fire had gone out of her. *She doesn't think it's him either.*

So now the big question remained—if this wasn't the bomber, then who was and when would he strike next?

Chapter 15

False Alert: A false alert is called by the handler because clues or handling mistakes caused the dog to indicate when there is no odor present.

Saturday, April 15, 11:15 PM
Outside Moorefield, Hardy County, West Virginia

Only the TV and the flickering fire in the hearth lit the living area of the farmhouse. The fire was less for ambiance than warmth as the night took on a chill, reminding residents that winter wasn't as far gone as they hoped. The flames threw dancing shadows against the walls but cloaked the corners in gloom.

The man wasn't nearly so entertained. He hadn't moved from the edge of the worn couch from the moment he'd turned on the evening news to catch up on the latest updates of his reign of terror, only to be met by a story focused entirely on someone else. This was what he got for spending the afternoon and evening testing the new drone.

Jonas Skinner. Who the hell was Jonas Skinner and why did they think he was responsible for everything he himself had done? So he'd settled in to watch and learn. A man couldn't make plans unless he knew what was going on around him.

Grudgingly, he could only agree with many of this supposed suspect's opinions and actions, especially as they didn't fall far from his own. But now the bastards had the wrong man in custody. It wasn't likely they would simply question him and let him go. From the moment those gates remained closed, Skinner's fate was sealed. He simply jammed a couple of nails in his own coffin when he fired the first shot. The hotheaded sniper then proceeded to blow a few extra holes in that coffin.

Skinner's angry face filled the television screen, and the man watching raised the glass clenched in his fist to him. *Well done, brother. You are an honor to the cause.* He tossed back the moonshine in a single gulp, then sat back contemplating the mason jar, half-filled with crystal clear liquid that was one of the last remaining artifacts of the family legacy.

To a Mountaineer, moonshine was one of the marks of manhood. Liquid fire in a bottle, a thunderbolt in a glass. Nothing could warm the throat right down to the stomach quite like his Daddy's liquor. Or go straight to the head. It was a truly glorious thing. And in the time-honored tradition, his Daddy taught him the family recipe, including the special little tweaks and secrets that made their moonshine revered across the county.

At least it was until the West Virginia Alcohol Beverage Control caught him selling it without a license and then turned him over to the IRS for not collecting and submitting the required federal taxes and fees.

Well, he'd shown the IRS what he thought about them.

He turned back to the TV to continue his study of Skinner. The truth was that Skinner was a distraction. Now that a suspect had been caught, unless they could prove he couldn't have been responsible, the media would eventually stop talking about the bombings, at least until the court case lit a fire under them again.

A slow grin spread across his face. Only one way to fix that. Nothing says innocence quite like a bombing when your number one suspect is already behind bars.

He knew just what to hit next. *Who* to hit next. Because this one was personal. Not just an agency. *A man.*

When you're in public service, you're there to help the public. Not to turn your back on them.

The person who turned his back on him would pay.

It was all *his* fault. He had the chance to save a farm and a way of life, the chance to be a hero. But he'd chosen not to.

Now he'd burn for that choice.

Chapter 16

Parkour: A training regimen using only the body and contact with objects in the environment for propulsion. Parkour—derived from the French word *parcours*, meaning "the path"—emphasizes using the obstacles to increase efficiency and speed. Parkour offers fun-filled agility conditioning for both humans and dogs.

Sunday, April 16, 6:24 AM
Kalorama Heights, Washington, DC

Dawn was just stretching her graceful fingers over the horizon in wisps of pink and gold as Meg rounded the corner onto S Street NW, Hawk heeling at her side and Brian and Lacey following close behind. Misery loves company, and as much as Meg despised getting up in the dark to jog with her dog before the sun came up, Brian hated it even more. So at least once a week, they made a date to run together for mutual encouragement. A favorite run was Rock Creek Park, just north of their current location, but it had been Meg's turn to pick this morning and she decided on a city route to fit in some urban agility training. The run kept them all in shape, but the agility training kept the dogs strong and toned and at the peak of fitness for the most difficult of searches and rescues.

Meg loved classic architecture, so she'd selected a run past some of the finest old houses in Washington, in an area that hosted a large number of foreign embassies, but had also housed five American presidents either before or after their time in the White House. Heading west, they drew nearer to Woodrow Wilson House, across the street on their left. The three-story, Georgian-style redbrick home was named for the twenty-eighth president of the United States, who lived there following his departure from the White House until he died in residence in 1924.

They turned left down 24th Street NW next and then angled onto the short connecting section of Massachusetts Avenue NW, running past the Croatian Embassy. In front, Saint Jerome sat frozen in patinaed bronze hunched over the Bible he would translate from Greek and Hebrew to Latin for the early church in 382 AD, his head clasped in a single huge hand. Meg's gaze stayed frozen on the statue for several beats as she contemplated the statue's outlook—she could never decide if he was thoughtful or agonized. Sometimes it simply depended on how the light hit the rivulets of verdigris running down the face and body of the figure, lending it the appearance of an abundance of tears.

Then they were around the corner and onto Decatur Place NW, the rising sun glinting through the trees. Meg ran steadily enough to maintain the pace for the length of the run, but hard enough that this close to the end, her lungs were working intensely and her muscles had the pleasant burn that spoke of a good workout. Thank God—if she was going to get up in the dark and torture herself for an hour, it should be worth something.

As they crested the small rise, they all sensed they were just about there. She bore down and pushed herself harder, Hawk easily keeping up with her, his muscles rippling under his glossy fur, his tail high with pleasure, and his eyes bright. As much as Meg hated jogging—while appreciating the edge it gave her in emergency situations—Hawk loved both the company and the exercise. He was in sheer heaven when Brian and Lacey joined them.

They turned north just past a Narnia-worthy lamppost with a big frosted glass light fixture and found themselves on 22nd Street NW. Meg dropped to a brisk walk and threw a look over her shoulder at Brian. "Still with me?"

"You bet." Brian's breath came in hard puffs and his cheeks were pink, but he had a triumphant gleam in his eyes. "Showed that mother how it goes."

"Always do." Meg slowed a bit more and shrugged out of the pack she carried. Just as the dogs had their agility training, she and Brian always conditioned carrying their full search and rescue packs so hauling them out on assignment was second nature. She pulled out a water bottle specially fitted with a small attached trough. She flipped the trough down and unscrewed the cap, water flowing into the reservoir. "Hawk, water." She held it out to him and he lapped thirstily. She glanced over at Brian, who was also giving water to Lacey. "Think we'll ever find these runs getting any easier?"

"In our dreams. They'll always be hellish. My father would say it builds character."

"We must have character spurting out our ears then," Meg said dryly. After Hawk drank his fill, she removed a second bottle of water for herself, downing half of it in a continuous series of swallows before lowering the bottle and backhanding her mouth. "Ready?"

Brian was just closing his own mostly empty bottle of water. "Sure am. Same bet as usual?"

"Slower team buys coffee? You're on." She ran a hand over Hawk's silky fur, meeting his luminous brown eyes.

He was loaded for bear this morning. "Get your wallet ready."

Brian squinted at her in mock outrage. "I recall you bought last time."

"We were robbed. You distracted Hawk on purpose."

"I did not. That wouldn't be very sporting of me."

Meg rolled her eyes. "It really wasn't. Was it worth it, just for coffee?"

"Coffee is the most important meal of the day."

"So you say, pretty much every morning. Okay, you take the left, I'll take the right."

Shouldering their packs again, they called their dogs and jogged over to the bottom of the regal stone steps. Spanning the steep, thirty-foot incline between this lower section of 22nd Street NW and the upper section lay one hundred feet of herringbone brick and stone steps with three terraces. Built as part of Washington's City Beautiful movement of the early twentieth century, which also involved the creation of the National Mall as it is known today, the Spanish Steps provided a pedestrian route between the two sections of street. It also provided an excellent agility training area for the dogs as each set of stairs was bounded by a curb, interrupted occasionally by massive concrete urns.

"Ready? Three . . . two . . . one! Lacey, curb!" Brian cut left just as Meg went right with the same command for Hawk, both of them heading up the stairs.

Lacey and Hawk bounded up onto the curb on their own sides, racing up the incline as fast as their owners, who were taking the steps two at a time. On the first terrace stood the first set of giant urns. Meg glanced sideways just as Hawk reached the top of the incline, pausing only slightly as he gathered himself and pushed off in a huge spring to land lightly on top of the urn, feet perfectly balanced on the rim. It was as if his feet only barely touched, making perfect contact before he leapt off, stretching out in the air like a black arrow, and then blasting forward up onto the curb that lined the next inclined set of stairs. It never failed to amaze her how steady he was on his feet, and how sure his footing. He never stumbled. Honestly, sometimes it made her feel clumsy scrambling after him.

She and Brian darted into the center to avoid a series of flower beds that ran up the two edges of the staircase in this second set of stairs. Shoulder-to-shoulder, they sprinted up the treads, easily outpaced by both dogs, who within seconds were at the second terrace level.

"Hawk, around!"

Hawk and Lacey cut across the terrace on their own sides and jumped up onto the stepped wall that followed a curving set of stairs to the upper level. These stairs surrounded a lion head fountain, water spewing from the lion's mouth in a steady stream to overflow a large scalloped shell and spill over into the reservoir below. Brian and Meg pulled up short in front of the fountain, watching the dogs and trying not to sound too winded. Meg dipped one hand into icy water still carrying the night's chill and ran damp fingers over the heated back of her neck.

Propping her hands on her hips, she watched the two dogs race along the wall, taking each upward step in flight until they hit the top level and leapt up onto the balustrade that separated the top terrace from the fountain below. Headed directly for each other on the railing, they jumped down onto the terrace, circled round each other and then took the other's upward path back down again. Circling down around the fountain, it was a race to see which dog would come to rest, sitting beside their handler, first.

It was close, but Hawk beat Lacey by about a half second. Unaware of the bet, each dog sat, their sides heaving, tongues lolling, and each sporting a huge canine grin. Power, balance, speed, exertion—with the exception of rescuing victims, this was their drug of choice.

Because it was Brian, Meg let exultation shine through her grin. "Looks like it's your turn, coffee boy."

Brian shrugged good-naturedly and squatted down at Lacey's side to give her an enthusiastic rub. "Good girl, good run. We'll trounce the whippersnapper next time." He straightened and turned to face the downward slope once again, pointing at the curb. "Now, downhill. Slowly."

Meg moved to the opposite side of the staircase. "Hawk, down the hill. Slow."

They walked down the stairs beside the dogs, who balanced on the narrow curbs, handling the sharp incline like pros, carefully placing one paw in front of the other without a hint of misstep on the smooth concrete. Reaching the bottom, they hopped down for praise and pats.

"How about that place on Connecticut?" Brian suggested. "The artisanal shop?" He put the word "artisanal" in air quotes.

"That would be nice. Give us a chance to cool down on the way there."

Meg and Brian fell into step together, their dogs naturally by their sides.

"So . . . I did something unsanctioned the other day."

Brian sent her a sideways glance, but years of camaraderie and trust meant he didn't need to ask.

"I e-mailed my old sergeant at the Richmond PD and asked to see him. I want to ask him a favor."

"This has to be case related."

"Knew I couldn't put anything past you." She paused for a moment, suddenly unsure about what she was doing. "Look, I don't have to tell you any more if you're worried about getting into trouble."

Brian let out a short bark of laughter. "Like that's ever stopped me. You know I'll go to the mat for you, just like you would for me. Out with it."

She tossed him a relieved smile. "Knew you'd want in. Sorry, don't know what came over me for a second there. So the whole thing started yesterday when I had a quiet word with Greg." She quickly summed up the evidence she'd learned about the explosive and its taggant. "I think this is related to a theft in West Virginia a few months back. An army reserve depot was broken into and some explosive material was stolen. It made the news briefly at the time, but then the story disappeared."

"So they never caught the guy."

"That's my take on it. I think it was our bomber planning in advance. He grabbed the C-4 and then sat on it awhile just to make sure his trail was cold. But I'm wondering if they missed something—a lead that didn't seem to go anywhere back then, but combined with our data and incoming tips, could lead us to him now."

"That makes sense. What can your sergeant do to help?"

"Any criminal activity inside the army is investigated by CID. He's ex-CID and he's still got buddies back in the department."

"So rather than waiting for the suits to make agreements about sharing case files, you're doing an end run around the red tape." He held out a fist and she bumped it in solidarity. "I like it."

"I think it'll work. He e-mailed that he's out of town but will be back on Tuesday morning, so I'll see him then. I'd rather wait and meet with him than do this by e-mail. I don't care so much about my getting into trouble, but I want my source left out of it. He's a great officer and about five years from retirement. I won't jeopardize that for him."

"You'll let me know what you find?"

"Of course. And I'll fill McCord in too. He'll have different investigatory channels and might be able to dig out something we can't."

When Brian remained silent, she glanced at him. "And suddenly you're quiet. What?"

"I just . . ." He paused, and Meg could see him fighting to put his feelings into words. "I just can't get over the fact that something about that guy puts my teeth on edge."

"You still think a reporter could be the bomber?"

"I don't know. It just seems too . . . convenient that the guy is talking directly to him and only him. If McCord was the bomber, he'd be in the perfect place to fake it. Write his own letter, send it to himself inside his own totally anonymous system, then be all 'Wow, look what I got!' when it arrives." He drilled an index finger at her. "You know it's a possibility. Don't let his pretty boy looks blind you."

Meg batted his hand away. "Trust me, I'm not. It's not his looks. It's him. I'm ex-cop. I've learned over the years to trust my gut, and my gut is telling me he's the real deal." She held up a hand when he started to speak. "I'll take it under advisement and be cautious. But I still think he could be useful and I can't stand sitting behind a desk, rifling through papers as the only way to track this guy down. I need to be out there doing something."

"I get that. Trust me, I get up every morning now dreading what the day will bring and how many others, getting up to do nothing more than have breakfast, take their kids to school, and go to work, won't ever be coming home again. I want this guy stopped as much as you do."

They continued down the sidewalk, the mellow radiance of early morning swathing the world in soft golden light. But the beauty of the day was smothered under the anxiety of waiting for a madman to make his next move. Meg felt like a coiled spring, wound too tight, simply waiting for the other shoe to drop. And it could happen any second.

How many would die this time?

Chapter 17

Decapitation Strike: A precise attack aimed at eliminating the entire leadership of an organization.

Monday, April 17, 1:45 PM
Tyler Mountain
South Charleston, West Virginia

Puffing and nearly out of breath, the man pushed up the last twenty feet to the crest of the ridge leading to Tyler Mountain. He bent over, bracing his hands on his knees, his lungs working like bellows. As he struggled to catch his breath, he scanned along the cleared track running eight hundred and fifty feet downhill toward the Kanawha River.

He'd chosen well; it was perfect.

The power transmission towers running up the hill, carrying high voltage lines from the power distribution node on the river's edge, up over the mountain and to the communities beyond, made it the ideal location. The land around the towers was cleared regularly, giving him a perfect view of the distribution center and Dow chemical plant on the north bank of the river, and then all the way across the river to South Charleston beyond. South Charleston—a suburb of Charleston, the capital city of West Virginia. South Charleston—his next target.

He shrugged out of his backpack and sat on the ground,

propping it between his knees. Bracing his feet on the down-hill slope, he rooted through the bag, finally pulling out the control unit. He turned it on, made a final few adjustments, and then looked east, toward Rollins Lane, where he'd left the drone a mere twenty minutes before.

He couldn't stop the grin from lighting his face. Frankly, he didn't need to—there was no one on this hill to even note his presence. This one he could simply sit back and enjoy without fear of discovery.

"Look out, below, 'cause here I come."

Monday, April 17, 1:56 PM
Krispy Kreme Doughnuts Parking Lot
South Charleston, West Virginia

Officer Trent Howard peeled back the tab on his sixteen-ounce coffee cup, snapping it into place before raising the cup to his lips for a long, slow sip. He closed his eyes, waiting for the hit of caffeine that was still minutes away; just knowing it was coming was a relief.

He was only seven hours into his twelve-hour shift, but felt like he'd already done two shifts back to back. A smile curved his lips at the thought of his wife and new baby, curled together in their bed as he left the house at six-thirty that morning. Their first newborn brought a lot of new experiences, most of them good, but the hardest for him was lack of sleep. It might be his wife getting up every two hours to feed the baby, but he woke up with her. Their son was now four weeks old, but a month into this new routine, Howard was wearing down. Family assured him they'd all get into a regular schedule soon, but it couldn't come fast enough as far as he was concerned.

In his line of work, sleepy and inattentive wasn't an option. As much as he hated to perpetuate the cop-at-the-doughnut-shop persona, coffee was currently his best friend.

And the sugar and fat from the doughnut didn't hurt either.

Returning to his squad car, he heard the usual squawk and chatter coming from his radio—dispatch calling, answered by officers on patrol. He glanced at his watch, deciding he could take another two minutes to lean against his door, soaking up a little sun while the caffeine slowly trickled into his bloodstream. Setting his coffee cup on the roof of his car, he reached into the brown paper bag he carried and pulled out a double-chocolate-filled doughnut. He bit in, sweetness and chocolate exploding over his tongue. He sighed in pleasure. Ten minutes from now he'd be wired and ready to take on the rest of his shift.

At first he wasn't sure what he was hearing—a faint, whirring buzz that seemed to come from the northeast. Jamming another bite of doughnut into his mouth, he turned, scanning the low roofs of the plazas that surrounded the coffee shop. In the distance, the vibrant green shoulders of Tyler Mountain rose into the blue sky beyond the flowing water of the unseen Kanawha River.

But there was something about that buzz that tickled cells deep in his brain. Like somewhere in his sleep-fogged mind, he'd heard it before. Not a lawn mower. Not a leaf blower.

What is that?

Trent stepped past his police car and stood next to the curb of Maccorkle Avenue SW as cars whizzed by. He nudged his sunglasses further up his nose and stared off into the distance toward the east as he pushed the last of the doughnut into his mouth, chewing mechanically.

He almost missed it, the tiny dot in the sky that swam into view, coming in off the river.

Connections slammed into place, making him jerk back from the road, already spinning toward his patrol car. The

buzzing of a small motor. A small, unmanned flying appa-
ratus in the air. Two bombings already in neighboring
states.

He yanked open the car door, diving in and jamming the
keys in the ignition. His surprisingly steady hand hit the
right spot on the first try and the car roared to life. Turning on lights and sirens, he roared out of the parking lot,
around the corner and onto Maccorkle, heading east. The
thump and splash on the roof of his car barely registered
as his nearly full coffee cup flew off. But the rush of adrenaline swamped any effect caffeine might have had.

*You're insane. You can't follow an airborne drone
through city streets and catch it.*

Maybe not, but he was going to try. And he was going
to get as many people as possible to help.

He picked up his radio mic, speeding through traffic
and weaving around cars that pulled out of his way with
only one hand. "Dispatch, this is Patrol 24, 10–8. I have
an 11–54, an unidentified flying object seen flying into
South Charleston over the Kanawha. I think it's a 10–79.
It looks like the drones used in the DC and Maryland
bombings." He automatically rattled off the radio codes
for a suspicious vehicle and a bomb threat. "Recommend
emergency evacuation of all federal, state, and municipal
government offices and buildings in South Charleston."

"This is Dispatch, 10–4. Report current location and direction of travel of 11–54."

"I'm on Maccorkle Avenue Southwest, just turning onto
E Street. The drone is headed southeast, toward downtown. Request all available units to report visual on
11–54."

"10–4."

Dispatch went silent and Howard jammed the radio mic
back into its slot. With both hands on the wheel, he hit the

accelerator hard, sorting through possible targets in his head. *They said a one-mile range, so has to be downtown. Government or administration. Post office. Police head-quarters. Fire headquarters. Division of Natural Resources. What about churches? Or banks? Too many banks to pro-tect them all.* A part of his brain considered and discarded the Dow chemical plant. *Past it already, thank God. If that had been the target, it would already be too late and we'd have a massive environmental emergency on our hands.*

The radio crackled to life. "Patrol 11 to Dispatch. I have eyes on the 11–54, 6th Avenue and D Street. Headed southwest."

Howard took a hard left onto 7th Avenue, still one block north and west of the drone's location. Tires squealed and cars pulled out of the way as he flew by. Even shooting through city streets at sixty-five, certainly faster than the drone could fly from his single quick view of it, there was no way he could match its straight trajectory over the city buildings when he had to follow the grid city planners set out almost a century before.

He took a hard right at D Street, the car shuddering when it nearly went on two wheels as he shot past the Criel Native American burial mound from 250 BC with-out a glance. The car's back end started to swing out and he white-knuckled the steering wheel, fighting for control and only barely winning. His heart pounded even harder now, the throbbing in his ears nearly blocking out the ca-cophony of other sirens as he bulleted down D Street. It was clear every available officer was converging on down-town.

City Hall. Had they thought about City Hall? Evacu-ated it? A stream of faces appeared in his mind's eye like a slide show. The mayor, his staff, the clerks. Good people who always had a kind word for those trying to make their way in this small suburb of the capital of West Virginia. *Who would want to kill these people?*

"Patrol 4 to Dispatch. The drone appears to be landing on the roof of 324 4th Avenue."

Howard's mouth ran dry. The Division of Natural Resources. They had seconds now, half a minute max. *Had word gotten through? Was everyone out?*

He had to slow slightly as another police cruiser coming from the south careened around the corner onto 4th Avenue, but then he followed, hammering the brakes almost immediately. The street was full of people still streaming out of the post office on the north side and the Division of Natural Resources on the south.

He'd done it. They were getting out.

He jerked to a stop on the side of the road behind the other cruiser and sprinted from the car toward the Division of Natural Resources, encouraging confused workers to keep going. "Keep moving, get as far down the street as you can. Keep—"

The roar of the blast came from overhead and Howard only had enough time to wrap his arms around an older woman, pulling her down to the pavement on her knees and curling his body over hers before the wave of heat hit.

Monday, April 17, 2:09 PM
Tyler Mountain
South Charleston, West Virginia

Success.

The single word beat victoriously behind the man's sternum, matching the beat of his heart. *Suc-cess. Suc-cess. Suc-cess.*

He swayed on his feet, nearly light-headed with the joy shooting like lightning through his veins. He was in control and they trembled at his will. Never before in his life had people truly feared him; but now they did, and it was a truly heady experience.

He'd heard the sirens, so they knew ahead of time the hand of doom was about to smite them, but there'd be no way to know what his target was and no time to figure it out. And now the Division of Natural Resources was gone.

In the distance, black smoke boiled in greasy billows from a location inside the heart of downtown. He couldn't see the actual building from this distance, but he knew he'd hit the mark. Wanting the cover of the line of buildings down the length of 4th Avenue, he'd come in from the northeast, skimming the rooftops. He couldn't have missed number 324; it was the only three-story building on the block. Guaranteed bull's-eye.

He could imagine his target as he must have been in his last moments. Sitting behind his desk, toiling away at the nonsensical red tape that was his entire existence. Probably searching for ways to make the lives of honest Mountaineers more difficult. Raising his head slightly at the sound of sirens in the distance, wondering what poor schmuck had gotten himself in trouble this time.

They're coming for you. . . .

The thump of something hitting the roof over his head, the squint of confusion. Then the whoosh of the explosion and the openmouthed, glassy-eyed expression of shock as the fireball raced toward him before consuming him in its hellish maw. Until nothing was left of his worthless self but carbonized bone and charred muscle.

With a jubilant laugh, he settled back down on the hillside. He could bask for another minute or two; there was no way anyone would be looking for him here . . . yet. They'd be scouring the town first and wouldn't look toward the hills beyond until eyewitness reports came in. So he had a few minutes to sit and watch the beauty of destruction he had caused.

He liked the feeling of control, of knowing that the power of life and death was cradled in his rough, work-weary hands.

He wanted to do it again. Soon.

But what should he cleanse next? The drone was starting to be notable, so he might only have one or two more opportunities to use it.

Go big.

Did he dare?

Few things would be bigger, or be a way to thumb his nose at the government, quite like this. It would take planning. It would take smarts. It would also take the kind of balls that few who knew him would think he had—because to pull this off, he'd need to be close, real close. Close enough to risk capture.

He grinned, feeling even more victorious than just a few minutes ago. *Three down and they still can't catch me or stop me. And if nothing else grabbed their attention, this certainly will.*

Time to move. He had the next strike to plan. And this one was going to put him in the history books for sure.

Chapter 18

Clear: A call made by the handler that a search area is blank.

Monday, April 17, 2:24 PM
Forensic Canine Unit; J. Edgar Hoover Building
Washington, DC

Meg looked up from the report she was reading as Hawk jumped up from where he snoozed beside her desk. His body was tight with tension, his tail held high as he stared intently toward the open door of the Forensic Canine Unit bull pen.

She laid a hand on the back of his neck, feeling the coiled muscles under soft fur. "What's wrong, Hawk? What do you hear?"

Brian and Rocco were on their feet then, while Lacey lifted her head from where it had rested on her paws, her ears quirked forward toward the open doorway. Only then could the humans in the room hear running feet.

Meg's stomach tied into a greasy knot, instinct already knowing what was coming.

Craig sprinted into the canine unit bull pen. "Another bombing!"

The remaining team hit their feet.

"Where?" Meg asked.

"South Charleston, West Virginia." Craig picked up the

remote to the wall panel and brought up a video feed. "This is live, courtesy of the local PD."

The video showed a small-town street with cars parked in diagonal slots along both sides. Fire trucks filled the road in front of the building. The ladder truck was already in use and firefighters at the top of the ladder directed a high pressure stream of water toward the top of the building.

Brian walked closer to the screen. "Are they so lucky the fire station is directly across the street?"

"Looks like it," Craig said. "Looks like the trucks only had to pull out to the far side of the street and set up. That would have saved considerable time."

"Do they need us to go?" Lauren asked. "Or do they have local search and rescue who can get there faster?"

"I don't think they need search and rescue at all." At Lauren's indrawn breath, Craig clarified. "From what I got from the fifteen-second conversation I had with Peters in the hallway, they think they got everyone out. They're doing a head count now."

"Got them all out after the bomb went off with no injuries?" Brian's tone was heavily laced with skepticism.

"No. Before the thing even landed. A really on-the-ball cop heard the thing flying in over the Kanawha River, connected it to the bombings, and radioed it in. South Charleston PD had every municipal, state, and federal office building evacuating while the drone was still incoming. It landed and went off, but there was no one inside to be injured. Property damage, sure, but initial estimates are no loss of life and only a few minor injuries—a twisted ankle on the stairs and being hit by debris from the blast in the street, that kind of thing." Craig studied the footage. "That's why there are so many people. It's not just the one building; it's the post office across the street and the city library next door. Once they were out, they stayed out."

Meg sat back down in her desk chair, her knees weak

with relief. *His first major failure. What fallout would that cause?* "How did they get them out so fast? They couldn't have had more than about two minutes' notice on it."

"They figure about two and a half. The PD took the easy route. They pooled their dispatchers and called one person per building, telling them to pull the fire alarm. That got everyone out. Explanations could come later."

"Smart thinking." Brian patted Lacey. "Down, girl." Then he stepped around her to study the video footage. Several cops milled around the area helping the injured or calming the upset. "That cop deserves a medal. Quick thinking may have saved a lot of lives."

"I'm sure we'll hear more about him or her in the coming days," Craig agreed. "It'll be nice to see something positive above the fold for a change."

"I can see it now." Using both hands, Brian drew the headline in the air as if it was a long banner. "FOILED! MYSTERY BOMBER CHEATED OF HIS TARGET." He grinned. "Yeah, that will be nice to see." His hands dropped to his sides with a light slap. "But you know what this really means?"

"Skinner isn't our guy." Meg leaned back in her chair and blew out a breath. "We're back to the drawing board."

"Back to the drawing board, but maybe not exactly to square one," Craig said. "We've covered a lot of ground since we focused on Skinner, and he even taught us a few things about that mind-set. I honestly think we're looking at this *kind* of guy, just not this *particular* guy. Think about all the things he said about the government."

"Every one of them rang true to what we've heard so far from our bomber," Meg said.

Craig nodded his agreement. "This kind of discontent is like a disease slowly spreading through the country. There are certainly more of them out there than I suspected. We have a much better understanding about where our guy stands mentally because of all the time we spent with Skinner."

"Our guy may not even know he's failed yet. But when he does, I have a bad feeling he's not going to take it very well," Brian said.

"Funny, I was thinking the same thing. Is this kind of failure going to prompt him to try for a bigger target? Or change his tactics since the drone is beginning to be its own calling card?"

"He hits a big enough target, he won't need to stop using the drone. The locals got away with it this time because it was a small, three-story building in a small city. If he hits a skyscraper in New York City, they won't have enough time to evacuate."

"He tries to go after New York City, the inhabitants will rip his country bumpkin ass limb from limb," Brian muttered loud enough only Meg could hear.

"So it's even more important we find this guy pronto," Craig continued. He looked back at the video footage. The crowd had calmed and order prevailed. In fact, there was an air of triumph, of nice-try-but-you-missed-us in the air. "Hey, I bet that's him right there."

"Who?"

"Look at the cop on the left there. The one who looks a bit sheepish as everyone is slapping him on the back or trying to talk to him. There's your hero. He looks like a regular guy, just out there doing the job. But he's one of us. He's going to help us nail this son of a bitch." He turned back to the team. "He just bought us a day or two of no fatalities. Let's not fail him by dropping the ball."

There was a chorus of agreement and the team returned to work with fresh enthusiasm.

Chapter 19

Fringing: The tendency of a novice or poorly trained nose work dog to indicate or alert when it is near, but not at, the actual source of the target odor.

Tuesday, April 18, 10:14 AM
Outside Moorefield, Hardy County, West Virginia

He'd failed.

Not one person died or suffered more than a minor injury in the attack. That meant his own personal target was alive and well, and probably entertaining everyone he knew with his tales of derring-do. It made him want to put his fist through a wall.

Then there was the newspaper. The *Washington Post* was spread across the kitchen counter, the headline screaming in sixty-point font: THWARTED—BOMBER HITS TARGET BUT MISSES VICTIMS. Under the headline was a four-inch square head shot of the cop in his uniform, as American as apple pie with his baby blue eyes, overly white smile, and uniform hat perched over sun-bleached blond hair. He looked like the goddamned captain of the football team.

He himself was just a below-the-fold footnote. The bomber who had killed and maimed was losing his edge. His bombs now came with their own built-in early warning system and, while still effective, he was missing the mark.

A single swipe of his arm sent the pages scattering to the ground. He stepped on the newspaper and ground his boot heel into it, hearing the satisfying rip of paper shredding.

He returned to the rough kitchen table, yanking out a chair with a screech of chair legs on floorboards, and threw himself down, studying the completed drone that stood on the table.

Leaning forward, he gave one of the propellers a flick with his forefinger, watching it spin. The other drones had been perfect for what he needed them to do—create as much damage as possible while he controlled from a distance—but that was no longer enough. He eyed the bulk of C-4 blocks strapped to the bottom of the drone, the dull silver of a series of blasting caps sunk deep into the plasticine-like material of the blocks. The detonation cord from the blasting caps was coiled on the table still and wouldn't be connected to the charge until he was on site. He didn't want a bomb of this size sitting live in his house overnight or in his truck while he was driving.

It was the biggest bomb yet, which meant he needed his biggest drone to carry it. Considering the weight of the frame and the bigger propellers and the additional explosive, his battery time was going to be under five minutes, so he was going to have to be close.

Close meant risking getting caught. He likely only had one shot left to deliver a bomb via drone, and he was ready to take that chance. He was willing to risk it all for a chance to take out the National Security Agency.

Go big or go home.

The NSA was a glorified bunch of snitches. Eavesdropping on phone conversations and ferreting through your e-mail or browser history. Telling the higher-ups so they could unleash the power of the government all over your ass. Sending you to jail for expressing your God-given rights to freedom and self-determination, rights they didn't seem to think you deserved.

So the snitches would pay. They'd pay for all the misery they'd caused. For all the families broken apart and the innocents sent to jail. For spying on their own people.

They'd pay with their lives.

Chapter 20

Heart Dog: A dog with a unique connection to its handler, often spoken of as a "canine soul mate."

Tuesday, April 18, 10:54 AM
Richmond Police Headquarters
Richmond, Virginia

It had been years since Meg stood in this sunlit foyer, but it felt like only yesterday. And now to stand here without a dog at her side left her feeling naked and alone.

The dark paneled walls were covered with numerous framed pictures and display cases—department photos, awards, trophies, portraits of police chiefs, and more—but her eye was drawn to a single display case on the far wall.

In honor of the fallen.

She was too far away to see the individual portraits and the engraved brass plaques, but she'd stood in front of the case often enough to know the faces and names by heart. The department's first line of duty death, Officer Thomas Kirkham, in 1869. The tragic loss of ten officers all on the same day in 1870, when a balcony in the Virginia State Capitol collapsed, killing the officers and fifty-two spectators. The oldest photo of an officer, Robert Austin, resplendent in official regimentals in 1898. All the way to the most recent death, in 2003, of Officer Douglas Wendel.

Almost unwillingly, her gaze drifted to the lower right-hand corner on the case, where she knew the picture would be. Where the only K-9 lost in the line of duty was pictured. Deuce . . .

She knew coming here would be hard because she couldn't come and not mark the passing of her own dog. She didn't even realize she was moving until she found herself in front of the case, her gaze fixed on that beloved face, intelligent dark eyes, and glossy fur.

Her fist closed around the pendant containing his ashes, the edges of the glass digging into her flesh as memory dragged her unwillingly back to that day. . . .

Sprinting flat-out down the darkened street, the sobs of the teenaged girl still ringing in her ears. Deuce running in front of her, his nose down as he focused on the scent trail. A single frantic swipe to wipe her eyes clear as rain pounded down on them, flattening Deuce's fur against his body and her uniform to her skin. Her gasping breaths fanning out in diaphanous clouds in the chill spring air.

This was their chance to get him.

A serial rapist was attacking young women out on the streets—the homeless, sex workers, and those simply in the wrong place at the wrong time and without the street smarts to recognize trouble until it was too late. Each girl had been left alive, but battered and often cut by the knife he held at their throats to force their silence until he was done, leaving behind only the hollowed out shells of the young women they'd once been. They would heal, but the scars he inflicted would linger forever.

His carelessness with the fragile spirits enraged Meg, who was close enough to her teen years to remember the bravado that often overlaid the uncertainty of not only who you were but who you had the potential to be. This man's attacks terrified and left these girls forever locked in cycles of self-loathing and shame.

Until tonight. Tonight he'd made the mistake of going after someone who not only had street smarts, but an indomitable spirit that wouldn't be cowed by one man's assumption of power over the weak. When Chelsea Sanders was attacked, she did everything right. She fought back, using the Kubotan on her key chain as she struck at his eyes and throat, landed a kick between his legs, and screamed for help.

He abandoned ship.

But before he got away, Chelsea committed one last act to seal his fate: She pulled the black knit balaclava from his head, revealing his face. And then the clever girl continued to scream at the top of her lungs, so he didn't think of wasting time using the knife on her, but instead melted away into the rain, leaving her sobbing with relief.

Chelsea couldn't realize the balaclava soaking up rain on the sidewalk was their most important evidence at that moment. Meg and Deuce, on duty in their patrol car only a few blocks away, were able to come quickly when responding officers realized they had a way to track the rapist.

Deuce took the scent, found the trail immediately, and they were off. He never faltered in his path, but followed surely through the dark, rain-drenched streets. They tracked the perp for blocks, never catching sight of him, but Meg knew they were close behind nevertheless. She kept dispatch notified of their position; more dogs and additional backup were coming and they needed to know where she was at all times.

The alley was dim, with only ambient light to illuminate its length between two tenements, leaving the recesses draped in inky darkness. Puddles gathered in the hollows of the cracked and broken pavement, reflecting what little light crept in from either end. High above, skeletal fire escapes scaled the buildings, ending about eight feet above the pavement. Dumpsters lined either side, providing ample nooks to hide, or a boost to a lower level balcony.

Deuce would have entered the alley at a run, but some sixth sense, a warning of impending danger, made Meg pull him back from the entrance. She crouched down beside him, running her hand over the wet fur, feeling the warmth of his body, and the heaving of his ribs as he panted. Her own heart pounded from the chase.

Her back pressed to the wall, Meg peered around the corner into the alley. All seemed quiet and still, but she couldn't tell if that was because the perp had passed through, or because he was hiding inside. The fire escapes were silent and empty.

She glanced up the street, taking in the length of the block. They could circle the block to see if Deuce could pick up the scent from the other end of the alley, but in that time, the suspect could escape from either end. She could wait for the incoming backup to arrive and someone else to close ranks from the other side, but if he had already gone through, he'd have more of a lead on them and the scent cone would disintegrate, washed away in the pounding rain. Going in, they risked meeting him with no backup; if they waited, they'd likely lose him, and then who would suffer as his next victim?

A no-win situation.

They needed to go in. She unholstered her gun in preparation. They'd walk the alley and if the perp went right through, then they'd pick up the chase back out in the open. She considered pulling out her small, sturdy flashlight, but thought better of being such an obvious target. They knew he was carrying a knife, but didn't know if he also had a gun. He might be the type of sick pervert who found a knife in close combat was more terrifying because a woman could cut herself on it simply by struggling. Meg couldn't make any assumptions.

She and Deuce started down the alley, Deuce in the lead. Behind a Dumpster to their left, the sound of skittering feet told her they'd interrupted a pack of rats scavenging for food. But Deuce was single-minded, his nose down, following the scent.

His posture told her they were getting close as his movements slowed slightly, his tail held stiffly as he concentrated. Meg peered into the darkness ahead. Several Dumpsters lined the right-hand wall, a foot or two of space between each of them. Assuming he was in the alley, it would be the perfect place to hide.

They'd have to check each one out individually. It would cost time, but if he was holed up with a gun, waiting for something to cross his line of sight, she and Deuce were sitting ducks.

With a hand motion, she told Deuce to heel and he stayed glued to her side. At each gap, she watched her dog for a signal that the perp was close. She checked each nook even without an alert just in case, peering around the corner, leading with her firearm clutched in both hands. As gap after gap revealed nothing more than empty spaces or tumbled garbage, she continued slowly and carefully.

She knew they were close when Deuce suddenly swerved toward the darkness between two Dumpsters. The space didn't look out of the ordinary. It was filled with piled garbage bags and a teetering stack of boxes balanced precariously near the opening. The smell of rotten food and God only knows what else made her eyes water and was nearly overpowering.

The man exploded out of the trash, dark and hooded, throwing his weight at the boxes so they toppled over onto cop and dog. The gun glinted darkly in the dim light and

Meg had just enough time to aim and get a shot off before his gun fired.

Then he was flying down the alley, heading for freedom.

Meg, miraculously, wasn't hit and scrambled to her feet. "Deuce, attack!"

The first sign that something was wrong was when Deuce stumbled fifteen feet down the alley. But he got his feet under him and put on a burst of speed before slamming into the man's back, his teeth closing over the man's forearm, the force of his body weight taking them both to the ground. The man screamed in pain into the pavement and fought the dog, who held on for dear life, but then Meg was there.

Deuce held on as she cuffed the man's hands behind his back.

It was only then, with the perp safely secured, that she commanded her dog to release him. But instead of letting go and sitting at attention as expected, he crouched on the ground, breathing hard.

"Deuce? Deuce!" Meg turned back to the perp. "Move one inch and I'll just shoot without a second thought." She moved to her dog, keeping the perp in sight at all times. Her hand came away wet with blood at the very first touch of his fur.

She'd escaped the perp's bullet, but Deuce had not.

She frantically radioed for assistance for Deuce, even as sirens screamed closer as her backup finally arrived. And there, huddled in the rain, chilled and drenched to the skin, her beloved dog drew his last breath in her arms. In an instant, all that warm vitality, fierce loyalty, and love vanished. She wept into his chilled fur as his body cooled, not wanting to let go, not yet, because letting go meant saying good-bye.

The other officers stood by awkwardly, not knowing what to do. It was finally her sergeant who pulled her away and quietly ordered the men to carry the dog to a waiting patrol car.

And just like that, Deuce was gone from her life forever.

Deuce's photo blurred as tears welled in her eyes, but she bore down, blinking and swallowing hard. She fixed her gaze on the wall above the cabinet and just concentrated on steadying her breathing. In ten seconds she had herself back under control and allowed herself one last look at his joyful face. She pressed her fingers to the glass. "I miss you, buddy," she whispered. "Every single day."

No one ever questioned what happened in that alley. The department gave her its full support. But she couldn't stop questioning her own decisions that night.

She'd left Deuce's bulletproof vest in the front seat of her patrol car. Most K-9s didn't wear their vests unless the situation called for it. The vests were heavy, hot, cumbersome, and tiring to wear for long periods. Vests were used at the officer's discretion. Time was at a premium that night, the pouring rain washing away the suspect's scent much too quickly, and rather than waste time and possibly lose the perp, they hit the scent trail immediately. She might have made the call differently if a gun was part of his modus operandi from the start, but he'd only been reported with a knife and the vests didn't protect the face and throat.

She more strongly questioned her own belief that she could handle the situation by herself, that she *had* to handle it on her own. How differently would the bust have gone down if she'd waited for backup? She'd never know, so she could only blame herself for the loss of her dog. Self-confidence in tatters, she resigned from the department, not believing herself fit for duty, and not willing to risk the life of the new dog they were already offering her.

Her fingertips slid from the glass and she turned away.

At the foyer doors, she stood still for a moment, her hand on the door pull, dragging in one more deep breath and letting it out. Then, squaring her shoulders, she went through, her back straight and her head high.

When Meg got to the open doorway of the office, she paused for a few seconds to look in. Behind the nameplate engraved with Sergeant Will Archer sat a man in his midfifties, even more bald than the last time she'd seen him, but still wiry as ever. He was hunched over his keyboard, slowly and precisely typing out what was probably his latest report.

Meg knocked on the door frame and Archer looked up. His face lit up at the sight of her standing in his doorway.

"You made my day when you e-mailed asking if you could stop by." He got up from his chair, crossed the tiny office in three strides, and had her wrapped in a bear hug within seconds.

After the sorrow of seeing Deuce's portrait, this was the balm her soul needed and she hung on for a second before letting go with a laugh. "Hey, Sarge."

"Come in. Sit." He ushered her in and shut the door behind her, then indicated the chairs across from his desk. "Can I get you a cup of coffee?"

"Only if you're trying to poison me. I haven't been away from here long enough to forget how bad the coffee is."

He chuckled and raised the mug that sat beside his mouse. "You're not wrong there. So if you didn't come for the coffee, what brings you?"

"As much as I'd love to stop by just to say hi to you and the guys, I admit I'm here to ask for a favor."

Archer hesitated in front of his desk for just a fleeting moment, then he took his chair. "This favor have to do with the bombings? I saw your picture in the paper."

"Yes, it does."

"What can we in Richmond do for you? Is there some indication the perp is from here?"

"Not at all. And I should say right up front that this isn't a Bureau-endorsed visit. This is me doing a little legwork on my own, because I think you might be able to help."

One eyebrow quirked in interest. "Intriguing. You know I'll do whatever I can. This guy needs to be stopped before more people die. What are you looking for?"

"A contact in CID."

Archer stared at her in surprise; clearly this wasn't the direction he saw the conversation going. Then he settled back in his chair, crossing his arms over his chest to study her. "You know I know people. What will that do for the case?"

"This evidence hasn't been released to the public yet, but the bomber is using tagged, military grade C-4."

Archer whistled. "You think the bomber stole the C-4 from the military, or got it on the black market after someone else stole it?"

"There was a theft from an army reserve in Wheeling, West Virginia, last November. I'm sure the FBI is thinking about it too, but you know how bureaucracy works. They'll have to apply for access to CID records, then the army needs to grant that access, then they have to track down the records—"

"And you're looking for a shortcut." Archer cut her off. "You want me to call in a favor to get those records now."

"I do." She gave him a wary smile. "Too much to ask?"

"I know you were at the first bomb site. Were you at the second?"

"We were, actually."

He winced slightly. "I can't imagine what that was like.

So, no, it's not asking too much. Not when you take into account what you've already seen and done for this investigation. Let me make a few calls. I've got a buddy who can help out and I can probably get you something within a couple of days."

Relief flooded Meg. "Thank you. I know this is asking a lot, and going above and beyond."

"Not really. Not when you consider what's going on. And you know how I hate bureaucratic BS."

She laughed. "Oh yes, I remember. I admit I was counting on it."

"So let's cut through some of that if it will help. We'll let the other guys go through channels, but I'll see if I can get you the information you need sooner. Just keep it to need-to-know for now and remember that it came from an anonymous source. I'm not paying him back by getting him into trouble with the brass."

"Deal." She relaxed back into the chair, feeling the tension leave her for the first time since she'd left Hawk at the obedience school with Cara and got in the car to drive to Richmond. "I hate how this guy makes me feel."

"Angry?"

"Helpless. I need to do something, but so far all we do is come in when it's too late. This will help change that."

"I make no promises, but hopefully it'll be what you need."

"That's all I can ask."

Archer scribbled a name and phone number on a Post-it note and handed it to her. "Here's his info. I'm not sure how he'll contact you but you'll hear from him somehow."

Meg dug into her pocket and pulled out a business card. "All my contact info is there. Whatever works for him works for me."

"I'll pass that along." He grinned at her. "Now that business is over, tell me all about your new boy and life in the Bureau. Hawk, right?"

"Yes, that's him." Satisfied, Meg sat back and allowed herself a few minutes to catch up with an old friend, knowing she'd done everything in her power to move the case along. For now.

Chapter 21

Rapid Dominance: A US military doctrine emphasizing a crushing display of force to intimidate an enemy.

Wednesday, April 19, 10:32 AM
National Cryptologic Museum
Annapolis Junction, Maryland

The man backed the truck into a parking spot farthest away from the museum, then scanned the lot—only four other cars, all at least fifty feet away, parked close to the front door. Perfect.

Pulling the bill of his cap down further over his forehead and the collar of his jacket up higher, he got out, carefully keeping the body of the truck between himself and the museum to prevent anyone seeing him. Unhooking the vinyl truck bed cover, he drew it back to reveal the crate beneath. Lifting the lid, he peered inside. The drone poised like a venomous spider, black as night, eight legs splayed and ready to spring.

He carefully lowered the lid. A quick glance over his shoulder showed him the forest line, a mere ten feet from the back of the truck, and the narrow utility road that wound through the trees. Time to get this show on the road. By midmorning the NSA building would be fully staffed; now was the time to strike.

He tugged on leather work gloves, carefully unloaded

the crate, then disappeared into the trees with it. It was large and incredibly awkward, but for a man used to hauling rock, digging post holes, and hefting one-hundred-pound sheep, it wasn't so hard to carry.

Minutes later, he was at his prechosen location, right under the overpass. He unpacked the crate, removing a small detonator remote and the radio transmitter, complete with a small color monitor to view the camera output. With infinite care, he lifted the drone from the box and set it on the ground. He did a quick check of the payload strapped to the bottom and connected the detonator cord so it was now able to transmit a charge. Time to rock and roll.

After one last loving glance at his creation, he jogged out from under the overpass and back into the trees. He'd selected a small clearing in the trees to fly from, close enough to the drone to be able to see it pass overhead, and close enough to the truck if a quick getaway was required. He'd never been so close to a target, and while he was adjacent to a freeway entrance, he knew very well the Fort Meade NSA building was heavily guarded by teams of NSA police officers backstopped by experienced security investigators. That was why drawing blood here would be such a feather in his cap. It was also why the deck was stacked against him. Every one of those officers would have a firearm, and the outer perimeter checkpoints were likely stocked with additional firepower in the form of sharpshooting rifles or automatic weapons.

He couldn't see his target through the trees, but he could see OPS2A in his mind—the tallest building in the complex and home to much of the NSA brass, a towering black monstrosity of glass and steel. The cold, faceless icon of a cold, faceless agency.

His plan was to fly in a U-shaped flight path and come up on the NSA complex from the back and to the west while he stayed safely out of harm's way to the north. He'd land on the northwest corner near a row of giant fans circulating air through massive ducts into the build-ing—where the building would be least stable—and deto-nate as soon as it made contact. All told, it was about three quarters of a mile and, at an estimated thirty miles per hour, would take about ninety seconds. He'd be back in the truck and leaving at a leisurely pace within two min-utes while all the attention was centered on the smoking wreckage he left behind.

No time like the present. He set the detonator remote on a nearby tree stump and reached for the transmitter. With a few quick adjustments, he brought the drone online. Next he brought the motors to life; even from this distance he could hear the whir of them spinning up. He increased the throttle and the elevator and it was airborne. He piloted it out from under the overpass and up one hundred and fifty feet, then forward, the pitch of the rotors' whirring rising as they settled into their full twenty-thousand-revolutions-per-minute capacity.

It was glorious. This feeling of freedom, of flying like a bird and seeing the world beneath the clarity of the sunlit sky. Of holding life and death in your hands. On the monitor, the drone glided over asphalt and treetops. Over the gleam of sunlight bouncing off windshields in the parking lot.

That was when he heard the first defensive response. Even from where he stood, the boom of multiple gunshots reverberated in the air. The drone stayed steady, so it wasn't hit, but it had been seen and they were trying to bring it down before it could reach its target.

He increased the throttle slightly. He didn't dare overtax the battery and leave himself short of power, but he knew he had a small margin of leeway. He was so close, he couldn't fail now. Not when the drone was sailing over the original low, sprawling NSA building far below and OPS2A was in his sights.

Heart pounding in his chest, but his hands dead steady, he guided the drone over the building, keeping as low as possible to use the building as cover from gunfire, and gently set it down on a clear section of roof.

In the distance, sirens were screaming from the complex itself. No time to waste. Picking up the other remote, he held his thumb over the control switch.

He hesitated for only a second before he depressed the button.

Chapter 22

Endgame: In chess, the stage of the game where few pieces are left on the board and strategy is influenced by the type of pieces a player has remaining.

Wednesday, April 19, 10:46 AM
National Cryptologic Museum
Annapolis Junction, Maryland

The button clicked as he depressed it, and he closed his eyes, waiting to hear the satisfying blast. He was so close he had hopes of feeling the shock waves pass by, sliding eerily over his skin and shimmering through the trees.

His breath came hard and fast, not from exertion, but from excitement. From anticipation. He'd never been this close before, been so much a part of the attack.

Any second . . .

But nothing happened. Only the sirens' screams streaked through the air.

His eyes flew open and looked down at the remote in his hand. The red light to match the one under the drone was illuminated, just as expected. Just as it was three times before.

He lifted his thumb and pressed down again . . . harder. *Click.*

Nothing.

Panic clawed at his throat, trapping his breath in his

lungs. He stabbed at the button repeatedly, frantically, his breath coming even faster now as his heart beat a staccato rhythm in his chest.

Click, click, click, click.

Still nothing.

His head whipped up. He had to get out of here. They knew they were under attack and now they didn't have the dying and injured to distract them. Now they had nothing in mind but catching whoever was behind it.

With a muffled curse, he jammed the remote into his pocket, bent to pick up the transmitter from the ground, and sprinted down the service road. Through gaps in the trees he could see the Cryptologic Museum and the parking lot. He could swear there were more cars now. *Where had they come from in only the last twenty minutes?*

He broke from the trees, searching wildly, looking for eyes staring accusingly at him, but the parking lot was empty of any living soul. He sprinted to the truck, pushing his hand into his pocket and past the remote to find the keys. He pulled them out, but his shaking hand was slippery and uncoordinated and they tumbled with a jangle to the asphalt below. He scooped them off the ground and jammed the key into the lock, wrenching open the door and throwing himself into the cab. The transmitter slid across the seat to fall with a dull *thump* to the footwell below. For the first time ever, he ignored the costly technology.

He was done with drones anyway. In all likelihood, he was done, period.

He rammed the key into the ignition and the engine started with a roar. In a panic, he came off the clutch too quickly and the truck bunny-hopped slightly as it lurched forward and then stalled. He swore viciously and turned the engine over again, forcing himself to keep his feet on both the clutch and brake as he took two deep breaths, reminding himself he'd lose more time stalling out the old piece of crap than if he drove with a little more care. He eased more slowly off the clutch and onto the gas and the truck rolled forward with only the smallest of jerks.

He followed the roadway around the curve, taking the corners too fast, but not daring to go any slower, even at risk of tipping the pickup. He barreled past the spy plane display and then out onto Canine Road without daring to stop at the stop sign. Alarms were still screaming from every building in the complex, but now police sirens were wailing, both from the complex and incoming from outside the facility.

It was only about seventy feet to the on-ramp for MD-32 northwest and from there two and a half hours to home. If he could make it to the highway, he could escape. He pressed down harder on the accelerator, the old truck vibrating beneath him. The trip here had been tooth rattling, but at this speed, it was going to be bone jarring. He'd risk that any day for the chance to escape.

The sound of sirens was coming closer and the flash of blue and red was suddenly visible ahead roaring off the freeway. He geared up and hammered the accelerator, praying for that tiny extra bit of speed, enough to get him past the cops and onto the freeway and out to freedom.

He shot onto the on-ramp just as the black and white cruiser was coming up the paired off-ramp. Keeping his eyes forward and his face relaxed, only his stranglehold on the steering wheel might have given him away. The cop sailed past him without slowing and then he was on the freeway, headed for freedom.

One quick backward glance told him how close his escape had been—the police cruiser was stopped crosswise over the road, blocking anyone inside the complex from leaving. So very, very close. Seconds had made the differ-

ence today. A few more and he'd have been trapped behind the barricade.

But even given his near escape, dread curled like a hard
ball in his stomach. His bomb hadn't exploded, which
meant that his fingerprints were all over it. He might not
be in the system, but if they ever caught him, there'd be no
way around his role in building the bombs.

He needed to go home, to really think about how to
deal with this new reality. If he was lucky, he'd have time
for one more strike. But he had to figure out where, and
how, and when.

It was time to go out in a blaze of glory and then disappear forever.

Chapter 23

Positive Reinforcement Training: A method of training emphasizing food treats, praise, or play to reward an animal for performing a behavior the handler wants.

Wednesday, April 19, 11:52 AM
Starbucks, 7th Street NW and E Street NW
Washington, DC

Meg peered through the window of the coffee shop until she spotted a tall, willowy redhead behind the counter inside. She rapped lightly on the window. All three baristas turned to the window, but the redhead smiled and waved back, holding up a single index finger. *Give me a minute.* Meg gave her a thumbs-up and led Hawk onto the small fenced patio that enclosed a half dozen tables and chairs. Hawk stopped briefly at the wide metal dog dish, giving it a quick sniff before taking a drink.

They settled at the empty table farthest from the door, Hawk flopping down on the sun-warmed pavement, giving a gusty sigh of contentment and resting his head on crossed front paws. Meg turned her own face into the sun, grateful for the warmth of spring and a few moments of peace.

The door opened with a squeak of hinges. "There's my boy!"

Meg opened her eyes to see Katie, their favorite barista,

setting down the coffee and sandwich Meg had ordered by mobile app when they were a few blocks away. At her appearance, Hawk bolted to attention, sitting tall and offering a single paw in greeting.

Katie bent down to shake it before running a hand over his head. "How's my boy today? Handsome as ever, I see."

"I swear he knows a block away when we're coming here. And on days when you're not working, he's positively disappointed."

"Well, he's in luck today." Katie straightened and thrust a hand into her green apron pocket, coming out with an oversized dog biscuit.

If it was possible, Hawk sat up straighter, his whole body vibrating with excitement.

Katie shot a quick look at Meg, who nodded her permission, then leaned over and held out the biscuit for Hawk, who didn't move but vibrated even harder.

Meg took pity and released her invisible hold on him. "Okay, Hawk, take it."

He rose up on his hindquarters, neatly plucking the biscuit away without touching Katie's fingers. It was gone inside of thirty seconds.

"Does he even taste it?" Katie wondered.

"He must, because he knows when he comes in and you're on shift, there's a treat in it for him."

"Always. Gotta head back in. Enjoy your lunch. See you next time."

"Thanks for bringing my order out."

Katie stopped with her hand on the door handle. "I always love a chance to visit with my favorite boy." She threw them a sunny smile and then disappeared into the café.

Meg picked up her coffee and took a long, slow sip. She didn't have much time, but had told Brian she needed out of the office for a half hour, so she was determined to give herself a few moments of relaxation. Those moments were too few and far between lately and Hawk needed it as much as she did.

By reflex, her gaze darted back to the door when it opened again and a dark-haired man stepped out carrying a take-out coffee. She would have looked away again, but something about him seemed familiar and held her gaze.

He wore soft, faded blue jeans, a red plaid shirt rolled up over his forearms, and hiking boots, but nothing leapt out at her to help her identify him. His casual clothing said he wasn't an on-duty agent. Maybe he was someone she'd seen in the shop on her regular stop-ins without really taking notice?

The man's gaze rested on Hawk, but then he looked up to meet her eyes and the sight of that gold-flecked brown clicked recognition into place. The lack of gear, helmet, and soot had disguised him, but she'd never forget those eyes.

She pushed back her chair and stood. "Todd Webb, right?" She held out her hand. "Meg Jennings, from the FBI K-9 unit."

He grinned and shook her hand. "No need for an introduction. I remember you very well. And your picture in the paper only reinforced that memory."

Meg tried not to cringe at the mention of that photo. "Don't remind me." She dropped her gaze, turning slightly to look out into the street.

He grabbed her arm lightly, causing her to raise her face back up toward his. "Wait a second." He looked down to study her expression, something that at her height didn't happen often. "You're embarrassed." Confusion flitted across his face. "Why?"

"It wasn't a good day; you know that as much as I do. I wasn't exactly in a good place at that moment, and I certainly didn't want to advertise it."

"You'd had a hellish day, were exhausted right to the bone, and were grieving the loss of innocent people who were gone before you ever had a chance to help them. That picture was nothing less than pure honesty captured in a single frame. As a first responder, you don't have to explain that to me."

She gazed up at him, surprised and, if possible, further embarrassed by his words of understanding. But nothing in his gaze said he was being dishonest in his opinion or that he was surreptitiously making fun of her.

She indicated the empty chair opposite hers. "Have a few minutes to join me?"

"I'd love to. I'm off today and was just running errands when I came in for coffee. Is this your usual stop?"

She nodded. "It's just down the street from the Hoover, so it's convenient. And it has a dog-friendly patio."

"I'll have to remember that."

They took their seats and Webb stretched out his long legs, crossing his ankles as he looked down at her dog. "Hawk looks no worse for wear after that experience."

"He was exhausted the next day and a little dehydrated, but we got him back on his feet quickly. We pretty much had to, with the second bombing coming so soon after the first."

Webb leaned forward, cupping his hands around his coffee. "They sent you in for that one too?"

His eyes were flat, but Meg could see the knowledge there. This was a man who knew all too well what fire could do to a human body.

"We scrambled within twenty minutes of the blast and flew there directly."

"They never had a chance. Between the bomb and the natural gas fire . . ." Webb's words faded away and she saw his eyes go unfocused for a moment, as if he was seeing the site itself.

"They really didn't. Thirty-seven lives gone like—" She snapped her fingers. Hawk's eyes opened to look up at her, but when Meg didn't indicate any command, he settled again. "It was horrible. We do live finds, or injured. We don't often do dead, and it's the first time Hawk's done a fire like that. That's more your wheelhouse than mine, so you know what it's like."

"Yeah, it's bad. Was he confused by the overload of smells?"

"Maybe a little. What he knew was that there wasn't anything that smelled like a human he could find. He didn't understand what had happened to the people that were actually still there. I don't know if he even knew they were human." She took a long sip of her coffee to give herself time to calm slightly. "Hell, I didn't understand it. Still don't."

"No sane person does. What about the kids we pulled out of the rubble at the Whitten Building? Heard anything?"

"Everyone we pulled out alive is still with us. You remember Jill?"

"Of course I do. She's the reason I asked."

"She's doing great. She's at George Washington Hospital. They had her in the ICU for a few days, but she's out now and is supposedly coming along quite nicely."

"I should stop by to see her. The poor kid is probably bored to tears in there."

Meg fiddled with the sandwich she had yet to take a bite of, the discussion about the bomb sites having taken away her appetite.

Webb seemed to sense a misstep. "But enough about all that. I'm sure you're steeped in this investigation twenty-four/seven."

"That's the truth," Meg muttered.

"So let's talk about something more interesting. Tell me about you and Hawk."

Meg's head snapped up. That was a change in conversation she hadn't seen coming. "You want to talk about my dog?"

"And you, but sure, why not? I love dogs. Don't own one because of my crazy schedule. I live alone and I can't leave an animal on its own for the twenty-four hours straight I'm on shift, but I had one as a kid and I miss having one underfoot now." He leaned down to pet Hawk, but froze, his hand two inches above the dog's glossy black head, Hawk's eyes locked on him. "Is it okay if I touch him? Is he working?"

"Not right now, but thanks for asking. Go ahead."

Webb stretched down farther, extending his hand toward Hawk's nose to let him sniff first before running his palm over the sun-warmed fur. Hawk's tail thumped several times against the sidewalk. "Such a great dog. And smart. I really appreciate a smart working dog. How did you get him? Did you train with him at the Bureau?"

"Not even close." Meg looked down at her dog, feeling a swell of affection for the gutsy little scrap of a pup he'd been and for what he'd grown up to be. "He was surrendered to my parents' rescue."

"Wait, your parents own an animal rescue?"

"Sure do. Just south of Charlottesville, Virginia. Mostly dogs, but they get a few cats now and then. We even had a couple of guinea pigs once, the odd rabbit, and a pig. They won't turn anyone away. If it's beyond their expertise, they'll find the right rescue or sanctuary and transfer them there. They live on the property, and one morning when they went out to the kennels to feed the dogs, they found a box on their porch. Inside the box was a very small and very sick black lab puppy. Way undernourished and suffering from a severe case of parvovirus, he was in pretty bad shape and they weren't sure that he was going to make it." She glanced down at the hardy, healthy animal at her feet and smiled. "But they didn't count on the bone-deep stubbornness of the little guy. Within two months he was a whole new animal.

"I was . . . between jobs at the time and happened to be there when Hawk arrived, and we took to each other from the very first meeting. He was a gift when I was in a very bad place." Reaching down, she stroked her fingertips over his back and he sighed in response. "In the end, we saved each other." She looked up to see Webb's eyes on her, compassion in their depths. "Sorry, that was probably more than you wanted to know."

"Actually, no. That sounds like the real story to me. Do you mind if I ask what put you in that place?" He held up a hand to stop her before she spoke. "And we hardly know each other, so if you don't want to tell me, that's okay too."

"I have a feeling that you actually might know a little about this. Ever lost a colleague on the job?"

His face clouded and she had her answer before he spoke. "Yes." His answer was short, tight, and without any elaboration. *Touchy ground.*

"Then you'll get it. I was with the Richmond PD as part of their K-9 unit. Deuce was my patrol partner and he was shot and killed while we were trying to apprehend a serial rapist. He brought the guy down, but he didn't make it." She took a deep breath to try to control her emotions as her voice wobbled. "He died in my arms."

Webb reached out and covered her hand with his. "I'm sorry. That must have been a heartbreaking loss for you."

Meg blew out a long breath and took a few seconds to pull herself together. It never ceased to amaze her how, even years later, Deuce's loss was a gaping wound that never truly healed. "I couldn't stay on the force. They offered me another dog, but I couldn't do it. I resigned and went back home to lick my wounds."

Webb had been about to take a sip of his coffee, but he froze with the cup at his lips, and then set it down untasted. "That's not being fair. You lost your partner, but you make it sound as if you wimped out and should have been able to do better."

"I bet the guys would have done better."

"The guys might have *looked* like they were doing better, but they would have been a mess. You were the smart one. You stepped back while you were adjusting to your new reality so no one, human or animal, suffered if you weren't at the top of your game. A man would just brute force his way through that scenario, and who knows what the fallout might be. You carry a gun, and control what could be a lethal weapon. That's a responsibility to take seriously."

She considered him for several seconds as the noise of street traffic and pedestrians rose around them to cover the silence. "You're pretty astute."

"I've been there." Again that flat tone of voice.

Moving on. "Well, within a week of Deuce's death, Hawk landed on our doorstep. He gave me something to focus my energies on at a time that I desperately needed a reason for getting out of bed in the morning. For the first week he needed almost constant care, and by the time he was more independent medically, we were bonded. I could tell right away that he was smart, but as he got better and gained weight, it became clear how really smart he was. Mom and Dad encouraged me to train him, but there was no way I could consider training him as a police dog. It was a journey for both of us, but we trained in search and rescue and certified in area search, trailing, and first responder disaster/human remains detection. Now, a few years later, he's a damned good tracker and SAR dog."

"You don't have to tell me that. He's kick ass."

"I like to think so, and that's all on him. In the end, the

animal community is pretty small, so I caught wind of some talk that the FBI K-9 program was looking to expand. I'd been working for Mom and Dad all that time at the rescue, but I was starting to get restless. The rescue was perfect while I was getting back on my feet, but truthfully I missed the life of catching bad guys. I felt like I was good at it and could contribute, so I figured *why not?* and applied. We tried out, were accepted, and the rest is history. I moved to Arlington with my sister Cara, who runs a dog-training school, and that's where we are now."

"Great story. A real left turn in your life, but it was kind of a right-place-right-time scenario that was good for both of you."

"It really was. But enough about me. Tell me about you. Did you always want to be a firefighter?"

Meg settled back in her chair and ate her sandwich while he entertained her with the story of growing up in a family of firefighters and never wanting to do anything else. When he told her about his connection with an animal rescue—this year's firefighter calendar where he was Mr. June—she laughed and told him she was going to have to hunt down a copy for herself and her sister because what's not to love about shirtless hot guys and puppies?

She jerked when her cell phone alerted an incoming text message. "Sorry, have to get this. Can't ignore anything right now." She flipped open the message and quickly scanned it, stiffening as she read.

"What's wrong?" Webb asked. "Has he hit again?"

"Tried to. The balls on this guy." She looked up to meet his eyes. "He went after the NSA."

"Damn, that is ballsy. You said 'tried to.' Did they catch him first?"

"Sadly no. According to my coworker, the bomb didn't go off, but they didn't catch the bomber either." She pushed back from the table and jumped to her feet. "I have to get back now. Hawk, come!"

"Of course you do." He politely rose to his feet as she gathered her things, thanked him for the company, and rushed off down the street at a jog, Hawk keeping pace at her side.

It was only as Meg was pushing through the doors of the Hoover Building that she realized she didn't even know what firehouse he was out of or how to contact him if she ever wanted to see him again.

Chapter 24

Scent Cone: Scent molecules disperse outward from the source in a conical pattern, forming a scent cone downwind of that point. An air-scenting dog normally works across or into the wind until he locates the scent cone. The dog's search behavior will change as he works his way along the cone until he reaches the source, which is the quarry he is searching for. The dog will then alert his handler of the find.

Wednesday, April 19, 1:39 PM
Outside Moorefield, Hardy County, West Virginia

The Mason jar rapped jerkily against the lip of the glass as the man poured moonshine with hands he couldn't still. Sharp-smelling liquor sloshed over the rim, streaming over his fingers and dripping onto the table below. He cursed and slammed the jar down on the table with a *crack* before downing the alcohol that made it into the glass in one gulp. Then he turned and hurled the glass at the fireplace.

It exploded in a spray of shards, falling like rain over the floorboards. The raging flood of anger dissolved, and he sagged into a chair, his body limp and his head lolling backward to stare sightlessly at the smoke-darkened ceiling.

It was over.

What started as a victorious reign of terror was turning

into a humiliating comedy of errors. First a bomb that gave too much of a heads-up so all the occupants—including his real target—escaped. Sure, there had been significant property damage and that was satisfying, but the media viewed it as a failure, so the general population did as well.

And then there was Fort Meade.

What the hell went wrong?

He'd find out exactly what happened when it hit the news, so he could only guess for now. Faulty wiring, loose blasting caps, a dead receiver . . . it could be any number of things.

He blew out a breath bitter with disappointment and reached for the moonshine. Maybe it would wash the taste of self-disgust from his mouth. He tipped the squat jar to his lips to drink directly from it. *Fort Meade. The end of the line. The end of his line.*

Sooner or later they'd come for him.

So now was the time to act. The bank was going to take his house and land. The animals were already gone. God knows, his family was out of his reach and had been for years.

His family . . . maybe that was the perfect bookend. To end at the beginning. A circle was beautiful because of the way the ends met in perfect symmetry. So perhaps it was time to return to the root of his destruction to make one final statement, a personal one this time. No more remote delivery. No chance of advance warning. This time, he was going to walk in the door and handle things his way.

The grinding pressure in his stomach loosened slightly at the thought. He had time, even if just a few days. Time to plan, time to improvise. Time to put the finishing touches on what would be his legacy in this world.

Then he would go out with a bang and his name would be remembered forever.

Chapter 25

Change of Behavior: Any of a number of behaviors—like turning of the head or a rapid change of direction—that are interpreted by the handler to mean the dog has detected a trained odor.

Wednesday, April 19, 6:24 PM
S Street Dog Park
Washington, DC

Meg stood in the shade of a blooming cherry tree, Hawk lying at her feet. He was off leash and free to run around the dog park with the other dogs, but as if he sensed her tension, he chose to stay by her side instead of playing. Bending, she ran a hand over his thick, sun-warmed fur. She couldn't blame him; she'd been decidedly on edge ever since the second unsuccessful attack. *After two failures, the bomber is going to need to prove himself, even if only to himself. He's a loose cannon now, and anything could be a target.*

The need to do something was nearly overwhelming. Meg hated inactivity, but they were still awaiting the analysis of the most recent drone strike to reveal that last, crucial link. On top of that, she still hadn't heard from Sarge's CID contact, and the silence was making her itchy.

Movement across the park caught her attention, and she turned to see McCord and Cody coming through the gate.

McCord scanned the park and when his head swiveled toward her, she raised a hand in greeting. He nodded hello and headed for her, dragging Cody with him. Cody, who would rather be frolicking with the dogs, pulled hard against his leash, his head craned toward the green space filled with playing dogs.

McCord gave her a sheepish grin as he approached. "I still need to talk to your sister. As you can see, Cody's under the mistaken impression he's in charge."

Meg laughed and bent to greet Cody. "He's testing you to see where his boundaries are. They all do; it's perfectly natural, but it doesn't mean we have to live with it." After Cody sniffed her politely, Meg gave him several long strokes. Then she turned to her own dog. "Hawk, say hi."

Hawk immediately sat up, looked at McCord, and graciously offered a paw.

McCord groaned. "You've got to be kidding me. Are you trying to rub in the fact that Cody is a hot mess?"

"He's not a hot mess, he just needs some instruction and to learn you're the master. Hawk, doggy greet." Hawk immediately sidled up to Cody, who started to leap around him like an excited rabbit, McCord holding on for dear life.

"Let him off his leash," Meg suggested. She waited while McCord unclipped Cody. "Okay, Hawk, play!"

Hawk tore off for the far side of the park, Cody hot on his heels, giving several high-pitched puppy barks of excitement.

Meg turned back to McCord and then only half succeeded at smothering a snicker at his drooped posture, the leash dangling from one limp hand to coil on the gravel at his feet, his eyes fixed on his retreating puppy. When he turned his head to fix her with a slit-eyed mock glare, she could only grin and shrug. "Sorry . . . You're giving me the most levity I've had in days."

"You're welcome." He coiled up the leash and jammed it in the pocket of his windbreaker. "I guess we could all use a break. So . . . where are you guys standing now that we all know your arrested suspect can't be the bomber?"

"Off the record?"

"You know those are a reporter's three most hated words, right?"

"Sure do. But you and I shouldn't even be standing here." She pinned him with a steady gaze. "Why are we standing here?"

"Because I texted you?"

"Nice try, McCord. You can do better than that."

"Because . . . well, some of the things you said last time we met here stuck in my head and made me realize that doing what you do must be damned hard."

"Sometimes it certainly can be. Sometimes it's also the most rewarding job on the planet."

McCord sat down on a circular bench surrounding a cherry tree. "Tell me about one of those times. So far I've mostly just got a handle on the worst part of your job. Put it in perspective for me."

Suspicion raised its scaled head and hissed as she blinked at him. "Are you writing an exposé?"

He raised three fingers to the level of his temple. "Scout's honor. Not unless you give me permission." His hand dropped but he gave her a sideways glance. "I do think you and the team would make a great article. No, scratch that, series of articles. Very inspirational."

"No, thanks. I don't do publicity."

"I think you need to think about it more." When she started to object, he steamrolled right over her. "But not right now." He patted the bench beside him. "Now sit. Please. I promise I won't bite." He raised a single eyebrow and the twist in his lips told her clearly a more risqué comment had come to mind, but he'd filtered it out of the conversation. "For now, tell me about the rewards of your job. Off the record. While all this crap is going on, I want to hear something positive."

Meg sat down on the bench, leaving several inches between them. Her eyes locked on Hawk's dark form as he raced across the grass, Cody behind him, barking like a loon, eyes bright and tail waving like a joyous flag. *Loosen up and give him a little. So far he hasn't given you a reason not to believe him.* "You've heard all the bad stuff from the last few weeks. How about a piece of the good? Her name is Jill and she was at the Department of Agriculture on the eleventh on a school field trip. Had you ever visited the Whitten Building before the bombing?"

"Yes."

"You know the World War One memorial down at the one end?"

He nodded.

"She was down there. She was under the balcony when it collapsed and was trapped under a ton of rubble." The tiniest of smiles touched her lips as she remembered. "Hawk found her. The fire department needed to dig her out, but she was panicky and had been sliced badly by exposed structural steel. Hawk was going crazy up above. He knew she was down there, knew she was hurting. So we sent him down through the rubble to her."

"Wasn't that dangerous?"

"Very. But he needed to do it, and she needed him down there. He kept her calm enough for the firefighters to muscle their way through the debris down to her. When they got her up, none of us were sure she'd make it. She'd lost consciousness and a *lot* of blood. But I got word yesterday she's out of the worst of the danger and is expected to make a full recovery." She smiled fondly at her dog, cavorting energetically with his puppy playmate across the play space. "Another save for Hawk."

"How many is that?" McCord asked. "If you keep track."

"Oh, I keep track. When so much of what we do involves death, the live rescues are notches on our proverbial belt. So far he's got fifty-two."

"That's amazing!"

"It's not bad at all. And considering he's only two years in the field, it's an impressive start. He's a smart boy, my Hawk, and a very hard worker. I usually have to make him stop because he'd go until he drops."

"I get the feeling you're well matched that way. So where is Jill now?"

"George Washington Hospital. She's out of intensive care, so that's good. I've thought about going to see her, but hesitated. What if I'm a bad memory that brings other bad memories back for her?"

"Not a chance. Especially if you take Hawk with you. I guarantee she'd be thrilled to see you both. You saved her. If you hadn't been able to find her, she might have bled out."

"I guess you're right. But she's already been through so much—"

McCord's phone alerted with a whistle. "Sorry, I left the alert on and the volume cranked so I don't miss anything." He pulled out his phone and quickly brought up his e-mail. "It's likely just another rant from my editor about the shrinking distribution size of the paper but . . ." His voice petered out as he stared at his inbox.

"What?"

"I have another message."

Meg sat up straight, as if he'd hit her with an electric cattle prod. *"From him?"*

McCord busily worked the keys. "It's a message from the SecureDrop system. It could be anyone, but that's how he's been contacting me. Give me a sec." More keystrokes and several new windows, then he simply sat and stared at the screen.

"Well?" Meg's voice rose an octave in that single word. "Is it him?"

"Yeah. Ready?"

She stared at him, stunned. "You're letting me see it?"

"You're going to see it sooner or later anyway. And after what you've been through, I think you deserve to see it. We're on the same team after all, right?"

"Yes. Just don't let my bosses hear you, a reporter, say that." She took a deep breath, then let it out. "Okay, let's see it."

"Done." McCord opened the message and held the phone between them where they could both read it.

> I made a mistake. When I wanted to smite my enemies I was decieved into thinking that fancy technology would increase the length of my reach and the power of my stroke. Insted my enemies avoided my vengence and are unpunished. The casualties of my carelessness were mostly ants who blew away as I flew by. I should have beaten them with their own weapons. But thats all in the past now. I dont be thinking you'll here from me again. I bet the minions of the Non Sequitour Ass-sniffers will hunt me down. The present I left on their doorstep will lead them to me. So I will make sure my last acts are suitable punishments. The pale rider is coming. Fear what he will do to yur cities.
>
> It was an educational jurney. I hope you learned something to Mister McCord.

Meg stared at the screen, her mouth going dry as sawdust. " 'Last acts'?"

"You can hear it. He's winding down. And going out with

a bang from the sound of it. 'And I looked, and behold, a pale horse: And his name that sat on him was Death, and Hell followed with him.' "

"I wouldn't have taken you for the biblical type."

"I'm not, but those early days in Sunday school have apparently stuck with me. It's Revelation, and he's referring to the end of days. The apocalypse. The personification of Death, coming to kill untold thousands."

"His threat about the cities."

"Maybe like McVeigh, he wants his name remembered for his deeds for all time. To do that, you have to make a splash. A bigger splash than perhaps he's already tried." McCord tapped the edge of his phone near the bottom of the message. "But notice this time he didn't actually sign off. It's like he's fading away into history."

Meg skimmed the letter again. "Who are the 'Non Sequitour Ass-sniffers'? And he spelled 'non sequitur' wrong."

"He's spelled a lot of it wrong. I think he's being clever there. See it? 'Non Sequitour Ass-sniffers'? See how it's capitalized? NSA. He's talking about his last attempt."

"It must be burning his ass to have failed like that. To open the door for the FBI to walk right through to find him."

"He's clearly expecting the trail to lead back to him. That's why he's going out with a bang." McCord turned off his screen and stood. "He's never going to be more dangerous than he is now."

Apocalypse. The end of days. Destruction. Death.

They rose as one, sprinting for the exit and calling for their dogs.

Chapter 26

Fire in the Hole: A warning originating with coal miners that a charge has been set and miners should clear the area because an explosion is imminent.

Wednesday, April 19, 7:35 PM
O'Donnell's Pub
Moorefield, West Virginia

The man propped his elbows on wood worn smooth by decades of arms resting on it and pints of beer sliding across it. He cradled a fresh glass of Mothman Black between his intertwined fingers, the dark brew topped with a foamy pale head. He took a long draught of the beer, then set it down on the bar with one hand, backhanding his mouth with the other.

This was it, a last night with the men of his town before he went down in infamy.

His eyes were drawn up and over the shoulder of the man behind the bar to the TV mounted on the wall. An aerial shot of the NSA compound filled the screen and then cut to a close-up of a man in a suit and tie talking to a reporter, the dark specter of OPS2A hulking in the background behind them, slightly out of focus yet unmistakable. He ground his teeth and hunched down further over his beer, his shoulders riding up near his ears.

The bartender, Joe, wiped a damp rag over the dull surface of the bar almost in front of him. Joe had been a fixture behind the bar for as long as he could remember and had served his daddy and his grandaddy before him. "You're quiet tonight," Joe said.

"Not much to celebrate."

"Couldn't talk them down?"

"The bank?" Hot anger shot through him at everything that was being taken away. "No. They're foreclosing at the end of the month."

"Shit, man. I'm sorry. Your family has owned that land for generations."

"Nearly two centuries. But they don't care about that kind of history. And they certainly don't think it deserves any kind of credit. I tried to tell them I only needed one more year to get back on my feet. But they won't go for it."

A man stumbled and collapsed unsteadily on the empty bar stool beside him, awkwardly elbowing him and jarring his hand so his glass tilted wildly. Beer and foam ran in a slow ooze over his hand.

He turned on the drunken man with a flash of bared teeth. "Watch what you're doing." He flicked his hand in the interloper's direction. Beer flew onto the man's shirt.

The drunk turned toward him, his small eyes narrowed and his crooked, yellowed teeth flashing behind an overgrown wiry beard. His breath carried the overwhelming stench of stale booze. "Fuck off. I'm here for a beer and don't need to hear from the likes of you." His lip curled as he hissed the last three words.

He froze at the implied insult, his heart rate spiking as adrenaline surged through his veins and his extremities went cold. "What do you mean, the likes of me?"

"Everybody knows all about you." The otherman's words were slurred, but carried clearly through the smoky bar. "You got caught peddling moonshine and uninspected meat by the IRS and the Ag boys. Half your herd of sheep ran off a cliff and you tried to sell it to the DNR as a bear attack, but they were on to you and your lies. You smuggled illegal sheep across state lines to get your stock numbers back up so they slaughtered every animal you had when they came down with scrapie. You're a fuckup. Your daddy and grandaddy would be turning in their graves if they knew what a fuckup you are. You can't do anything right. But at least you'll be doing it somewhere else soon enough."

He stood up so abruptly his bar stool teetered momentarily and then toppled to the floor with a crash.

"Hey, hey! Not in my bar!" Joe tossed down his rag and put a big meaty hand on the chest of each man and pushed back, hard. But with the bar blocking him, he didn't have much leverage. The other two men simply sidestepped out of his reach.

Fury filled him. All he wanted was one last night surrounded by his neighbors. The people he'd risked everything for. And instead, they'd shown their true colors. He grabbed the newcomer by his shirtfront and dragged him so close his putrid breath nearly made his head spin. "You have no idea what I do right. You're so blind, you can't even see what's in front of you on CNN. And you're so deaf, you can't hear when someone speaks for you." He gave the man a shove as he released his shirt, grimly satisfied as the man stumbled backward, crashing into another patron further down the bar.

He glanced back to see Joe, mouth slack and eyes wide, staring at him wordlessly from behind the bar. He picked up his glass and drained it in four swallows, then slammed it down on the bar so hard he heard the glass crack. "Thanks for the drink, Joe."

He stalked across the bar to the door, feeling Joe's eyes on him with every step.

Chapter 27

On Scent: Homing in on the source of an odor.

Thursday, April 20, 7:03 PM
Jennings residence
Arlington, Virginia

Meg opened the door to find Clay McCord standing on her doorstep. "Hey, thanks for coming."

McCord stepped through the doorway and then out of the way as she closed the door behind him. "You were very mysterious on the phone. 'Come now, don't tell anyone, and bring anything you might need to do research.'" He patted the leather messenger bag that hung from his shoulder. "Do I need a password to enter?"

"Definitely not. But what we're doing is off the books, so I didn't want it to be at your office or mine. Come on in."

McCord toed off his shoes, then followed her through the front hall and into an open concept kitchen, dining, and living space. His eyes were first drawn to the pile of dogs flopped on the sofa—two of which he recognized, the greyhound he did not—before he noticed the tall brunette in the kitchen. He actually did a double take, looking from Meg to the woman and back again.

Meg noted his surprise and laughed. "Clay, this is my sister, Cara. Cara, this is Clay McCord, the reporter from the *Washington Post* I've told you about."

McCord and Cara shook hands. "I've heard about your magical powers with dogs," McCord said. "Fix mine and I might want to marry you."

Cara's laugh was nearly identical to Meg's. "I've heard about Cody. He sounds perfectly delightful and perfectly normal. I've got a puppy class starting next week," she said in a singsong voice.

"As they say on the Internet: 'Shut up and take my money.' How do I sign him up?"

"There's a registration form on my website. Before you go tonight, we'll get you set up."

McCord cast his eyes heavenward. "It's a miracle."

"It's consistency and rules, and I'll teach you how to do it all."

"Thank God." He looked from one woman to the other. "Has anyone ever told you ladies you look like twins?"

"It's been mentioned a few times," Meg said dryly. "Like anytime anyone meets us together. Cara's a year and a half younger, but you'd never know it by looking at us."

Cara slipped her arm through Meg's, a devilish grin lighting her face. She dropped her voice as if sharing a confidence in a crowded room. "When we were in high school, we'd occasionally sit in each other's classes for fun. We'd wear the same pants and leave class halfway through, swap sweaters in the washroom, and then go back to the wrong class. We never got caught."

"We came close. Remember the time Mr. Eldridge nearly caught you but you talked your way out of it?" Meg turned to McCord. "She's got the best memory and reasoning skills of almost anyone I know. She can get herself out of almost any jam."

"So why aren't you in law enforcement too, then?" McCord asked Cara.

Cara cast a look over her shoulder at the dogs, a loving smile curving her lips. "Because the animals always come first with me. They make me happy and they need me. It's fulfilling to take an animal who might be lonely, or scared, or sick, and help them become loved, well-behaved companions who will enrich someone else's life."

"Not to mention, she's always been my secret law enforcement weapon." Meg motioned to the living room. "Let's sit down and I'll catch you up. You've shared your leads with me. Now it's my turn." Moving to the couch, she gave Hawk a gentle shake. "Hawk, shift over."

He immediately shuffled sideways on the couch, the other two dogs raising their heads as they were jostled. Cara took an oversized armchair and propped her stockinged feet up on an ottoman. Saki, seeing her chance, jumped off the couch and up onto the ottoman, lying down with her head in Cara's lap. She gave a deep sigh of pleasure as Cara automatically started to stroke her wide, square head.

"Come on, Blink, you too." After Blink and Hawk settled at the end of the couch, Meg sat down and patted the cushion beside her before pulling the laptop on the coffee table closer. "Sit here so you can see this. Cara and I have already been through it."

McCord's gaze flicked to Cara. "Your secret weapon?"

"And if you breathe a word of it to anyone, I'll deny it to my dying day. This stuff isn't to be shared, but I know from past experience that Cara can see patterns that would take me weeks to work out on my own. We know what we've got here, but we're not sure where to take it. This all has to be on the QT."

"How did you get this information?" McCord pulled out his own laptop, setting it on the coffee table beside Meg's and booting up.

"I called in a favor." She turned to meet his eyes to be absolutely sure of his sincerity. "Your word that this goes nowhere. Also your word that you sit on this story until we've got him. We can't afford any leaks to tip him off. Once he's in custody, you can run with what you know, which is far and away more than anyone else. You'll have a great head start."

"Deal. And don't forget who you're dealing with. I'm the king of anonymous sources. If you can get me something to run with, they'll never find out where the information started."

"Good enough. I have a friend who is ex-CID. I wanted him to get me in contact with someone who is still in CID because we got some information back about the C-4 used in the bombings. I went after this when the evidence results were in from the first bombing only, but we've since had it confirmed that the second and third bombings have identical signatures. What's special about this C-4 is that it's marked with a military taggant."

"Military grade C-4. I assume it's stolen?"

"That's what I wanted to investigate. There was a theft from an army reserve in Wheeling, West Virginia, last November and I wondered if it was linked. So rather than waiting for the FBI and the army to make connections, I went for the back door."

"The contact inside CID."

"Right. It wasn't even really clear what happened that night. News reports said explosives were stolen, but didn't specify what kind or how much. I figured going to the source was the best way to find out." She brought up a file on the computer. "He just sent me the entire case file."

McCord gave a low whistle and angled her laptop so he could scan down the screen, giving a running commentary as he read. "C-4 packaged as M112 demolition charges. Two M183 demolition charge assemblies stolen." He glanced up at Meg. "That means the C-4 was packaged as one and a quarter pound elongated bricks. Sixteen M112 charges make an M183 assembly. So the guy took thirty-two bricks of C-4. That's enough to do some serious damage."

"We had to look all that up," Cara said.

"I was overseas in a war zone with our boys for years. I picked up a few things."

Cara tipped her head in a silent acknowledgment of his experience.

He turned back to the laptop. "The reserve depot is only open from eight to four, Monday to Friday, and isn't manned during off hours. The only security is a fence and motion-sensitive cameras mounted on the outside of the building. So the guy got in overnight when the place was locked and dark. Track marks show he came in on foot from the west and scaled the fence. Security footage showed a hooded figure wearing gloves and carrying tools. He broke a window to get in. . . ." McCord paused for a moment as if not believing what he was reading. "Then used a saw and a pry bar to cut through the ceiling of the weapons vault?" He looked up. "Gotta give the guy points for ingenuity. Such a simple solution—brute force. But still easier than going through the vault door."

"It looks like the vault was constructed of steel and plywood and wasn't nearly as sturdy as one would hope when you're storing this kind of weaponry," Meg said. "Pretty poorly done."

"Bet they've already reviewed their systems. Okay, so the guy gets in and gets out with two cases of C-4. Leaves the tools, but goes back over the fence with the C-4. Good thing that stuff is stable as hell unless a charge is applied. He would have had to throw it over the fence."

"That's what we thought. Then he carried the cases to a vehicle, which is why he didn't take more." Meg pulled up another window, showing a pair of buildings, just to the west of the crossed runways of an airport. "Here's a map of the reserve. See how it's located right next to the Wheeling-Ohio County Airport? Security cameras show that he got in just before two AM, so the airport was also dark and uninhabited. CID found evidence to the west of the reserve on Short Creek Road"—she ran a fingertip along the meandering line of a county road to the west of the forest that bordered the reserve to the south and west—"of a truck parked on the side of the road. Unfortunately, being November, the ground was pretty solid, so they weren't able to get any definitive evidence as to the brand of tires."

"So he carried the boxed C-4 back to his truck and drove away."

"In any of about six ways in all directions, north, south, east, and west. But we may have gotten lucky. This is a pretty remote area, but there are several army buildings in the area and, like the reserve, they all have security cameras. There are several post offices, a couple of bars and convenience stores, all with security cameras. So CID got all the video from that night and captured any images they could in a window following the time the reserve security cameras show him leaving the building.

"They timed his escape and then padded it for thirty minutes on either side just to be sure and then added the travel distance from Short Creek Road to the location of each security camera. Even though the traffic level was exceedingly low, they still came out with eleven possible vehicles."

She quickly started flipping through a series of fuzzy black and white pictures of trucks, cars, and SUVs. None of the plates were clear, but in most, a small portion of the plate could be discerned. "The only good thing is that every single one of them is a West Virginia plate. But not one of them was a full plate and some of the vehicle makes couldn't be determined, which means they were looking at possibly thousands of vehicles of which one could be the real match.

"They tried to follow it further, but without any evidence to corroborate—fingerprints, fibers, definitive boot or tire tracks—they couldn't make any connections leading to a short list for which they could reasonably argue for a warrant. In the end, the trail went cold."

"So how do you think I can help?" McCord asked.

"Because we now have this." Meg pointed at a stack of file boxes across the room. "I went back to the Hoover Building tonight while Cara was combing through this file. I picked up all the files that I and my two colleagues have deemed possible suspects based on interactions with the targeted departments. I also knew where another few groups were keeping files on suspects and I grabbed them too. I don't have all of them at this point, but I'll bet I've got most of those that have been short-listed so far."

"Ah." McCord leaned back into the couch cushions, throwing one arm up across the top of the couch. "So you want to see if there might be any crossover between the huge list of possible plates and the smaller list of possible suspects."

"There's not even any guarantee he's in that box, but the Bureau has gone through a *lot* of files and I think there's a chance. Of course, if our guy is anything like Skinner, he might not even have a valid license plate. But my gut says his vehicle was on the road that night and these all look like legitimate West Virginia plates."

"He may hold some of Skinner's beliefs, but denying the legitimacy of the federal government might not be one of them. There are lots of people who begrudge having to pay the government a red cent, but do it anyway because otherwise their lives will be beyond difficult."

"Very true," Meg said. "Now, what I need from you is a contact at the DMV. Someone who, if he can't get access to the West Virginia files, knows someone who can."

"Done." McCord sat upright and pulled his cell phone from his pocket. "Can I tell them why I need it?"

Meg looked at Cara, whose face mirrored her own doubt. "I don't know. This should really be off the books."

"It will be. But if you want to light a fire under someone, you need to give them a reason to pitch in. I won't lead with it, but I'll keep it in reserve in case I need it." He opened up his contacts information on his laptop and started scrolling.

Twenty minutes and the promise of two bottles of Johnnie Walker Platinum Label eighteen-year-old scotch later, he had his contact in the Virginia DMV sweet talking a buddy in the West Virginia DMV into giving them a hand for the price of one of those two bottles and the knowledge he was helping stop the bomber.

Thirty minutes after that, they had an impressive list of names.

"One thousand, two hundred and fourteen names," Meg said.

"But only fifty-two to compare them to." Cara raised her coffee mug in a mock toast. "Could be worse."

"Sure could be." McCord pulled his laptop toward him. "I told you it was worth it to take the time while we were waiting to make an electronic list of the FBI's possible suspects. Now it's just a matter of running the search." His fingers flew over the keys, merging the two lists and searching for duplicate entries. "And there we are. What do you know? Only got one name in common." He turned his laptop so both sisters could see.

"Daniel Mannew," said Cara. "And the vehicle fits. CID suspected the perp drove a truck from the chassis size indicated by the wheel marks. This guy is the registered owner of a 2005 Chevy Silverado. Only vehicle registered to him."

Meg started digging through the boxes. "Mannew . . . I'm pretty sure I've seen that file. I'm pretty sure I put him on the list." She kept flipping and flipping. Nothing in the first box. She moved onto the second. She found his file a third of the way down and slid it free.

"Those are all his dealings with government agencies?" Cara's widened eyes were locked on the file. "It's got to be nearly an inch thick."

"Some people go out of their way to be miserable and to make other people miserable." Meg carried the file to the coffee table, opening it to the stack of papers inside. "Keep in mind too that these are federal records only. We'll have to talk to the West Virginia Division of Natural Resources to see if he had a beef with them." She shot a sideways glance at McCord. "Got a contact there?"

He shrugged. "I'm a helpful guy, but I have my limitations. Given time, I could track down someone at the DNR, but no one at my fingertips after hours like this. Which reminds me. I may actually have something for you there, even though I'm not sure of the specifics." He opened a file on his laptop. "We all remember message number two, right?"

"The 'you disrespect me, sir' message?" Meg clarified. "Sure do."

He scanned the text on his monitor until he found the lines

he was looking for. "Remember that bit about 'Public education is the cornerstone of conflict management efforts'? And 'Application of aversive conditioning techniques may provide immediate relief for agricultural damage and provide public satisfaction that a problem is being addressed'? And then he talked about the best answer being a bullet?"

"That never made any sense to me," Cara said. "But I always thought his sudden switch to grammatically perfect spelling was a little odd."

"That's because he lifted those lines. I looked it up. They're direct quotes from a DNR brochure about black bear management. Which makes me think when we find out what his issue was with the DNR, assuming there's still some trace of it considering the office got bombed, it's going to be around bears. His solution? Shoot them. Their solution must be to find other more peaceful ways to all live together. Now, let's see what the feds have to say about him."

"And what he has to say about the feds." Meg handed out sheaves of papers to McCord and Cara and the search began.

"I've got letters to the Department of Agriculture," Meg said. "What's 'scrapie'?"

"Scrapie?" Cara echoed. "Used how?"

"He says he's from West Virginia, a farm outside Moorefield, near the Virginia border. His entire flock of sheep was euthanized because several of them had it. Guess it must be bad, because they killed all of them, apparently to keep it from spreading around the county. But he wasn't insured, so he lost everything. He wants to sue for damages."

"I found it," said McCord, scanning his laptop monitor. "It's some sort of infectious neurological disease. Related to mad cow."

"We've all heard stories about farmers losing their whole herd because of mad cow disease," Cara interjected. "Must be the same thing here. One animal gets it and they're all killed to contain the spread to neighboring farms and beyond. He wrote a letter saying he wanted to sue for damages, right? What does it look like? Similar writing style?"

"Meaning terrible spelling and all that? Yes. By the way, he signed off as Danny Mannew, instead of Daniel, so keep that in mind while you're looking."

"I have a letter to the IRS that's also signed off by Danny Mannew. He's complaining about being nailed for selling moonshine without a license. Apparently two West Virginia Alcohol Beverage Control Administration guys caught him trying to sell to a local barkeep and then posed as buyers themselves. He's calling it entrapment."

McCord rattled the papers in his hand. "This report goes along with the scrapie situation. Apparently the Department of Agriculture thinks it all started when he illegally brought in cheap, unregistered sheep from out of state. They were infected and that brought down the whole herd."

"Ouch." Cara winced.

Meg's cell phone rang and she reached across Hawk and Blink to pick it up off the arm of the sofa. She glanced at Cara. "It's Craig." Then for McCord, "My boss." She took the call. "Jennings."

"We've got something."

The urgency in Craig's voice had her heart kicking double time. "What?" She held a finger to her lips and then put the phone on speaker so everyone could hear.

"We just got a call into the tip line," Craig continued. "Some barkeep had a guy in his pub last night, someone he's known since the guy was a kid. It never occurred to him that he might be the bomber; he just seemed like a regular guy, down on his luck lately, but a regular guy. But last night he got into a dustup with another patron and something about his reaction didn't sit right. He was threatening the other guy, telling him that he had no idea what he was really doing. The bartender started putting it all together—he's apparently had trouble with the IRS lately, as well as the Department of Agriculture and the Division of Natural Resources. He asked that we go easy on him, if that's who it is. He's someone who's had a hard life and the barkeep's known the family for decades."

"Craig? Is the guy's name Mannew?" She spelled it out for him.

There was dead silence for the span of three full heartbeats. Then, "How the hell did you know that?"

McCord's shit-eating grin summed up her feeling of victory.

In a few quick sentences she summed up her off-the-book activities.

Silence reigned for another few seconds before Craig spoke. "I suppose I should be chewing your ass out for going outside Bureau ranks for this, except that you've just given us enough to get a search warrant to go after the guy almost immediately. Stay available. My bet is that first thing tomorrow they'll send in a team, and if he rabbits, I want us on-site right from the start. And, Meg?"

"Yes, sir?"

"Get those damned files back in here so no one knows you took them out of the building."

"Yes, sir."

There was a *click* as he unceremoniously hung up on her.

McCord's grin melted away. "Uh-oh. Are you in trouble?"

"Not to worry. You just heard the last of it. Craig will cover for us and will bury how it was done. For him, getting the right answer is worth ignoring how we got there at this point." She started piling papers back into the file. "Great work, guys. Without this connection, it might have taken at least an extra twenty-four hours to put it all together from the tip, and that could have given him more than enough time to rabbit, as Craig so succinctly put it. Now we have a chance to stop him."

Chapter 28

On Source: The alert by a scent detection dog when it is at the source of odor.

Friday, April 21, 8:40 AM
Hardy County Courthouse
Moorefield, West Virginia

Danny quietly slipped down the darkened halls of the old courthouse, his gaze skimming over features he hadn't seen in years. It was a building he wished he'd never set foot in.

This was where his downfall had started. Where his bitch of an ex-wife divorced him and got full custody of their two kids, leaving him with few rights and even less money. Worse, she then took the kids and left the state. He hadn't seen them since.

Judge Harold Eggers was responsible for all of it. He could have stopped her, or at least lightened the custody payments and required her to stay in state. But no, he gave her everything, leaving Danny with nothing.

Time for payback.

He'd sent a last note that would have the feds looking at big buildings in even bigger cities. But for him, this was personal. A way to come full circle. For him, this was as big as it gets.

He was going to start over.

He thought of the cave, deep in the mountains, where he'd hidden the money. The bank would foreclose on the farm and the contents—whatever little was left at this point—but they never knew about the rifle, so they wouldn't miss it.

It was his great-great-great-grandfather's .53 caliber, used during West Virginia's time in the Union Army during the Civil War. A beautiful first model Burnside, it had an intricate, factory-engraved frame with a burnished wood stock so satiny smooth it gleamed. Several months back, he'd taken it to a well-known collectors' gun shop in Pennsylvania. He'd driven a hard bargain that day and had come out twenty thousand dollars richer.

Rather than trusting the money to a bank, he'd stashed it in the rafters with the C-4 until a few weeks ago, when he'd hidden it deep inside a cave almost no one knew about. It had financed the equipment he needed to buy to build the drones and now it was his ticket to a new life. They'd taken everything from him and he'd done his best to take back some of his own. His only way to win was to close out this portion of his life and escape to freedom as a new man with a new identity.

But first he needed to settle one final score.

He ghosted past the closed doors of the county clerk's office. He knew Jimmy was in there; he'd unlocked the building already, but the office wasn't officially open for another twenty minutes. But ever-trusting Jimmy paved the way for him to slip in the side door. This was Hardy County—some neighbors still didn't lock their doors at night, so leaving the side door of a county building open a few minutes early didn't require a second thought.

Next he passed the glossy wood panel doors of the courtrooms. Number three was Eggers's courtroom, always had been. Danny pulled on the heavy handles and the door opened silently on oiled hinges.

God forbid a squeaky door interrupt the judge at work.

Morning light streamed into the empty courtroom. Court wouldn't be in session until ten o'clock, bringing the bailiffs and defendants and prosecutors. But, for now, the big room was silent, his steps whispering along the tile floor.

His gaze was fixed on the narrow door behind the big wooden bench with the gavel—the judge's chambers. Eggers would be arriving soon. An early-to-bed, early-to-rise type, it was well known that Eggers liked to work in his office for an hour before the start of court, and then vanish as soon as the day was over to indulge in a glass of the local 'shine at his favorite bar down the street.

Danny was counting on having a few moments alone with him. A few moments was all he needed.

He let himself into the room, slipping the backpack from his shoulders to the floor. He removed an ax handle from the pack.

He was rewarded fifteen minutes later by the sound of footsteps in the courtroom. Seconds later the door opened and he only needed one quick look at the wide, bald head to bring the ax handle down hard.

After that, it was only a small matter of removing the bandanna and zip ties from his bag to gag Eggers and then bind his arms and legs to his fancy antique wooden desk chair. Just before he pushed the backpack full of C-4 under the desk at the judge's feet, he pocketed the detonator remote. Then he waited.

It wasn't long before Eggers's eyelids fluttered and then slowly blinked open. The look of confusion, followed by alarm and then fear, gave Danny the most satisfaction he'd felt since the IRS bombing.

"Remember me, Eggers?" he goaded softly. "Remember the man whose life you tried to ruin? Well, I'm back and now you're going to pay. But before that happens, I want you to understand exactly why you're going to die." He leaned in closer, close enough to see the dew of sweat gathering on the older man's forehead. "Because you *are* going to die."

Eggers tried to call for help from behind the gag, but all that came out was a gurgle. He struggled against his bindings, but Danny had pulled them too tight to have any give.

"You started it all. If it hadn't been for losing everything in the divorce, I'd have had the money I needed when the farm ran into trouble. It was bad enough losing my sheep to the bear, but the DNR not paying for them forced me to go out of state for new stock. Who knew they'd be sick? Then they were all dead, and just like that, a hundred and fifty years of family farming was gone." He pointed back to the heavy oak door leading to the courthouse. "It all started right here. It's all going to end here."

He nonchalantly strolled around the desk and rolled the chair out just far enough for Eggers to see the bag underneath. "See that, Judge? That's all the C-4 I've got left." He feigned an expression of shocked innocence. "Oh, didn't I tell you about that?" Innocence melted away to reveal pure malice. "That's what I have left after blowing up the Whitten Building, the IRS office, and the DNR. You're going to be my crowning glory to all of this. One more bomb and I'll be gone in a puff of smoke. Hope they can trace you through your DNA, because that's all that'll be left of you."

Eggers started struggling as if his life depended on it, and Danny, sick of the game, pulled the ax handle from behind his back and clipped him across the head again, leaving him stunned and drifting in and out of consciousness. "So long, Judge. See you in hell."

He threw open the window and pushed out the screen, then hopped down to the grass below, pulling the sash down behind him. He jogged across the lawn and into a small stand of trees at the back of the building. Ducking behind the trunk of a large oak, he peered back toward the courthouse.

He'd picked this spot earlier because it had a straight line of sight into the judge's chambers. As much as he needed the judge to die, preferably taking the whole damned court-room with him, he needed to see it happen. After two misses, he wasn't about to drive off into the sunset and trust that this bomb did its job. This time he needed to see the detonation and was willing to waste precious moments to experience the thrill. Then he could move on.

Behind the glass, the judge was groggily coming to. It took a moment, but then memory and clarity returned and he started to struggle frantically. Smiling, Danny could imagine the muffled screams of terror from behind the gag.

The explosion was staggering—the flash of light, the ca-cophony of sound, the thump of the shock wave hitting Danny, even sheltered behind the tree. He allowed himself one quick look at flames licking through the broken walls of the building and roiling black smoke billowing skyward, and then he was running, sprinting for his truck left a few blocks away.

Victory fueled his steps, and his eyes fixed on the green hills rising in front of him.

Fresh air. Open sky. Sunshine. No responsibilities.

Freedom.

Chapter 29

Clue Searches: Each searcher looks for items the subject has left behind, such as clothing, candy wrappers, cigarette butts, keys, or backpacks. Handlers are trained to look up, to each side, and behind for clues while their dogs search for the subject's scent.

Friday, April 21, 8:57 AM
Mannew Farm
Outside Moorefield, Hardy County, West Virginia

"We're getting close according to the GPS." Beside Meg in the SUV, Craig peered up the narrow mountain road, lined with sparse scrub on one side and a brutal drop on the other. "Keep your speed steady though. All the cars in front of us will be doing the same. Better to come in slow and quiet than quick and hot, giving the perp warning." He turned around in his seat to check if Brian followed in his own SUV, carrying Lacey, Lauren, and Rocco. "Brian's still with us."

"How far out are we?"

"About half a mile. But otherwise literally in the middle of nowhere. In the middle of silent nowhere."

Mannew's farm was located well inside the United States National Radio Quiet Zone. While emergency and CB radios were allowed, for inhabitants in the area it was the choice of cable or satellite communication or the silence of the mid-nineteenth century. The team had even had to change out their regular gear; K-9 handlers carried a satellite phone instead of their usual standard issue radio.

A dark smudge over the mountain to their right caught their attention.

"What's that?" Craig swiveled in his seat, putting down his window. The soft breeze that wafted into the car was laden with damp earth and fresh green life, but laced with the unmistakable scent of wood smoke. He stuck his head out to gaze up into the sky. "Shit."

Suddenly the driver in the lead car ahead of them hit the gas, speeding away from the group. It took only seconds for the cars trailing behind to do the same.

Meg followed suit as Craig settled back into the seat, his face grim. "They've seen it too. It's definitely fire. And from the size of that smoke trail, it's an inferno."

Meg's gaze stayed locked onto the rough dirt road as they sped along it, bouncing over dips, all while keeping her eyes away from the nearly sheer drop to her left in hopes of staving off the gut-wrenching fear. But she couldn't help glancing at the tiny wood and wire fence marking the precipice that wouldn't stop a child's wagon from going over. And then down, down, down. She didn't want to think how far.

She clutched the steering wheel tighter, her knuckles going dead white, and fought not to hyperventilate. Craig didn't know about her fear of heights; only Brian knew, although she suspected Lauren had guessed and guarded her secret. It was crucial that he not learn or it might affect the cases he assigned to her. Miraculously, she managed to speak with her voice sounding completely calm. "He's burning down his farm to cover his tracks?"

"That would be my guess."

"I can't take my eyes off the road. How's Hawk? It's got to be pretty bumpy back there."

Craig peered through the metal mesh into the back. "He's lying flat with his legs braced to keep from sliding."

"That's my smart boy. Hang on, this is a wicked bend."

Meg muscled the SUV through a hairpin turn that sharply angled up Sugarloaf Knob, then glanced in the rearview mirror to see Brian and Lauren still safely behind them.

They climbed the steep incline as fast as they dared. In the distance, down South Branch Mountain, lay the town of Moorefield, settled in 1777 at the convergence of several branches of the Potomac River on its way downstream toward Chesapeake Bay. Except for a quick glance, Meg kept her eyes firmly on the road and the bumper of the vehicle in front of her as they jerked along. A particularly hard lurch had Craig lunging for the handhold on the door and then peering into the back to check on Hawk again.

"He's okay."

"I hate this road." Meg's words came from between clenched teeth. "The last thing we need is one of the dogs getting hurt before we even start."

The smudge over the hill was getting darker now, charcoal clouds filling the sky to the west.

Craig fiddled with his satellite phone, resetting his map for their current location. "One more curve and we're"— he cut off as the SUV gave a tremendous lurch and Hawk gave a small yip from the back—"just about there."

They took the last curve too fast, leaving Meg fighting inertia to keep from fishtailing around the bend. Then they were shooting into a farmyard and pulling to a stop in front of a split rail wooden fence. Meg swallowed a sigh of relief and nearly had to peel her own fingers from where they'd seized around the wheel.

At the far end of the enclosure, the barn was engulfed, flames rising high and sparks exploding into the sky to dance in the hot air vortices, while below, the barn's timber framing glowed an unholy reddish orange. Nearer, the farmhouse was also in flames, smoke pouring from open, flame-licked windows. Inside the front door, an inferno roared and swirled, consuming everything within.

FBI agents piled out of vehicles. Already in bulletproof vests, guns drawn, they ran toward the house to see if there was hope of recovering any evidence. But they drew up short, driven back by the blistering heat. With shouted commands, they split up to search the property.

Meg pulled her Glock from her belt holster and saw Craig do the same on the far side of the SUV. They jogged over to Brian and Lauren, standing outside Brian's SUV, their faces lit by the glow.

Brian's gaze was fixed on the house, the flames lighting his face in tones of gold. "He burned it all. Any evidence we might have found, it's all gone."

"It's doubtful he's even here," Meg said. "No reason to start a show like this and then stick around. He knew it would attract attention." She met Craig's eyes. "He's ending it all now. Whatever he's doing next, he's on his way to do it now. He knows it's all coming down around him."

Craig nodded in agreement. "From the moment the NSA bomb didn't go off, he knew we'd have evidence to nail him. The question is—what's his endgame?"

As if on cue, Craig's cell phone rang. Further out, around the house and property, several other phones started to ring. Craig's face was grim when he answered the call. "Beaumont." He listened intently for a moment, nodding in agreement with the person on the end of the line. "We'll be there as soon as we can. We're close, so within a half hour. Don't let anyone on the property. We need it pristine." He ended the call and swiveled to look down into the valley, his hand shading his eyes from the morning sun. "Goddammit."

Meg tried to follow his gaze. "What happened? What are you looking for?"

"Look way down into Moorefield. See that tiny stream of black smoke? Someone just blew up the Hardy County Courthouse. The explosion happened in one of the judge's chambers and they think he went with it." Craig turned to look at his handlers. "No way that's a coincidence when Mannew probably just set his farm on fire."

"He's tying up loose ends," Lauren said.

"But that's hardly an 'end of days' target." Brian stared harder at the tiny town below, as if concentrating would make the situation clearer. "We thought he'd try for a sky-scraper or sports stadium or arena."

"Maybe you're thinking too big. Maybe it's *his* end of days," Meg said. "He's done two federal targets and a state target. Maybe to end everything off, he wanted to go personal. Wanted to take out something with special meaning to *him*. If a judge is dead, maybe he felt he'd been wronged by that judge at some point."

"A man was seen running away from the bomb site, so I think you're probably right." Craig watched several senior agents hurrying toward him. "We're going in to see if you can track him. Load it up, we're headed back." He turned to meet the agents and they quickly exchanged information.

"Tracking Mannew is one thing, but a starting point would be even better." Meg scanned the farm, squinting through the acrid smoke: rusted barrels, an overturned wheelbarrow, piles of broken wood . . . an old shirt tossed over the split rail fence? She needed to move fast before the fire got any closer to it.

She took off across the open yard, ignoring Brian's questioning yell. Grabbing a splintered piece of wood from a jumbled pile of boards, she inched closer to the barn, turning her face away from the blistering heat, holding out the stick to slip it under the shirt to snag it and draw it away. She missed on the first try as she was nearly doing it blind, the smoke from the blaze making her eyes tear. Flaming timbers crackled over her head and sparks rained down, but she didn't back away. Turning into the heat so she could see what she was doing, she successfully caught the shirt and was able to whisk it up and away. Keeping the shirt balanced on the end of the wood, she jogged back to the cars, feeling the cool relief of the mountain air as she moved further and further away from the fire.

"Look what I found!" She brandished the shirt in Brian and Lauren's direction. "This is our way to track him. Get out the gloves and the cases. We're taking some of this with us. He thought he was stumping us burning down his house and barn. But he didn't take our dogs into account. That will be his downfall."

Chapter 30

Mantracker: The tracking dog works from a scent article belonging to the subject, such as a piece of clothing or an item touched only by the subject. From this article, the dog picks up the subject's scent and uses it to find the subject's path.

Friday, April 21, 11:58 AM
Outside Perry, West Virginia

"Slow down!" Craig leaned forward in his seat, squinting into the distance. "There they are, off to the right." He swore quietly. "They could have at least tried not to advertise that his car's been found."

Meg couldn't miss the flashing lights on top of the deputy sheriff's police car. "Mannew can't spell, but that doesn't make him an idiot. He's going to be looking for any sign we're on to him. Now he's probably moving faster."

Meg pulled off to the side of the gravel road behind the deputy's car, her gaze flicking to the rearview mirror to see Brian pull off just behind her, Lauren visible through the windshield in the passenger seat.

Mannew was in the wind.

Each handler carried a small water-resistant plastic case containing a torn piece of the shirt from the farm. Each case was carabiner-clipped to their packs and could be easily opened and offered if needed to give the dogs the scent again. At the remains of the courthouse, Meg, Brian, and Lauren had given their dogs the scent and they'd immediately started tracking Mannew. From the way the dogs had immediately taken to the trail, they knew they had the right target.

The dogs tracked him over the fences and through the six backyards lining Eisenhower Street. After that, Mannew had gone over the level crossing at the train tracks. He'd hit a muddy spot by the train tracks, so they knew he was wearing some sort of deep-treaded hiking boot. Clearly, this was part of his plan from the beginning and he was prepared to make his escape on foot. Well, they were ready to track him, whatever his plans.

The trail had gone stone cold behind a farm equipment repair shop just off Jefferson Street. They didn't need a forensic expert to tell them the tire tracks belonged to a pickup truck and Mannew had fled. A block west was Old West Virginia 55. From there he could have taken WV 28 south, US 48 west, US 220 north, or WV 55 east.

He could have gone anywhere.

The local sheriff, who knew Mannew personally from previous run-ins, immediately put out a BOLO on his vehicle—an eleven-year-old white pickup truck—with the associated license plate, with instructions to consider other plates as well in case he'd stolen a set or two to throw trailing law enforcement off the track. He'd also supplied them with Mannew's driver's license picture so they could recognize him on sight.

Fifteen minutes later law enforcement got a lucky break when a call came in from a trucker with a CB radio who reported passing a white pickup on WV 55 headed east, and the chase was on. An hour after that, a Hardy County deputy sheriff radioed in he'd found Mannew's abandoned pickup just off Trout Run Road, a single track gravel road that wound through the mountains nearly twenty miles due east of Moorefield. The K-9 teams were standing by, and arrived about forty minutes after the reported sighting.

Handlers and dogs all piled out of the SUVs, Craig's arms full of maps.

As the handlers pulled out their packs and watered their dogs before starting, the deputy approached. "Glad you folks were so handy for this. He's maybe got an hour lead on you, but that's all. When I arrived, his truck was still pretty warm, so he hadn't been gone for long. I did a quick look 'round while I was waiting. It looks like he went due west, headed straight for Trout Run."

Meg closed Hawk's water bottle and snapped the trough back into place. "Trout Run?"

"Local creek. He's a country boy and he knows K-9s have been involved in the case. He likely wanted to hide his tracks."

"Creek is a good way to do it," said Meg. "But unless he walked for miles in it, we'll find him coming out somewhere."

"Problem is Trout Run has three or four feeder streams in this area. And due east is Pond Run and its handful of feeders. He'll be crossing more than one stream."

The deputy's laundry list of challenges was starting to get on Meg's nerves. Did he think they were rookies? "More challenging, but not beyond us."

Craig was spreading out a map on the hood of the deputy's car, using rocks to hold down the edges where they danced in the cool spring breeze. "It explains why he picked this area to dump his truck, assuming he knows it."

"He knows it all right," the deputy said. "Grew up here. Never lived anywhere else."

"Then a gold star goes to Sheriff Granger, who was sure

he wouldn't take the pickup far now we know who's responsible," said Craig. "It's too recognizable in this area and people would be looking for that vehicle specifically. He suspected Mannew'd try to get some distance between Moorefield and himself, but then would dump it because it was too risky to be seen in it. I thought he'd go southwest and get lost in the Alleghenies and the million acres of the Monongahela National Forest, but Granger called it right. He concentrated on small roads, off the beaten path, and headed right into the heart of the Quiet Zone. Communication is at a minimum in this area, so not as many ways to get the word out that a search is on in the first place. And the people who come here, they want to live this kind of cord-cutting quiet life. They're not glued to their TVs and radios and Internet. So Mannew could pass right through this area unnoticed because people don't know to look for him. Except for that one report, we've lost Joe Public as our eyes on the ground, I'd bet."

"And considering our location, he's likely headed straight over the border to Virginia." Hands on hips, Meg studied the mountains to the east. "How far is it from here?"

Craig used his thumb and forefinger to measure the distance on the map and quickly compare it to the scale. "About two and a half miles as the crow flies. Which doesn't seem like much, but you know the rough rule of hiking— one hour for every two to three miles, depending on the load you're carrying, and an hour for each thousand feet of elevation." Craig straightened and swept an index finger across the mountain that rose above them. "According to the GPS we're sitting at about fifteen hundred feet above sea level. That mountain ridge is nearly three thousand feet above sea level. Head further north and it's over three thousand feet."

"We can't discount it," Lauren said, "but it's more likely

he's gone southeast than northeast. Granted, he may be betting on us making that call and then missing his trail altogether."

Meg gave a dismissive half snort of disgust. "Then he doesn't know us very well. No assumptions."

"Never."

Meg shouldered her pack and looked down to Hawk at her side. He was staring up at her, ears perked, looking like a coiled spring. Brian and Lacey, and Lauren and Rocco were also ready. "We're going up." She turned to Craig. "Can you coordinate from here?"

"Sure can. The sheriff's office gave me all the maps they had on hand because they said satellite mapping of an area this remote is pretty hit and miss. And the deputy is here to share his knowledge of the area. We're good to go. Whatever support you need, you'll have it. Just let me know."

"Thanks."

"Keep an eye out for snakes," the deputy advised helpfully. "Sunny day, they'll be out and about."

"Good to know. Okay, let's move." Meg unclipped the case containing the tattered piece of Mannew's shirt from her pack, opened it, and offered it to Hawk to smell as Brian and Lauren did the same for their dogs. "Hawk, find it. Find."

Hawk put his nose down to the ground and in seconds had the scent and was circling the front of the truck. He headed into the forest lining the road, with Brian, Lauren, and their dogs hot on his heels.

The dogs were absolutely sure in their tracking and only displayed the usual small back-and-forth weave as they crisscrossed from one edge of the heaviest of the scent trail to the other. The air inside the forest was mostly still, with only the slightest of breezes, optimum conditions for tracking as the shed skin cells the dogs followed had mostly fallen straight down onto the path Mannew had taken. Sunlight filtered through the new leaves above their heads and the land rose only slowly at this point, so the team moved at a comfortable jog.

But they hit a wall when they broke from the trees into a narrow gully and the scent stopped dead at the stream. High with spring rains, the water ran fast, nearly over-flowing its narrow banks.

Brian cursed under his breath as all three dogs cast about for the scent, which was washed away in the tumbling water.

"We knew this was coming," Meg said, one hand shading her eyes as she scanned further upstream. Nothing. "We'll have to cross at the best spot and then come back and try to find the scent again. We'll likely have to split up."

"He could have waded up or down this stream for half a mile or more." Lauren stared at the icy water. "I hate tracking with wet feet. Waterproof boots never keep that kind of water out."

"Trust me, we all hate it." Meg pointed twenty feet further upstream. "Let's cross up there; that section looks easier. There are some rocks we may be able to use to try and stay out of the worst of it."

When they got to the spot she'd chosen, Meg bent and submerged an index finger in the tumbling water, her body shuddering at the extreme chill. "Just a warning, that's *cold*. It'll be running down from the mountains, and it was a bad enough winter there's likely still snow at the higher elevations." She stood and studied the half-submerged, slimy, moss-covered rocks that sparsely peppered the width of the stream. "In we go."

She and Hawk went first, Hawk stepping enthusiastically into the stream, seemingly unaffected by the temperature. Meg stepped out onto the first rock, making sure it was solid before trusting her weight to it. Her gaze flicked to the far side, only ten or twelve feet across, before she stepped to the next rock, and the next.

She got cocky on the second to last stepping stone, stretching her long legs to reach it and pushing off with a little too much force. She landed on the slanted rock and it shifted under her foot, her boot skidding over the slippery moss. Arms windmilling to keep her balance, Meg stayed upright, but didn't have a hope of staying out of the water.

With a splash, both boots landed in the water. She stifled a small shriek and leapt for the far bank, landing just as Hawk gave a massive, ear-flapping shake, water spraying in all directions. She gave him the side-eye. "Thanks, buddy. You couldn't have waited ten more seconds for me to get clear?"

Hawk simply gazed up at her with laughing eyes. He was on the hunt and there was nothing he loved more.

They moved out of the way so Lauren and Rocco could cross. Lauren was doing great until she hit the same stone, then she too went into the creek, cursing under her breath.

Brian didn't even try; he simply waded through after his dog. When the two women stared at him silently, he just shrugged. "What was the point? I'd rather be wet up to my shins than all the way up to my ass when I slipped off and fell in."

"You have a point," Meg said dryly. "Okay, let's split up. Lauren, you go north from here. Brian, you and I will go southeast and we'll split up further in that direction when we hit the next tributary. Stay on the sat phone and when anyone finds anything, give GPS coordinates so we can double back to where you are and come after you if you've moved on." She quickly contacted Craig, giving their current coordinates and their plan to pick up the trail again. Then they set out.

It was in an area where the forest crept close to the

creek when they heard a rustling in the undergrowth to their left, near a large log. Meg and Brian exchanged suspicious glances, and she could tell he was thinking the same thing she was—snake, and not just any snake, a timber rattler or a copperhead, sunning itself on the log and now slithering through the underbrush. They picked up their pace; that was a critter they didn't want their dogs to meet, with no antivenom on hand. Come to think of it, they didn't want to meet it even if they had antivenom on hand.

She and Brian were only together for just over five minutes when the stream they were following forked, one branch going south, the other east. Brian pulled his satellite phone from the holder on his belt and reported in that he would take the more southerly fork, while Meg took the east. With a nod to each other, they split up.

Now alone, Meg felt more in tune with her dog. She didn't mind searching with a group, but she always felt Hawk worked better with no distractions, when he could get into the zone. He led the way, head down, his glossy black coat shining in the brilliant sunlight, tail high, muscles rippling under his fur as he trotted along. A dog in his element. But still no trail to find.

She kept him fairly close to the stream, knowing Mannew had to climb out at some point, so the bank would be their starting point. It was a long way to wade through icy water, but if the man was determined to stay lost, then cold feet were the least of his concerns.

She knew when Hawk picked up the trail again simply from his body language. He slowed and started to cast about in undulating waves, his muscles tense with concentration as he wove back and forth. He had the edge of something, now he needed to find the main trail. "Find, Hawk. Find Daniel Mannew."

Hawk picked up the main scent and abruptly angled

away from the creek just fifteen seconds later. Meg knew the scent was strong because Hawk deviated from his path only very slightly and ran even more quickly than before. Meg pulled her phone out and reported in breathlessly where they were and that they were moving fast. Craig acknowledged and then called Lauren and Brian back in to follow as reinforcements. Meg knew Brian was maybe only ten minutes behind her, but Lauren was more like thirty or forty minutes away. Meg couldn't wait for them though. For now, they were on their own.

They settled into what Meg knew would be the longest part of this search—catching up. Hawk had the scent, but Mannew had a solid head start on them. However, she had every confidence she and Hawk were in better shape than he was. A sheep farmer was used to hard work and heavy lifting, so he wasn't going to be a pushover, but he wouldn't likely be used to long distance pursuits. Meg and Hawk were very, very good at that.

"Just you wait, you bastard. You're ours now," Meg growled under her breath.

All around them, the smell of spring was in the air— damp earth and wildflowers, last fall's decomposing leaves, and new grass. Birdsong floated on a light breeze, and the occasional scurry in the foliage suggested squirrels or chipmunks.

The dichotomy of spring, new life, and a manhunt for a killer was not lost on Meg.

They covered ground quickly. Hawk never lost the scent for more than ten or fifteen seconds when Mannew would climb boulders or make sudden switchback changes. Meg would occasionally stop to give Hawk a drink from the portable water bowl she carried; he could push on for long stretches, but staying hydrated was crucial. She updated her position with Craig and learned that while Lauren was far behind, Brian and Lacey were keeping up with her and were less than a mile away. She couldn't wait for them, but if help was needed, Brian's backup would be timely.

At the beginning, Mannew's trail took them through dense forest, in many places following no established path. However, much of the time Meg could have tracked Mannew on her own, based on boot prints left in the dirt, disturbed leaves or undergrowth, and broken branches. Speed was clearly Mannew's priority, not stealth. He had his eye on the prize and that prize was the backwoods of Appalachia.

After tracking him for over a half hour, Meg and Hawk found their path veered out of the dense forest and onto a rough, rarely used trail. But even one so rarely used afforded a clearer path and allowed for a faster chase.

The first sign of trouble was when Hawk slowed and lifted his head from the trail, tipping his nose into the wind as if scenting something else nearer, stronger. Meg was instantly on alert. When tracking in the wild, you never knew when you'd cross into an animal's territory. It could be a coyote or a wolf or—

A bear.

Shit.

A yearling bear cub, easily forty or fifty pounds in size, wandered into the path twenty feet in front of them. Hawk instantly braced all four feet, dropping his head, his lips curling back to reveal his teeth as he let out a low growl.

"Hawk, no." Meg laid a hand on his back, feeling the tightness of the muscles beneath. She scanned the trees around them. Nothing was worse than coming between a mother bear and a cub; it was a recipe for disaster. And who knew if this was the only cub? Litters could be up to three or four. This was clearly a cub born last year, and one look at those paws convinced her that a single swipe could fatally harm Hawk. They didn't want a fight; they just wanted to get past. But should they wait or go around him and risk running into Mom?

The cub decided the issue, casting one disinterested look in their direction before ambling off into the bushes, likely in search of food.

Time to abandon the search for a few minutes. "Hawk, come." Meg jogged up the path, Hawk at her side, scanning for any dark shapes or sign of movement in the trees. Nothing . . . thank God.

They slowed a minute later and Meg let Hawk take the lead once more. If he picked up the trail again because Mannew had stayed on this path, then no harm done. If not, she'd have to refresh the scent for him and they might have to backtrack a bit, but if that was the case, they'd have to be very careful.

"Hawk, find Mannew. Find."

He put his nose back to the ground and within seconds had the scent again, and they were off.

Around twenty-three hundred feet, the path inclined steeply and the terrain changed. The forest started to thin out, with more dead trees opening the canopy above, or clusters of boulders that kept even the toughest tree from taking root. The dirt trails of the lower ranges slowly became rocky and difficult, and the climb slowed.

Shading her eyes with her hand, Meg eyed the peak towering overhead—Miller's Knob. At its highest point, it rose to nearly three thousand feet, about five hundred feet higher than their current elevation. Both woman and dog were breathing hard; for all their training, this was tough, taxing work. But she felt like they were closing in on their suspect. Hawk wavered less and kept up his pace, despite the exhaustion, which told her the scent trail was growing stronger and narrower, signaling they were approaching their target.

She watered Hawk, then downed an energy bar and

guzzled half a bottle of Gatorade before she repacked her S & R bag and seated it over her shoulders again while studying the rocky mountainside rising above them.

"Time to end this. Hawk, find."

They headed toward the peak, following trails that switch-backed to follow the natural ridgelines of the mountain. It was a hard, steady climb, but determination pushed them forward. Their breathing became heavier with exertion as they moved upward, but Meg never needed to encourage Hawk. He drove himself, sometimes looking back at her as if to say, "Come on, hurry up!"

As they neared the top, Meg muted her phone, feeling them closing in on their target and not wanting it to ring, warning him of their arrival.

Up to this point, tracking a suspect was very much like tracking a missing person, but now the two tasks diverged. Normally, if they were tracking a lost child or hiker, she'd be calling the person's name every thirty seconds. Instead, silence and surprise were imperative in this situation. Using hand signals, she kept Hawk closer to her and paused every fifteen or twenty feet to listen intently. Hawk, familiar with this aspect of the search process, often looked back to her for instruction and would stand very still during those listening moments. But only the sound of their own labored breathing reached her ears.

They crested the ridge after climbing for over an hour and a quarter. Instead of a single high peak, Miller's Knob was part of a fifty-mile ridge that ran down the length of Great North Mountain. It was covered with scraggly trees, and huge chunks of bedrock jutted from its uneven surface, marking the rough border between West Virginia and Virginia. Yet, there was still no sign of life. Had he already started down the other side? Meg didn't think so from Hawk's behavior. He was casting about as if he'd lost the scent or was confused in some way. They might need to backtrack downhill, reestablish the scent trail, and go from there. Perhaps this wasn't exactly where Mannew came through? Or perhaps he'd retraced his footsteps?

Meg crouched down beside Hawk under the shade of a young sapling, slinging her arm around his neck, giving them both a few seconds to rest, panting quietly. She stroked his fur, grown warm from exertion, and he leaned against her slightly, as much for support, she knew, as just to maintain their connection.

She eyed the panorama spread out before them, the bottom dropping out of her stomach. A steep downward mountain path was better in her mind than a sheer drop, but their altitude still made her queasy. The wind was vicious this high up and it whipped around them, moaning mournfully.

It was then that Mannew appeared along the ridgeline to their left. He wore dirty jeans, a plaid shirt, and a nylon jacket. Backpack straps cut across his shoulders.

Meg didn't dare move. Her sidearm was at her hip, but he was only twenty feet away, having missed them crouched low as they were, half hidden by a boulder. He was coming right toward them, mumbling about impassable trails.

The advantage of surprise was needed while she was still below his line of sight. She pulled her sidearm, aiming for his torso.

"Daniel Mannew, stop."

Mannew's head came up, his eyes wide as he searched for the voice, his gaze finally dropping to Meg, who continued, "You're wanted for bombings in the states of West Virginia, Maryland, and in the District of Columbia. Put your hands where I can see them."

She didn't see the rock he must have picked up to carry as he walked until it was too late. He started to raise his hands, as requested, his hands moving from his hips up to his shoulder. Then he drew back his right hand and hurled something at her. The rock caught her forehead with stinging pain; she ignored it, pushing to her feet. She fired one shot at Mannew's back as he ran back the way he'd come. Not having caught her balance, she knew the shot went wide, missing him completely.

She tore after him, hearing Hawk follow right behind her. Mannew had a good twenty feet on her and he ran along the ridgeline, ducking around boulders and in and out of trees, his eyes cast over the edge looking for a way down.

Something warm and wet trickled over her left temple and she swiped at it with her left hand. It came away wet with blood. So he got in the first hit. The only blow that really counted was the last, and that one would be all hers.

Meg realized why he'd likely doubled back. There was no path down from here, only a long rocky drop to the forest, more than a hundred feet below, leading to possible death, definitely broken bones.

Meg awkwardly ripped her satellite phone off her belt with her left hand and hit a single key to speed dial. "Suspect is in sight. I repeat, the suspect is in sight. I am in pursuit at the top of Miller's Knob." There was no way she'd be able to put it back on while running flat out over rocky terrain, so she clenched the phone in her fist.

Hope soared in Meg's heart when Mannew stumbled, going down on one knee. She poured on every last ounce of speed she had. This was her chance.

His upper body turned to face her. That's when she saw the gun in his hand.

He fired.

Meg threw herself down, desperately hoping the shot would go over her head. But when pain lanced through her knees as they hit the rocky ground, she instead heard a sound that made her blood go cold—Hawk's high pitched yelp of pain.

She looked around frantically, but couldn't see her dog. Had he gone over the edge? *Was he shot?*

The sound of rocks tumbling attracted her attention back to Mannew as he'd gained his feet again and was getting away. She had to go after him. If she let him go, how many more would die? But she felt frozen, like her heart was ripped from her chest and lay somewhere with her wounded dog.

She prayed he was only wounded. After Deuce, she couldn't consider anything else. "Hang on, Hawk, I'll be back for you."

She bore down, taking her terror and rolling it into fury, letting that fury give her wings. Her own safety seemed like an afterthought as she sprinted after Mannew, years of training kicking in as she pursued on autopilot. Her gaze locked on him like a laser, she didn't even see the terrible drop that lined the path. Her only goal was to stop him. No more deaths, no more injuries. Not on her watch.

Enough.

When she calculated she was close enough, she pulled up short, planted her feet, dropped the phone to steady the gun in both hands, and took the shot. He was bobbing and weaving, so it narrowly went over his shoulder, but it made enough of an impression that he slowed. The gun locked on him, she jogged up to him. When she got closer, she realized why he'd stopped—they were coming to a stony outcrop, a series of rocky vertical towers that jutted out over the landscape, stories below. Just the impact of a bullet might be enough to lose one's balance and go over.

There was no escape from this point. This was likely the way he'd come before, but had turned back to unexpectedly meet them, and she'd unknowingly driven him back into the dead end. He'd no doubt hoped to spot an easier way down or to take her out with a bullet before he ran out of path.

"Turn around, Mannew. Hands where I can see them."

He spun around, the fury in his eyes nearly a living beast, but kept his hands at his sides, his fist white-knuckled around the grip of his handgun. "You're that bitch from the picture in the paper. You tried to take the attention off me. You and that dog."

Cold sweat dripped down Meg's spine. She'd assumed he was aiming that shot at her. But if he'd recognized her on sight, maybe Hawk was his target all along. Panic spiked, but she battled it back down, stuffing it away for when her life didn't depend on keeping her head. When Hawk's life didn't depend on it. "I didn't ask to be in the paper. Someone took that picture without my knowledge. Put the gun down, Mr. Mannew, and this will go easier for you."

"To do what? Put me in jail? I just wanted to take care of me and mine. I just wanted you all to leave me alone." His voice started to rise and take on an edge. "Was it too much to ask for?" he ended on a roar.

"Mr. Mannew, put down the gun or you'll force me to shoot. And let me assure you, I will hit my target."

"Don't tell me what to do!" Mannew bellowed. He took a threatening step toward Meg.

Meg's finger tightened on the trigger. She was losing control of the situation. Scratch that—she never had control. How do you control someone who's crazy? She was running out of options. It was him or her, and she wasn't going to lose this one.

"Mr. Mannew, it's not too late. Put down the weapon and we can work this out."

"You know who it's too late for?" he shouted, spit flying from his mouth and his skin flushing a dull red. His gun hand started to vibrate. "It's too late for—"

With an almost unearthly growl, Hawk came out of the bushes to Meg's left like a dark rocket, launching himself, teeth bared, at Mannew's gun hand. His teeth clamped down around the bare skin of his wrist, his fangs sinking into flesh and grinding over and between bone. Mannew screamed in pain and the gun went off, the bullet drilling into rock only a foot in front of Meg, sending up a shower of shards. Hawk bit down harder, jerking his head from side to side, and Mannew screamed again, involuntarily releasing the gun, which skittered along the rocks and disappeared out of sight behind them.

Meg snapped out of her shock at seeing Hawk, her eyes cataloguing everything at once. He looked uninjured except for a bloody furrow running along his right hind leg, but from the leap he'd just taken, it must not have been serious. Dragging her gaze from her dog, she scanned for the weapon, but it was gone, likely over the edge.

She needed to get her dog away from that madman. "Talon, off! Down!" Meg commanded.

But Mannew had a handful of Hawk's fur as they struggled for balance and the upper hand. Hawk's furious growl alone told Meg he wasn't going to let go, not while Mannew had hands on him. They staggered backward, the heavy weight of his backpack overbalancing Mannew, his feet slipping on loose bits of rock. Shock registered on his face, then terror as he hung momentarily suspended.

Man and dog disappeared from view.

Meg's terrified scream met only open air. *"HAWK!"*

Chapter 31

Indication: A trained behavior or a reinforced response by which a dog notifies its handler of a find. It is the dog's way of saying, "Eureka! I found it!"

Friday, April 21, 2:32 PM
Miller's Knob, Great North Mountain
Outside Perry, West Virginia

For a split second, sheer terror froze Meg to the spot. *Hawk . . . gone?*

But then adrenaline kicked in with a rush that nearly left her light-headed. *Can't assume. Have to check.*

She half ran, half stumbled to where she'd last seen Mannew struggling with her dog, took a deep breath, and peered over the edge of the precipice.

Vertigo tugged at her at the sheer drop—easily sixty feet straight down into boulders and unforgiving forest. She bore down, forced the spinning to stop, forced herself to really look into the abyss.

No way to survive the fall.

Meg felt hysteria building. *Not again. Not another lost in the line of duty.* She reached up, her hand closing on the necklace around her neck, crafted from Deuce's ashes. *Can't do this again.*

She forced herself to calm down, giving herself a mental shake, preparing herself to confront her worst fears.

Meg got down on her belly and commando-crawled forward to be able to look right over the edge. She held her breath, trapping the moan fighting to escape . . . and looked. Then blinked and looked again. Harder.

Nothing.

What the hell?

"Hawk?"

In response, a low whine and frantic scrabbling met her ears.

Not dead.

"Hawk!" She cupped her hands over her mouth and yelled it this time. She pulled herself to her knees, wrapped the fingers of her left hand around a sturdy root, and leaned out into thin air. And nearly let out a startled scream.

They were on a narrow ledge, twenty feet below. Hawk lay flat on his belly, all four feet braced, his teeth buried in the shoulder of Mannew's nylon jacket. Mannew himself was three quarters off the ledge, both feet dangling, with only his hands for purchase. And if he didn't get back on the ledge soon, he was going to go over and risk taking her dog with him again.

It was such a temptation to tell Hawk to release, letting Mannew simply fall to his death within thirty seconds. The dog had clearly halted his fall and risked his own life to save that nasty piece of—

She forced herself to focus. "Hawk, hold." She hauled herself back up and scooted further along the ledge to a small outcropping that gave her a full view of the ledge below. She leveled her gun at Mannew, aiming for the middle of his back, knowing a single shot would end it. And send him straight down to the bottom of the outcrop. "Mannew, you're done. Pull yourself back up."

"Get him off me!"

"I tell Hawk to let go and he will. You'll fall and I'll

only need to rescue him because you'll be nothing more than a bloody smudge on the rocks below. If I think you're going to try to go off and take Hawk with you, I'll give the command. Make a choice, Mannew. He's going to live either way. I don't give a rat's ass about you."

Pounding footsteps to her left announced Brian and Lacey's arrival. "Meg! I heard gunshots." He was out of breath, barely getting the words out. "What happened? Where's Hawk?"

"On a ledge down below with Mannew, who is currently making the most important decision of his life." Meg raised her voice so he couldn't mistake her words. "Choose, Mannew, or I'll choose for you."

Mannew's hand slipped a notch and Hawk had to dig in further. The abrupt move put too much pressure on the jacket and it made a distinct tearing sound. If the jacket tore, there'd be nothing anyone could do.

"Let me up!" Mannew bellowed, as if feeling his own mortality starting to slip through his fingers.

"You're going to have to help him. Try anything, one single thing, and I'll end you. Hawk, pull! Come on, boy, pull!" She kept her gun trained on Mannew as he got one foot on a tiny outcropping and with a tremendous groan, hauled himself up, assisted by Hawk, who even though exhausted, dug deep, his legs shaking with the effort as he pulled backward, dragging the man up an inch at a time.

Meg waited until she was sure Mannew was safely on the ledge, and then called out, "Hawk, release." The dog promptly let go. "Down boy. Stay." Hawk lay flat on the narrow ledge, panting, but kept both eyes trained on Mannew, who sat back against the rock and turned to the dog. Hawk bared his teeth and growled low in his throat in warning.

"I have my gun trained on you, Mr. Mannew, so I suggest you don't move. Once again, if I think you're a threat, I'll shoot. The FBI wouldn't have a problem with it because that's a highly trained dog, and he's worth a lot to them. You're not worth anything at all." She didn't take her eyes off Mannew for one second. "Brian?"

He knelt down beside her. "I'm here. What can I do?"

"Have your satellite phone on you?"

"Sure do."

"Please call Craig and let him know the situation. Tell him we're going to need a helicopter up here for a cliff-side rescue. Make sure they know they'll need a K-9 harness for one of the rescues. Someone could rappel down, but it would take too long to get here. I don't want that monster sitting with Hawk any longer than necessary."

"Done."

Brian made the arrangements quickly, complete with GPS coordinates, and then ended the communication, waiting for Craig to get back to them with confirmation. "We're all set. He's going to call in the West Virginia State Police's aviation section. They'll be here the fastest and without stepping on any toes."

They sat quietly for a moment, Meg's gun steadily trained on Mannew as he and Hawk stared each other down, both holding absolutely still. At the same time, Meg felt Brian's gaze on her. Finally, she couldn't take it anymore. "Why are you staring at me?"

"Sometimes you're a scary woman," Brian said under his voice. "You know, if I went for girls, it would probably be sexy as hell."

She choked back a laugh, but spared him a lightning fast glance and a cocked eyebrow. "Thanks . . . I think."

Friday, April 21, 4:02 PM
Miller's Knob, Great North Mountain
Outside Perry, West Virginia

Tension thrummed through Meg like a live wire as she watched the West Virginia aviation trooper secure Mannew into the harness at the end of the thirty-foot hoist cable. Hawk hunched miserably at the far end of the ledge—while he was used to helicopter travel, he was used to being on the *inside*, not underneath the screaming of the rotors and the wind they produced.

Meg tried several times to call down to him, but knew her words were lost in the vortex of air spinning around her. As much as she hated being near the edge, she forced herself to remain in his sight, using hand signals to communicate. *Down. Good boy.* But she was worried about the splatters of blood she could see on the rocks around him. She knew the femoral artery couldn't have been hit, or he'd already be gone, but she wanted him treated *now*. Who knew how badly he was hurt at this point.

But protocol demanded the human be rescued first. Meg was willing to defy protocol to save her dog, but part of her knew leaving Mannew there jeopardized the FBI's case against him and would likely get her suspended. So she had to stand back and let the staties do their job, even if that meant leaving her dog alone on the ledge for minutes longer than she was comfortable.

The trooper gave a thumbs-up to the hoist chief in the chopper and he and Mannew started to rise slowly into the air. Good thing everyone in the chopper was armed. The moment Mannew was aboard, he'd be contained and restrained. If he tried anything up there, no one would have any compunction about controlling him in whatever way was necessary.

Brian joined her at the edge to watch with her. "Hanging in?" he yelled over the maelstrom.

"I'll be a hell of a lot better when my dog isn't standing on the edge of a cliff." She looked around him. "Where's Lacey?"

He pointed back about thirty feet where the German shepherd sat, partially shaded by the few trees hardy enough to grow up here. Her eyes were fixed on Brian and she looked ready to bolt for him if he got too close to the edge of the cliff. "I don't want her near this drop." He gave her the hand signal for "down" and she reluctantly dropped to the ground.

They both looked up in time to see Mannew pulled into the helicopter. As the hoist chief held the line, another trooper cuffed Mannew, sat him onto a bench seat, and secured the handcuffs to a chain. There was no question of his guilt, and Daniel Mannew would never see daylight as a free man ever again.

Meg felt a small amount of her tension fade. One down, now the more important one to go.

The hoist chief secured a second harness to the clip on the front of the trooper's harness, one without the distinctive leg loops and heavy shoulder straps for human rescues. The K-9 harness was heavily banded around the chest and torso areas, with two sturdy attachment points across the animal's back. The chief slowly lowered the trooper and harness down once more. The gusting ridge wind tugged at the helicopter and Meg could see the pilot fighting to keep the Bell 407 steady.

Despite the wind, the trooper dropped down precisely onto the ledge and quickly unsnapped the harness. Meg gave Hawk the hand signal for "up" and the dog climbed awkwardly to his feet. Even from the top of the overlook, she could see his whole body shaking, but couldn't tell if it was from pain or the stress of the attack and rescue. Nevertheless, he stood stock still as the trooper stripped off his FBI K-9 vest, buckled the harness around him, and then strapped on a muzzle. Bending low, he attached the K-9 harness to the two steel clips at his shoulders. When he slowly straightened, Hawk hung from the harness at waist level. Looking up at Meg, the trooper gave her a smile and a nod. *Everything's okay.*

She gave him a small wave back, with a smile she hoped didn't show how scared she was.

Looking up at the chopper, the trooper gave another thumbs-up and then they were rising into the air. Meg kept her gaze glued to Hawk's as they swung, seeing confusion and then fear at the unfamiliar sensation in his eyes. But he never struggled; he just relaxed into the lift, keeping his eyes on her the whole time as they came closer and closer.

Meg raised her hand partway, wanting to reach out and touch him as he went by, even though she knew a good fifteen feet separated them. Her hand dropping limply to her side, she settled for vocal encouragement. "Good boy, Hawk. Good boy!" From the perk of his ears, she knew he heard her this time.

Suddenly, the brutal wind caught at the helicopter, jerking it up and away from the cliff, and Hawk and the trooper danced and swayed in ever-widening swings at the end of the cable, in danger of starting an out-of-control spin. The trooper held on to Hawk with a death grip as, above, Meg could see the pilot fighting with the controls, trying to compensate for the vicious gusts coming over the ridgeline.

Finally gaining control, the pilot swung them up and

away from the edge of the outcrop and out of danger of smashing against the rocky wall. Clear of the power of the ridge winds, the hoist chief pulled Hawk and the trooper up steadily. It seemed like hours later, but was only a matter of moments before they pulled Hawk and the trooper inside the cabin. The trooper gave her a thumbs-up and then the door slid shut and the helicopter flew off, banking back the way they'd come, sunlight glinting off its windows.

The air suddenly seemed oppressively silent and still after the roar of the engines.

The weight of Brian's hand landed on her shoulder and she looked up. "He'll be okay. Lauren and Rocco will meet the helicopter at the helipad, and she'll make sure Hawk is taken care of."

"I don't want a country vet to look after him if he needs surgery. They're good vets, but just don't have the facilities we have at home. If it's bad, I want to get him back to my own vet."

"Of course. But let's see what's going on first. I had a good look as he went up and I don't think it's that bad. It looked like a long shallow flesh wound. I don't think the bullet penetrated, just skimmed the surface."

Meg let out an embarrassed laugh of relief and scrubbed her hands over her face. "I didn't even look. I didn't want to break eye contact with him."

"Of course not, and that's what he needed. On the other hand, I was free to look at whatever I wanted." He slung an arm over her shoulders and turned her away from the edge. "Come on. Craig is going to meet us down on Forest Road 92 and he'll get us to Lauren and Hawk. Easy downward hike; I bet we can be there in twenty or thirty minutes tops. Come on, Lacey!"

Lacey scrambled to her feet, waiting for them with bright eyes and a wagging tail up the path.

Meg let out a long, exhausted breath and looked up at Brian as he walked beside her. "You're right. I've had enough of this madman and the chaos he's caused. Let's go home."

"I couldn't agree more."

Chapter 32

Reward: Anything that a dog dearly enjoys can be used as a reward, including a tennis ball, stuffed animal, a stick, or food.

Sunday, April 23, 11:14 AM
George Washington Hospital
Washington, DC

"Come on, Hawk. It's just down this hallway."
Meg's nose wrinkled involuntarily as she passed one of the open rooms, Hawk trotting easily at her knee. Hospitals had a smell all their own—that overriding antiseptic odor, as if they were trying to hide the smell of death and decay that likely haunted the hallways. They overcompensated, and now it was just too . . . clean.

Meg didn't like hospitals. In her experience, nothing good ever happened in one. Sure, babies were born, but no one in her circle of friends or family had experienced that blessed event yet. Her only frame of reference was desperate rescues of injured victims and her mother's terrifying breast cancer diagnosis at such a young age. And then the treatment. Surgery, chemo . . . so many visits. Her mother was the strongest woman she knew and she looked death in the eye, daring it to take her because hell, no, she wasn't going without a fight. It was a battle Eda Jennings had won, but still, her oldest daughter didn't like hospitals. Even if one had saved her mother's life.

But still she came. When you do search and rescue, part of you becomes attached to the person you've saved through the intensity of the moment and the intimacy of the rescue itself. If she could manage the time, Meg always spoke with her survivors one last time before they went their separate ways. It was a reminder to her of the good they could do. The effort was always worth it.

She glanced down at Hawk, critically eyeing his gait. Brian had been correct in his spot analysis of Hawk's injury. The bullet had skimmed along the outside of his hindquarter, slicing a shallow furrow through fur and skin. Hawk also had some scrapes and bruises from the fall to the ledge but, all things considered, had come through the experience in better shape than Meg anticipated.

A vet at a local emergency veterinary hospital in Harrisonburg, Virginia, had cleaned and bandaged the wound. Now Hawk sported a light blue elastic bandage with navy paw prints that wrapped around his belly and behind his right leg to cover the whole hip area. Hawk was under strict instructions to not take part in any rescues and to limit outdoor time in an attempt to keep the wound clean for a full fourteen days as it healed. Even with only minimal painkillers, his limp was barely noticeable.

Meg looked back up to scan the room numbers as they slid past, and then stopped dead as a man suddenly appeared up the corridor exiting a room. Hawk automatically stopped to stand quietly at her knee.

Todd Webb met her gaze from twenty feet down the hall, one corner of his mouth quirking in a surprised smile. He raised a hand in hello, sidling around a nurse pushing a wheelchair with a blond boy holding a stuffed lion nearly as big as he.

"Hey." His smile went right to his eyes, but then cooled slightly as he took in the cut at her temple. "You've had an exciting few days. You okay?"

"Yes. It looks worse than it is."

He dropped down to a squat to run one large hand over Hawk's back. Hawk responded by nudging him excitedly with his nose and fiercely wagging his tail. "How badly is he hurt? The newspapers said he was shot."

"He was, but the bullet only grazed him. It looks nasty, but it's just a flesh wound and won't take more than a couple of weeks to heal. He seemed a little stiff yesterday, but has been moving more comfortably today."

"Good to hear." Webb straightened. "You're here to see Jill?"

Meg laid a hand on Hawk's wide head. "We are. Things have been a little . . . crazy lately, so this is the first time I've made it here."

"You caught the guy who put her here. She's going to think that's the best reason ever for a delayed visit."

"It was nice of you to stop by."

"Was happy to. She's a scrappy little kid who's had a hard time, but she'll make it. I didn't want to overstay my welcome and it was getting a little crowded in there, so I didn't stay long. I'll try to stop by again sometime. Well, I won't hold you up. But . . ." He shifted his weight from foot to foot for a second or two. "If you're free, I'd love to see you sometime. Assuming I'm not overstepping or anything."

"That sounds lovely. Maybe dinner instead of coffee with an abrupt exit this time?"

He laughed. "Somehow I think that's always a risk with you. Which I get because when I'm on shift, that's always a risk with me."

"I knew you'd understand." She dug in her pocket and pulled out a business card. "Call me."

He gave her a salute, raising two fingers to his temple, the card tucked between them. "Will do. Enjoy your visit." He gave Hawk a pat, and then continued down the hallway, whistling a jaunty tune.

Meg stood and watched until he rounded the corner and disappeared from view. "Come on, Hawk, let's go see our patient."

Jill's room was near the end of the hallway. "Here we are. Room four-oh-five." Meg knocked on the closed door.

A woman's voice called, "Come in."

Meg pushed open the door and allowed Hawk to precede her into the room. It was a typical hospital room—a single bed anchored the center of the space with a rolling table, a visitor's chair occupied by a middle-aged woman, a small bedside table covered with an explosion of flowers and cards, and a single window framed by curtains in pastel stripes to match the bed's privacy curtain, which was currently pushed back to the wall. A small girl was in the bed, and a man sat on the edge of it, his back to Meg. The girl was dwarfed by the enormous fuzzy brown bear that lay beside her on the bed. A gift from Webb? Or the man on the bed?

The girl gasped when she saw Hawk, causing the man to twist toward the door. Meg nearly stopped dead in surprise as Clay McCord turned to face her, but kept moving and allowed the door to close behind her.

What is he doing here? The only possible reason rose to mind and her temper spiked from zero to sixty, as much for herself as for him. Had she fallen for his act, giving up information so he could take advantage? Ignoring McCord's presence, she approached the woman in the chair, holding out her hand. "Mrs. Cahill, I'm Meg Jennings. We spoke on the phone."

"So nice to meet you." Her gaze dropped down to Hawk,

concern clouding her expression. "Your dog. He's been hurt?"

"Just a little mishap on Friday when we caught the bomber, but it's nothing serious. It's a lot of bandage, so it looks worse than it is, but it's really just a tough spot to keep covered. Give him a week or two and he'll be good as new." She took a step closer to the bed. "Jill, do you remember me? Hawk and I found you at the Whitten Building."

Jill angled her pale face up toward Meg, but there was no recognition in her eyes.

Meg gave her a graceful out. "It's okay if you don't recognize me. I was kind of in the background. Do you remember Hawk? He climbed into the rubble with you and stayed with you until the firefighters could get to you."

Jill didn't say anything, but nodded enthusiastically, her eyes fixed on Hawk.

"Would you like to visit with Hawk?" Meg turned to Mrs. Cahill. "Would that be all right? He's very clean, just had a bath this morning, and he's very gentle. He won't hurt her."

"Hurt her? He saved her life. Of course that would be all right." Mrs. Cahill glanced from the dog to the bed to the dog again. "Can he get up on the bed with that leg? Jill's doing much better but isn't supposed to get out of bed without the nurses. She'd love to spend some time with him, but won't that hurt him?"

"I'll help him get up."

The woman beamed at Hawk and then stood to approach him. "Can I touch him?"

"It's absolutely fine to touch him. He's very friendly." Meg looked down at Hawk. "Hawk, say hi."

Hawk promptly looked toward Mrs. Cahill, sat down, and raised a forepaw to her.

She laughed and graciously shook it. "Such lovely manners."

Meg slid a long look toward McCord, who was still turned to face her. "If you don't mind?"

McCord looked slightly taken aback at her stiff formality, but stood and moved out of the way, allowing Meg to pat the side the bed. "Hawk, up!"

Meg only had to give minimal help as he leapt lightly onto the edge of the bed and lay down beside Jill, his shoulder at her hip. She threw her arms around him and buried her face in the fur of his neck, the gigantic teddy bear instantly forgotten in the presence of a warm, friendly dog. "I remember you. You saved me."

Mrs. Cahill went to the bed to stand with her daughter, running one hand down Hawk's back, smiling as his tail thumped against the bedding.

Meg turned to McCord and jerked her head toward the far end of the room to stand right beside the door, but where she could still keep an eye on Hawk. He wouldn't hurt Jill on purpose but sometimes his enthusiasm got away from him.

"What are you doing here?" she hissed, keeping her voice low so it wouldn't carry. "If you think you can exploit me to find a good story to write—"

"Give me a little credit, will you?" His tone became defensive. "Yes, I admit I didn't know about her until you told me her story, but after everything wrapped up, I was done looking at the bad and wanted to concentrate on the good. So I thought I'd come and introduce myself to Jill. Nice catch on Friday, by the way. You and Hawk are an amazing team." His gaze settled on the cut at her temple, his brow furrowing in confusion. "What happened to you?"

"I got too close to the rock aimed at my head. Stop trying to change the subject." Meg sidled closer to McCord so she could drop her voice even further. "You *did* come here to write a story."

"Okay, I'll admit—"

"I knew it!" Her eyes narrowed to slits as she drilled an index finger into his chest. "You newspaper reporters are all alike. Heartless bastards just living to chase a headline. Even to the extent of exploiting children. I thought you were different. Guess I was wrong." She turned away, disappointment rising in her chest like a wave. After working with him during this case, she thought he was better than that. That while most reporters couldn't be trusted, he was the exception. Finding out she was wrong was a blow that stung more than she anticipated. *Stupid, Meg. When will you learn?*

"Wait." He shot out a hand and grabbed her arm, hard. When she winced, he loosened his grip, but didn't let go, slowly tugging her back toward him. "You're not being fair. I'm not exploiting a child, for God's sake. Yes, I'm an investigative journalist. Yes, my bread and butter depends on finding stories, the bigger, the better. But at this point in the game, I get to pick my topics. And if I want to write a human interest piece about the spirit the bomber couldn't break to counter to all the horrific bomber articles I've written, then that's my choice. Especially when that spirit belongs to a very brave ten-year-old little girl and I have parental permission. Her mother loves the idea. Not because of the notoriety, but because her daughter nearly died and this is the best way she can think of to thumb her nose at a man who would kill without thought or a scrap of remorse. It's a way for them to get some of their own spirit back."

He released her arm and then rubbed at her biceps, soothing the pressure point. "I suggested the article use just a false first name to keep her anonymous. The idea is to tell her story, describe her struggles, highlight her successes, and showcase her hope. Have you talked to Jill? She's a remarkable child. She feels sorry for Mannew, that he would have so much hate inside him to strike out like that. And this experience has changed her. She wanted to be a veterinarian before, but now she wants to go into social work. To be able to work with people like Mannew and make a difference in their lives *before* they get to that point. Isn't this a story to share with the nation? With those who were affected by Mannew, hurt by him? To show he may have knocked us back a step, but he can't even beat a ten-year-old girl. *That's* the story I want to tell." He stepped back, resignation etched deep into the lines around his eyes. "And if that makes me a heartless bastard, then so be it."

He started to turn away, but this time she caught his arm to echo his action. "Wait." She searched his face, looking for some indication he was lying, pulling a reporter's trick and trying to put one over on her. But his gaze was clear and direct and she could discern no deception. "You really mean that, don't you?"

"Yes." His eyes were guarded, cautious, waiting for her to strike again.

She swallowed hard, deciding if she'd be an idiot to stick her neck out for him. With him. *Take a leap for once.* "Then I'm sorry I jumped to the wrong conclusion. At the PD and at the Bureau, we're taught reporters are . . ."

"The enemy?"

"Yeah, pretty much. That you guys will go to any length for a story and will blow a case wide open in the middle of the investigation for your own glory, possibly giving the perp the heads-up and allowing him to get away, sometimes literally with murder. Or theft. Or terrorism."

"That's not the way I operate."

"And I've known that all case long. Some of my colleagues wondered if you might have been the bomber, sending yourself coded messages to put yourself in the spotlight. I've been the one telling them I thought you were on the level. And then I saw you here and totally overreacted. I'm sorry. Can I blame it on too much stress and not enough sleep lately?"

He had the grace to chuckle and let her and her short, exhausted temper off the hook. "Sounds perfectly reasonable to me."

They turned back to the girl on the bed, laughing with her mother as she accepted a long, slow lick from Hawk.

"I'd still love to do a story on you and Hawk," McCord said, sotto voce.

She sent him a slitted side glance. "Now you're pushing."

"Can't blame a guy for trying. And continuing to try, especially at times when you're feeling like you owe me one." He crossed his arms over his chest, and while his eyes never looked away from the girl and the dog, one eyebrow cocked in challenge. "You just wait; I'll wear you down yet."

"Good luck with that. You got my picture in the paper, that's more than enough for me."

"We'll see. You sure he's okay?"

"He will be." She dropped her voice so there was no chance mother or daughter could hear her. "Mannew only grazed him. Even though I had a gun, he clearly thought Hawk was the bigger threat, the one that needed to be taken out first. He came close, but not close enough."

"Thank God."

"Amen to that. And in the end, Hawk took him down." She sent him a sly, sidelong glance. "I'll tell you the full story later if you promise it never makes it to print."

He stared back, but something in her expression must have told him she'd drawn her line in the sand. "Fine," he muttered, and turned back to the bed.

Hawk licked Jill's cheek again, and she let out a high-pitched giggle, the sound lightening the hearts of the adults in the room.

"Ya done good, kid." McCord gave Meg a gentle nudge in the rib with his elbow. "As I said, you and that dog are a heck of a team."

"He does all the hard work."

"Nah. You want people to think that, but I know better. It's teamwork through and through, and the sum is much greater than the individual parts."

"Still gunning for that story, aren't you?"

"Right there? Nope. Just telling it like I see it."

They turned back to the bed and the picture of peace and hope before them. There would be more violence to come, more stories to cover, and more lives to save.

But for now, everything was right with their world. This was what they loved best and worked for.

This was their reward.